Praise for best-selling author Melanie George

LIKE NO OTHER

". . . a bright story with a lively freshness that marks [Melanie George] as a talent to watch."
—*Romantic Times*

"Sparkling wit and charming characters."
—*Affaire de Coeur*

DEVIL MAY CARE

"[The devilish Sinclair brothers] are lethal as well as divine."
—*The Belles and Beaux of Romance*

"Devil May Care is paradise found!"
—*Midwest Book Review*

HANDSOME DEVIL

"Ms. George is a master of sensuous dialogue."
—*Winter Haven News Chief*

"A treasure, a triumph, a treat for the heart!"
—*Old Book Barn Gazette*

THE DEVIL'S DUE

". . . a thrilling roller coaster ride of an adventure story . . . so hang onto your hearts and get set for a memorable, fast-paced tale that puts Melanie George on your must read list!"
—*Romantic Times* (Top Pick)

". . . it's a winner, with one of romance's feistiest heroines and most alluringly brooding heroes."
—*Booklist*

THE MATING GAME

MELANIE GEORGE

ZEBRA BOOKS
KENSINGTON PUBLISHING CORP.
http://www.kensingtonbooks.com

ZEBRA BOOKS are published by

Kensington Publishing Corp.
850 Third Avenue
New York, NY 10022

Copyright © 2002 by Melanie George

All Kensington titles, imprints, and distributed lines are available at special quantity discounts for bulk purchases for sales promotions, premiums, fund-raising, and educational or institutional use.

Special book excerpts or customized printings can also be created to fit specific needs. For details, write or phone the office of the Kensington Special Sales Manager: Kensington Publishing Corp., 850 Third Avenue, New York, NY 10022. Attn. Special Sales Department. Phone: 1-800-221-2647.

First Printing: April 2002
10 9 8 7 6 5 4 3 2 1

Printed in the United States of America

To the wonderful readers on my list who have always been so supportive of me. This one is for you . . .

CHAPTER ONE

Hot, consuming desire.

Eve writhed with it, her body slick with sweat, a wild hunger building inside her, the roaring of her blood keeping tempo with the pounding surf as the perfumed night wrapped her in its sweet embrace.

Flames of liquid seduction licked over her, silken shackles binding her wrists, imprisoning her within the kiss of a darkly savage fire. She asked for no quarter. None was given.

Instead, she embraced the heat, drowned in it, let the blaze sweep her away. Her eyelids fluttered open. She wanted to see the face of the fiercely beautiful buccaneer who had captured her—whose love had set her free.

Passion glazed his deep blue eyes, as dark as the heart of the ocean. Passion she knew and understood. How she had longed for this moment. This man was her heart.

Her very soul.

He cupped her breast, playing with the aching peak,

the torture lingering and exquisite. His head lowered and he drew the tight bud into his mouth. She moaned, a deep, guttural sound pulled from a place she hadn't known existed.

He left no flesh untouched, soothing each spot with his lips, his tongue, the glide of his skin over hers its own pleasure. She pressed her hips to his, the need for completion making her frantic.

He slipped a finger between her wet folds and staked claim to the swollen nub, stroking, teasing, flicking until bright slashes of color burst behind her eyes.

When she thought she could take no more, he moved between her thighs, wrapping her legs around his waist, fear and excitement warring within her as he eased his hard length into her and—

"Hard length? Geez, Mal, can't you just say penis for once?"

Mallory jumped as her sister's voice blared in her ear, her fingers convulsing on the keys of her laptop, her concentration effectively shattered.

Mallory briefly closed her eyes and took a calming breath, knowing she would need every ounce of fortitude she could muster.

Then she turned to find Genie's head poised over her shoulder, green eyes scanning the words Mallory had just typed, her sister's lips moving as she read.

"I have a doorbell, you know," Mallory said pointedly.

"And I have a key." Genie dangled Mallory's apartment key in front of her. "You gave it to me, remember?"

How could she forget? Genie used it with relish. It didn't matter if Mallory was home or not. Nor did it seem to matter that Genie lived just around the corner with their mother. It was as if her sister was attempting to set some kind of record for how little time she actually spent at home.

Her sister plunked down in the chair next to Mallory's desk. Four small hoop earrings graced Genie's left ear, and four hoops and a gold stud adorned the right. Her lipstick was blue to match her nails. At seventeen, Genie still reveled in her role as a nonconformist.

"Well?" her sister prompted, snapping the wad of gum in her mouth.

"Well what?"

"Can't you say penis?"

Mallory mustered her patience. "No, I can't."

"Why not?"

"Because I write historical romance novels, and that word is not appropriate."

"Well, can you say—"

"No."

"What about—"

"No."

"Then, how about—"

"*No!*"

Genie held up her hands. "Man, you're uptight. Take a pill, will ya?"

Mallory sighed. "I'm sorry, Genie. I'm just very busy right now."

"What else is new?" her sister muttered, a hint of bitterness in her voice.

Mallory felt a twinge of guilt. She knew she had a tendency to block everyone out when she was in the middle of one of her novels—and the past few years it seemed she had been in the middle of one on a constant basis.

It had not escaped her notice that her sister had

become more belligerent; Genie's troubles had steadily escalated with each passing year. She had been caught shoplifting on several occasions and had nearly been arrested for illegal gambling a month earlier.

The thought made Mallory look closely at her sister. Genie gnawed one blue nail—a clear harbinger of trouble looming on the horizon. "Has something happened, Genie?"

"What makes you think something's happened?" her sister returned defensively.

"I don't know. Call it a feeling." A sinking feeling that Mallory wished wasn't such an accurate barometer.

Her sister looked as if she might continue the pretense, but then she shrugged. "All right. I do have a small problem."

Genie's definition of "small" was generally at odds with everyone else's definition.

"Go on."

"Well . . ." She drew out the word. "I thought I had—" The phone rang then, cutting Genie off.

Mallory's gaze moved to the caller ID, instantly recognizing the number. Karen Warner, her editor. Mallory hesitated, not in the mood to discuss how her manuscript was progressing, since it wasn't progressing all that well.

The answering machine picked up, and Karen's Boston-born-and-bred voice filtered into the room. "Hey Mal, thought you might want to hear about the unusual phone call I received this morning from a fan of yours—a male fan—and an interesting one at that."

An interesting male. It seemed a contradiction

in terms. She had begun to think she could only find one of those between the pages of a romance.

"Even if he is a bit eccentric," Karen added.

Ah, there was the catch.

"But he's British and wealthy, so who cares?"

That piqued her interest.

"Call me back as—"

Mallory picked up the phone. "Karen? Don't hang up." She sent her sister an apologetic look that promised she would only be a minute.

"Were you screening your calls again?" Karen asked. Clearly, the woman knew her too well.

"Me? Of course not. I, ah, just came in from a walk with the dogs." Mallory glanced down at her two Pekingese pups, Duke and Daisy, sleeping soundly beneath her desk between a clutter of books and papers. "Now, who is this wealthy Brit?"

"His name's Dexter Harrington."

Mallory furrowed her brow. "Who's Dexter Harrington?"

"You don't know who Dexter Harrington is? Really, Mallory, you have to get out more."

Now there was a news flash, Mallory thought, rolling her eyes.

"Dexter Harrington is a titled aristocrat whose family made their fortune in coal before the turn of the century. He graduated top of his class at Oxford and is purported to have an IQ upward of two hundred, which almost guarantees he's nuttier than a box of Goobers. But the man's got cheek bones you could slice cheese on and a smile that has been registered by the F.B.I. as a lethal weapon."

"That certainly is a recommendation," Mallory murmured drolly. "How do you know so much about him?"

"Don't you ever read *Newsweek*?"

With what five minutes? Mallory almost replied. Her life seemed to move from one deadline to the next, interspersed with calls from her mother to complain about Genie and calls from Genie to complain about their mother. Yes, hers was indeed a charmed life.

"Anyway," Karen went on, "he spends most of his time holed up in his family's estate in Wales and can be more elusive than the Loch Ness monster from all accounts." She sounded almost giddy as she said, "Do you want to take a guess at what he does for a living?"

Not really. "Why does a rich aristocrat have to do anything for a living?"

Her editor's impatient sigh coerced Mallory into playing along. "Hmm. Is he a little old man who lives in a shoe whose wife left him with so many children he doesn't know what to do? Or does he huff and puff and blow people's houses down? Or perhaps he's a butcher, a baker or a candlestick maker?"

"Will you be serious?"

"Fine. I give up. What does the British aristocrat whose family made their living in coal do for a living?"

"He's a scientist."

"How lovely for him."

Then Karen finished, "Specializing in *human sexuality*."

Now things were heating up. "A sex scientist?"

"That's right."

Mallory detected a distinct hubba-hubba lurking behind Karen's words, which probably stemmed from the fact that her editor was nose deep in romance manuscripts on a daily basis, giving her a therein-lies-a-story mentality.

Mallory, on the other hand, relied on her overactive imagination to draw a mental picture of a man who was a cross between Dr. Feelgood and Dr. Strangelove. She made a face. "So what did he want?"

"Well, the call was actually from his secretary, Cummings—all very pip-pip and tallyho—who inquired as to how he might get in touch with one Zoe Wilde, the scalding kettle of passion."

Mallory chuckled. "Scalding kettle of passion, hmm?" Zoe Wilde was Mallory's pen name and alter ego. "Call Guinness. That's one for the record books."

"Of course, I couldn't give him that information, so he asked me if I would be 'ever so gracious as to put forth the earl's request.' "

Mallory shook her head. A rich, eccentric scientist had a request. This might top the seventy-year-old drunk who flashed her every morning when she went to pick up her bacon, egg and cheese sandwich at the corner diner and the Cro-Magnon men at the construction site across the street who assumed her day wasn't complete without regaling her with whistles, hoots and the ever popular "hey, baby." Mallory was beginning to believe a real man was a thing of the past.

"So what was the earl's request?"

Karen did not hesitate to reply, "That you come to England immediately."

For a full ten seconds Mallory's facial muscles refused to function. Then her lips formed the words, "You're kidding, right?"

"I know it sounds crazy—"

"*Sounds* crazy? It is crazy. What in the world would make this guy think I would ever consider such an outrageous thing?"

"Oh, I did leave that part out, didn't I?"

"What part?"

"The part about his project, and paying you handsomely for your time, flying you first class, and allowing you the use of his extensive library, ten thousand books from what I understand. Pretty impressive."

"Project? What kind of project?"

"I don't know. His secretary said it was confidential."

The guy had a screw loose. He expected her to jet overseas at the drop of a hat without telling her anything about what he wanted?

"He said he'd explain it all when you got there," Karen added, as though intuiting Mallory's thoughts; a proclivity that was starting to get a little creepy.

"I guess he's going to have a long wait, then."

"You always said you wanted to go to England. Well, here's your chance."

"And I'll get to England." *Someday.* "But not via Lunatics Express. I can't believe you'd even suggest this. Have you forgotten that I have a book to finish?"

"Of course I haven't forgotten."

"I hear a distinct 'but' behind those words."

"Well," Karen drawled, "what a coup it would be if you could get this guy to tell you his life story when no one else has been able to get the time of day from him. Unauthorized biographies are hot property right now. And the guy's a British aristocrat. Maybe he knows some gossip about the royal family. You could be the next Kitty Kelly."

Mallory pulled the receiver slightly away from her ear and stared at it, hoping her incredulity would teleport across the wire. "I write romance novels. What do I care about his life story?"

Karen went on as if she hadn't spoken. "They say he's developing a new Viagra-type pill, but this one is geared toward women. Just imagine the press you'd receive having that information before anyone else."

From the sublime to the ridiculous at warp speed. "Not interested."

As usual, Karen heard only what she wanted to hear. "I'll give you some time to think about it before I call the earl's secretary back with your final answer."

"That is my—"

"Oops. Have a meeting. Gotta go. Call me later." The next sound Mallory heard was a dial tone.

"Go to England," she muttered, dropping the phone into the cradle. "Ridiculous."

"Who's Dexter Harrington?" Genie asked, reminding Mallory of her presence.

Mallory shrugged, more than ready to dismiss that particular topic. "Just some wealthy British scientist who is obviously delusional."

Genie stared at her quizzically.

"Never mind. Now, where were we?"

The reminder of their interrupted conversation made Genie gnaw on her nail again. "I have a small problem."

"That has been established."

"Well, maybe a little bigger than small."

No news bulletin there. "How much bigger than small?"

Her sister looked uncomfortable.

"Bigger than a breadbox?" Mallory prompted. Genie nodded.

There was that sinking feeling again. "Exactly how big, Genie?"

A sudden pounding at the front door halted Genie' reply as a new voice blared, "Yo, Genie, youse in there?"

Genie's gaze darted to the door and then back to Mallory, as she answered sheepishly, "That big."

Mallory groaned inwardly, recognizing the masculine voice that called out in a tone that was not as lilting as springtime in the Highlands, but as coarse as a Mafia boss whose cheeks were stuffed with cannolis.

Bruno the bookie.

And neighborhood leg breaker.

As a child, Bruno's favorite toy had been thumbscrews and he had been known to ponder that all-important question which had taxed many a man with an IQ of six: When it rains, why don't sheep shrink?

Mallory finally realized what she was sinking in. Quicksand. "What did you bet on this time?"

"Well, I coulda sworn that Sassy's Spitfire, the long shot at Belmont, would beat Monica's Misfortune. The odds were ten to one." She shrugged. "Guess my luck ran out."

"Yo, Genie. I knows you're in there. Now stop stallin'."

"I'll hide in the linen closet," Genie said, jumping to her feet. "You get rid of him."

"Now, wait a minute—"

Pound. Pound. Pound. "Youse better open up or else I'm gonna unleash a shit storm of whup ass on this door."

Whup ass. What a lovely way to start the day. "All right," she told Genie. "Hide."

Her sister sprinted into the closet as though she possessed bionic limbs, the words "We can rebuild her. We have the technology," popping into Mallory's brain.

She glanced down at Duke and Daisy, both of whom sprang up on their two-inch bowed legs and began to bark vigorously, looking like two gyrating Twinkies. Their bark had never sent fear into the hearts of men. What she wouldn't give for a tape recording of snarling pit bulls at that moment.

"Stay here, you two," she told them, rising from her chair. "I'll be right back." They looked at her with identical expressions of *Oh-no-you-don't*, which was followed closely by *Foiled again*, when she closed her bedroom door.

"Okay, youse Ginellis. I'm countin' to tree an' then I'm comin' in!"

Reluctantly, Mallory started across the room, hoping Bruno would be barreling full tilt toward the door when she opened it, which would, in turn, set him on a straight trajectory for the window.

She smiled, picturing him flying through the glass. Too bad the awning from the Indian restaurant on the street below her window would break his fall. The idea of seeing the man in a body cast appealed to her.

Mallory swung the door open at the exact moment Bruno angled his shoulder to ram it. He lost his balance and collapsed in a heap of gold chains and cheap silk suit. Not exactly what she had hoped for, but amusing nonetheless.

He glared up at her. "Youse did that on purpose."

Mallory stared down at him dispassionately. "The word is you, not *youse*. Singular as opposed to plural."

Bruno dusted himself off and rose to his stocky five-foot-six height. He was a barrel-chested bully with no neck, his beefy arms permanently pressed outward. He looked like one of the gangsters who had gunned down Sonny Corleone at a toll plaza on the New Jersey Turnpike.

"Don't gimme no lip," he grunted. "I ain't in the mood."

Mallory folded her arms across her chest. "What do you want, Bruno?"

His bilious gaze dipped to her breasts, which diverted his pea-sized brain and relocated it behind the zipper of his pants. "Why d'ya play so hard to get, baby?"

He needed a reason? Besides the fact that his breath smelled like garlic and his face looked as though the L-train had run over it. Repeatedly.

"I repeat, what do you want, Bruno?"

He edged closer to her. "If youse is nice to me, maybe I'll think about reducin' your sister's debt."

"I'm not for sale." Mallory dug into the pocket of her favorite faded blue Levis and pulled out a ten and two twenties. She slapped the money down in Bruno's hands. "That should hold you over for a few days."

"Fifty lousy bucks? You kiddin'? Your scrawny-ass sister owes me twenty thousand, three hundred eighty-one dollars . . . and twenty-six cents. Interest compounded daily. We both know she ain't got it, which means *you* gotta pay."

Mallory reeled. Twenty thousand, three hundred eighty-one dollars . . . ?

She told herself to breathe. "If you knew she didn't have the money, why did you let her bet?"

"Yo, am I my brudder's keeper?" His brow puckered, making him look like a walrus in the throes of labor. "Or would that be sister's keeper, even though we ain't related?" He shrugged. "Don't make no difference. She still owes me twenty thousand, three hundred eighty-one dollars—"

"And twenty-six cents. I know." Mallory shook her head. "I don't have that kind of money."

He pushed his face close to hers. "You know what happened to the last person who didn't pay up?"

Mallory didn't know—thankfully. It was one mental picture she could well live without. Unfortunately, she had other mental pictures to fall back on, all too clear memories of Bruno's handiwork. He might be a dumb stick, but he didn't need a degree from Harvard to know how to wield a bat with unerring accuracy.

"I'll get the money," she promised. "But you have to give me some time."

"You got tree days." He held up two fingers. "And I'll be back to collect." Then he swaggered his bulk out the door. Mallory decided not to tell him about the toilet paper stuck to the bottom of his shoe.

She heaved a sigh and leaned heavily against the closed door. "You can come out now, Genie."

No response.

Mallory walked over to the linen closet and found the door slightly ajar. She looked inside. No Genie. Then she noticed the window in her spare bedroom was open and realized her sister had ducked out using the fire escape.

Genie would be back; that was a given. So, too, was the fact that her sister would invite herself in, using Mallory's spare key.

Mallory went to close the window. An open window in New York was an engraved invitation for robbery, rape, homicide—and sometimes not all at once.

As she was leaving, she glimpsed the framed picture of herself, Genie and their mother on the bureau. She picked it up, studying their happy faces, arms wrapped around each other's waists. It was an old picture—and one of the last shots of all of them together and smiling.

Her mother had a beautiful smile, full of warmth. Yet she rarely smiled anymore, and the warmth seemed to have left her the day her husband walked out the door and never returned.

Perhaps if Mallory allowed herself to look within, she might discover her own scars, that her father's actions had shaped her life as much as the rest of her family's.

Maybe that was why she preferred made-up characters to the real thing. She could mold them to suit her needs. They were never ordinary or cruel. Never cowardly or dishonorable. The men were always heroes, and the endings happily ever after.

Carefully, she replaced the picture and scooped her trusty Magic 8 ball off the corner of the bureau, remembering all the questions a young girl had once posed, searching for answers when there had been no one to give them.

Mallory shook the ball, watching the little cube roll around within the murky liquid. "Will my family ever be happy again?" she asked tentatively.

The cube rolled to a stop. *Outlook hazy.*

What had she expected? Miracles were reserved for other people.

She wondered if she dared ask another question. She nibbled her lip, fearing the response, yet fearing the unknown even more. She shook the ball again. "Will I be able to come up with the money Genie owes Bruno?"

She held her breath, waiting for the cube to come to a stop. When it did, her heart dropped. *No.*

"Hmm. Travel to England to be the plaything of a disgustingly rich, sex freak earl with a BS in erogenous zones who's writing his doctoral thesis on the G-spot, or stay here in New York and risk mugging, being thrown in front of a speeding train, bombing, deadly mosquitoes and biological warfare. I can see how this decision would be difficult for you, bubbee."

Mallory stopped pacing and turned to face her best friend since birth, Freida, tough-as-nails-Jewish-American-princess, Feldman. If anyone looked less like a Freida, it was the golden girl standing in front of Mallory, whom she called Freddie—much to the dismay of Mrs. Feldman.

She and Freddie were a study in contrasts. Mallory was barely five-three to Freddie's five-nine. Mallory had an olive complexion. Freddie's skin was warm brown year-round. Mallory had been cursed with long, straight black hair while Freddie had been blessed with wavy, blond locks perfect for a L'Oreal commercial.

Freddie's God-given endowments also included endlessly long legs, an ample bust, a Colgate smile, and a husky voice that could seduce as easily as it could reduce a man to a burning pile of rubble with the utterance of one wrong word.

"I didn't say I wasn't considering the idea," Mallory told her, wishing it was a lie. But the truth was, her options were at an all-time low.

She had been wracking her brain all afternoon, coming up with very few ideas. She thought of selling something, but she didn't own anything that would bring in that much cash. And her checking account was in no better shape.

Who would believe the semi-successful romance novelist, Zoe Wilde, had a sum total of only four thousand dollars in the bank? And most of that money was earmarked for rent and bills.

She had had more cash until Genie had been caught shoplifting—for the third time—and Mallory had to post fifteen thousand for bail or leave her own sister in the slammer.

"Don't look at the earl's offer as a job," Freddie drawled, admiring her manicure. "Look at it as sex for hire."

"Will you be serious? If I don't give Bruno that money, Genie will be up to her knees in concrete."

"Or under it with Jimmy Hoffa."

"Thank you very much for making a bad situation look that much worse."

"I'm Jewish. It's in my blood to be cynical. It comes from hundreds of years of enslavement and persecution."

"Could we stick to the subject? How am I going to get my hands on that much money so quickly?"

"Rob a convenience store? No." Freddie shook her head. "Forget that. They wouldn't have enough cash. You'd need to knock off a bank. Your mother blends in well, so my advice would be to let her go inside and hold up the teller while you wait in the getaway car."

"Oh, there's a novel idea. My mother and I can share a jail cell."

Freddie made a face. "I shiver to think of sharing a cell with my mother. I'd have to listen to her berate me for the next ten to twenty because I didn't marry Marty Klein, the deli king. Twenty-two stores in the tri-state area. You'd think with all that money the man could get himself circumcised."

"Could we get back to the issue? Bruno. Money. Brass knuckles."

"Couldn't you just ask Bruno for an extension?"

"I'm sure he'd be amenable to that. Then he'd bust only one kneecap for collateral."

Freddie looked aghast. "And leave me to wheel you around? I think not. Let's just solve this problem quickly and easily. I'll loan you the money."

Mallory had already contemplated asking her friend for a loan. Freddie was a trust fund baby who had never had to work a day in her life while Mallory had had to scrape for every dime. She knew that given time, she could pay Freddie back, but it would feel too much like taking charity.

Mallory sighed. "I appreciate it, but no. I can't expect you to fix this problem."

"So why not just take the sex professor up on his offer, then? Lord knows you could use a good lay."

Leave it to Freddie to be blunt. "This is strictly business."

Freddie cocked a perfectly plucked blond brow.

"Oh? Well, if that's the case, what do you have to worry about?"

What, indeed, Mallory thought.

Yet, were she honest with herself, she would confess to a certain degree of curiosity about the man who had made such an outrageous request. She figured it had to be the mystery he presented, like being a contestant on "Let's Make A Deal" and wanting to know what was behind door number three.

It was a rather sad commentary that the earl's unorthodox offer was the most interesting thing that had happened to her in a long time. Her personal life had deteriorated to the point that listening to a lecture on the history of fertilizer would be considered exciting.

She could write about scaling Mt. Everest, but had she ever done it herself? Had she ever explored the pyramids? Seen the white cliffs of Dover? Tossed a coin into the Trevi Fountain? Eaten fondue in Switzerland?

No, no, and no again.

"So what does this hunka-hunka burning love look like?" Freddie inquired. "Personally, I'm picturing Johnny Wad in a tweed coat."

Mallory figured with her luck Dexter Harrington would resemble the Son of Sam and was probably plotting to perform experiments on her straight out of Hitchcock.

"I don't know. I searched for a picture of him on the Internet, but all I could come up with were a few web sites with some of his published papers."

And what papers they had been!

The Physiology and Pathology of Penile Erection.

Of Rats and Men: The Comparative Approach to Male Sexuality.

The Mechanisms of Human Female Sexual Arousal.

And her all-time favorite and most frightening: *Schizophrenia and Sexuality.* What one had to do with the other she didn't want to examine too closely.

After that bit of enlightenment, she should have been on the phone with Karen demanding that she tell the earl's lackey unequivocally that his employer could keep his first-class plane ticket, the substantial money he had offered her for her valuable time, and his library with nearly ten thousand books, and take a flying header off his paperwork about *Cognitive and Affective Contributions to Sexual Functioning.*

The reality of her situation, however, currently loitered across the street calling out to a teenage girl sashaying past, who, Mallory noticed with a smile of satisfaction, flipped him the bird over her shoulder.

New York girls, two. Bruno the Jerk, zero.

Now, if only Mallory could dismiss Bruno that easily. Since the possibility seemed highly unlikely, she had to consider the only option presenting itself.

The earl's offer.

If she took Dexter Harrington's mysterious job, she could pay Bruno off with the advance she would require the earl to give her, proviso number one, and still keep her pride intact—as well as Genie's limbs.

Mallory made her decision. What other choice did she have? Unless the bookie fairy magically appeared and made Bruno disappear in a puff of smoke, he would be back.

To coin *The Godfather*, she had been made an offer she couldn't refuse.

"I'll go."

Freddie merely stared at her.

"Did you hear me? I said I'll go."

"I heard you."

"And? Have you nothing to say?"

"Yes—but I'm waiting to hear God's voice coming from a burning bush as this is a day of miracles."

Mallory ignored her friend's unappreciated witticism. "I want you to come with me." Freddie was a bulldog when it came to men. Should things get out of hand with the earl, Freddie would treat him to a bris—Feldman style.

"Come with you? To the land of tea, crumpets, and Sir Elton John?"

Mallory nodded. "We always talked about going to England together. Now we can." Whether the earl liked it or not. Proviso number two.

Freddie leaned back against the sofa cushions and regarded her for a long moment. "You know, bubbee, you can't always use me as a crutch. Some day you'll have to stand on your own little size-five feet."

"I'm not using you as a crutch." But a small voice asked Mallory if she wasn't doing just that. "And my feet are a five and a half."

"I'm just pointing out the possibility of your suffocating dependency on me."

Mallory treated her friend to a withering glare.

Freddie shrugged. "All right. I'll go. I could use a change of scenery. But I refuse to travel with you looking like that."

Mallory glanced down at her worn-in jeans and extra large light pink T-shirt with dirty doggie prints on it, acquired when Duke had decided to sunbathe in a mud puddle in the park and who then turned mutinous when she tried to coax him out of it. Still, she said, "Like what?"

"With you wearing clothes that are two sizes too big. Your randy earl would think you had some genetic disease."

"He's not my randy earl."

A wicked grin lit Freddie's face. "But he could be."

CHAPTER TWO

Mallory smiled numbly at the expertly coifed stewardess as she disembarked from British Airways Flight 178, which she had renamed Flight 666, plane ride from hell.

She dragged her wheeled carry-on behind her, feeling as if the downtown bus had run over her, backed up and run over her again for good measure.

Three torturously long hours their flight had been delayed at Kennedy, sitting on the runway. Mallory had passed the time staring out at the tarmac, an endless sea of black punctuated with yellow hyphens that seemed to curve upward into smiley faces, mocking her.

The delay had given Mallory too much time to think about what she was doing. Doubts about her sanity had settled in, so that by the time they were taxiing down the runway, Freddie had been forced to physically restrain her to keep her from flinging herself out the emergency door and onto the tarmac she knew so well.

Mallory's first bleary-eyed glimpse of London had been a blanket of darkness and little pinpoints of light, which could very well have been caused by the headache building behind her eyes. She felt grumpy, rumpled, and completely out of sorts by the time they touched down.

They deplaned at Terminal 4. Heathrow still bustled, though it was nearly midnight. Everything seemed surreal, eerie, reminding Mallory of that Stephen King movie, *The Langoliers.*

She looked over her shoulder and out the window to make sure there wasn't some invisible entity swallowing great chunks of the earth and leaving a yawning chasm in its wake. Reassuringly, all appeared the same.

Dark.

She glanced covertly at Freddie. After spending nearly a full day traveling, Freddie still appeared perfectly kept while Mallory felt like a rung-out dish mop with breasts. She couldn't turn a head at that moment if her hair were on fire. She resisted the childlike urge to stick her tongue out at her friend when she wasn't looking.

"So where is the coital guru?" Freddie inquired, her gaze roaming. "I don't see anyone panting or wearing a wrinkled overcoat."

"I wish you would stop that."

"I can't help myself. You know what a perverse sense of humor I have."

Mallory knew.

"May I at least know what this carbon-based sex machine looks like?"

Good question. Mallory had neglected to get a description of Dexter Harrington. "I don't know exactly."

"That's wonderful. We travel to a third world country and you don't know what our friendly fleshmonger looks like? The local pervert could lead us out of here like sheep, take us to some seedy motel in Stalkerville, tie us to a bed that squeaks, and ravage our taut, nubile bodies—not that I'm against the idea, mind you."

"First of all, England is not a third world country. And secondly, *I'm going to strangle you.*"

Freddie gave her that blinding *Cosmopolitan* smile. "Will that be before or after the ravaging?"

"Ms. Ginelli?" a deep voice cut in.

Mallory didn't realize someone was speaking to her as her brain was calculating the repercussions of beating Freddie with her own shoe.

Freddie nodded at a spot behind Mallory. "You're being paged, bubbee."

Knotted muscles caused Mallory to swing around with a jerk, her purse walloping the man standing behind her. "Oh! I'm sorry!"

He rubbed his arm and smiled. "No apologies, dear girl. I startled you."

He spoke with a crisp English accent, and she realized with a start that this man must be Dexter Harrington. Relief coursed through her.

Her mental picture had been all wrong. He was not some fiend with "sex" tattooed across his forehead in big letters and drool dribbling down his jaw. His eyes were not bulging like Dr. Frankenstein's assistant, Igor. And he completely refuted Freddie's prediction that he would sport a hump and stand out like a Baptist Minister at Mardi Gras.

Instead, his features were rather pleasant. Tidy, short brown hair. Friendly mocha latte eyes. His teeth were an orthodontist's dream, straight and white. A square jawline bespoke a sensible nature. And he had a lean build. He stood only an inch or so above Freddie, who, Mallory noticed, eyed his lower region rather blatantly. Mallory jabbed the heel of her shoe into her friend's foot.

"Ow! Why did you—"

She spoke over Freddie's complaint. "Nice to meet you, Mr., er, I mean Lord Harrington." She extended her hand.

A warm hand clasped hers. "The name is Cummings."

Cummings? As in the earl's secretary? The purveyor of her services? Annoyance twanged Mallory's nerves. Had she traveled all this way and suffered the agonies of Flight 666 to be greeted not by Dexter Harrington, but by his hired help?

As if reading her mind, Cummings said, "The earl had business to attend to and sends his apologies for not coming himself."

"I understand."

"Here, let me." He took her carry-on bag.

"Hi." Freddie stuck out her hand, not one to be ignored. "I'm Ms. Ginelli's assistant shlepper and persona non grata, Freddie."

Cummings shook her hand and, surprisingly, did not linger like most men. "Nice to meet you. Freddie . . . what an unusual name." Before Freddie could formulate a reply, he said, "Please follow me," and began walking away.

Freddie frowned. "What did he mean by *unusual?*"

Mallory shrugged. "I don't know. What do most people mean by unusual?"

"Was that some read-between-the-lines British slur on my name?"

Mallory hid a grin. Clearly her friend was perturbed by more than Cummings's innocent comment. Freddie had just gotten her first dose of that awful medicine called indifference.

Cummings didn't know it yet, but he had just been consigned to eternal damnation because he had not drooled like Pavlov's dogs at the sight of Freddie.

Mallory suspected Cummings was the type of man who looked below the surface and sought inner beauty instead of external beauty. Now, *that* was unusual.

With a start, Mallory realized they were still rooted to the worn blue airport carpeting while Cummings was fading into the distance. In a walk-run, they charged after him.

"Nice ass," Freddie felt inclined to point out before adding, "for an uppity English guy."

Mallory flashed her friend an annoyed look. "Have you no shame?"

"None whatsoever," she replied. Then she sighed. "Too bad he's only a secretary. He's probably gay."

"Just because he's a secretary doesn't have to mean he's gay."

"Well, it doesn't give him high marks on the heterosexual scale either."

"What century are you living in? There are male nurses, male librarians, male hairdressers."

"True. And they're all doing the wild thing with each other."

"When did your brain shrivel to the size of a walnut? Don't you know a closed mind is an empty mind?"

"Okay, Miss We-Are-the-World, do you know any *females* who date one?"

"No, but—"

"I rest my case."

That should have ended it.

But it didn't.

Freddie pointed to Cummings. "Look at how the man walks."

Mallory told herself to pretend she had a delayed reaction to cabin pressure and had temporarily lost her hearing, but self-preservation had deserted her when the flight from hell had taken a detour over the Bermuda Triangle.

"What's the matter with how he walks?"

"It's too upright." Feldman logic at its finest.

"As opposed to other Homo sapiens who slither across the floor on their bellies?"

"His shoulders are all thrown back like he's got a steel rod up his—"

"It's called good posture."

"He's too stiff."

Mallory shook her head. "Just because his tongue didn't roll out of his mouth and puddle on the floor when he saw you does not mean the man is gay."

Freddie ignored her. "What real man likes romance novels anyway? If that isn't a fagola meter, I don't know what is."

Mallory realized there was no reasoning with her friend. Besides, she was too tired to argue. Eventually, Freddie fell silent.

Mallory's feet throbbed as though she had

walked thirty-seven miles in heels by the time they reached the outside of the airport. Now she understood what the man across the aisle from her on the plane had meant when he said Terminal 4 was on the fringe of the outer limits, a universe unto itself. If that wasn't the truth.

Cummings gestured to a stunning slate gray Rolls Royce parked at the curb. A man in a pristine black jacket and pants leaned against the driver's side door. He doffed his black chauffeur's hat, revealing a bald pate. "Welcome to England, Ms. Ginelli."

"Thank you . . . ?"

"Wheatley, miss."

"Thank you, Wheatley." Did anyone have a first name? "Please call me Mallory."

Wheatley bobbed his head, then asked for their luggage tags and disappeared inside.

Cummings opened the back door to the Rolls. "After you, ladies."

As soon as they had settled into the plush interior of the car, Freddie, always on the offensive, bluntly asked Cummings, "Are you gay?"

Mallory groaned.

Cummings raised an eyebrow, amusement lurking in his gaze. "No, are you?"

"Me?" Freddie looked as if Cummings had just accused her of shopping at the Dollar Store. "Of course not!"

"I guess that settles it, then."

Before Freddie could pose a more provocative question than her last, Mallory said, "How long have you been with the earl, Cummings?"

"About fifteen years now. We went to Oxford together."

She could almost hear Freddie's brain whirring

as the question departed her friend's lips. "*You* went to Oxford?"

"Indeed," Cummings replied, clearly not intending to elaborate further.

"If that doesn't beat all," Freddie hooted. "A male secretary romance reader with a degree from Oxford. Now I've heard everything."

"Yes . . . I imagine you have."

Freddie's smile turned upside down. "Now, listen you—"

Mallory quickly clamped a hand over her friend's mouth before a litany of four-lettered words poured forth. "Excuse her. She drank too much on the plane."

Cummings's expression clearly articulated his doubts about the validity of her explanation and conveyed that he suspected insanity ran in Freddie's family.

He spared Freddie one last glance before settling those sharp brown eyes on Mallory. "I'm sure you're curious as to why you've been summoned."

Summoned? Had she been summoned? She decided not to argue the point. "It has crossed my mind."

"The earl will explain it to you in due time." He leaned forward and added, "He's very happy you came."

Happy? Mallory didn't know how she felt about that. If he was so happy, why hadn't he met her at the airport? On the other hand, she didn't want him to be *too* happy. This was strictly business. She hoped.

The driver returned then, and they started through the airport maze. Fuming, Freddie stared out the window, her gaze narrowed. Mallory knew her friend hadn't finished with Cummings. Not by a long shot.

They all lapsed into thoughtful silence. Mallory tried to keep her eyes open; but the pill Freddie had given her to relax her taut nerves finally kicked in, and soon her eyelids drifted shut, leaving her only dimly aware of strong arms lifting her out of the car and cradling her against a broad chest.

CHAPTER THREE

A chattering noise roused Mallory from her blissful slumber, disturbing her sweet dream. Darn mouse. She thought she had seen the last of him when the new tenants moved into the apartment next to hers. They were Swiss and fond of cheese.

"Shush, mouse," she muttered sleepily, snuggling deeper into the fluffy pillow beneath her head and wriggling farther into the featherbed under her body.

She rubbed her cheek back and forth against the pillowcase, thinking it was the soft shirt of the mystery man in her dream. The vision was so vivid, she swore she could smell his subtle cologne.

The chattering increased.

"Cut that out, will you?"

Instead of complying, something furry touched her face and then plopped across it. Too big to be a mouse. Had to be Duke. Whenever he knew she was waking up, he showed his affection by trying to smother her. Just like a man.

"Get off, Duke."

He didn't budge.

"Oh, for heaven's sake!" She took hold of him and moved him to her chest, wondering about the strange feel of his fur.

She lifted her head, shook away the dark curtain of hair covering her face . . .

And found herself eyeball to eyeball with a hideous lion-faced creature who chose that moment to screech.

"Rosie!" a male voice barked, rising over the din of Mallory's hysteria.

The small monkey catapulted from her chest, jetted across the carpeting, and flung itself at the man standing in the threshold. The monkey wrapped its long, thin arms around the man's neck and hid its face in his shirt.

"Hush, my girl," the man soothed—the monkey! Mallory's terror was clearly unimportant.

Two things were patently obvious in that moment.

One, Dorothy was not in Kansas anymore asleep in her bedroom in Auntie Em and Uncle Henry's ramshackle farmhouse.

And two, the towering giant staring at her was not the Wizard of Oz.

Perhaps that was why she couldn't stop screaming.

The man strode forward, picked up the glass of water beside her bed . . . and tossed the contents in her face!

Mallory sputtered and wiped the water from her

eyes. "Why you big je—" Words backed up in her throat as she got her first good look at her attacker.

To say his face was a chiseled masterpiece and his body a monument to male perfection seemed inadequate somehow.

In fact, he could pass for Kevin Sorbo from "Hercules" if he would remove that ridiculous, and askew, bow tie and the tweed coat with the patched leather elbows and those hideous thin-rimmed spectacles that made him look like some turn-of-the-century . . . scientist.

Freddie's words came back to her.

I'm picturing Johnny Wad in a tweed coat.

No, this man could not possibly be Dexter Harrington. She wouldn't believe it.

"My apologies, madam. I was merely trying to alleviate your bout of histrionics. Your caterwauling was scaring my monkey."

That comment shook Mallory from her daze. "Your monkey scared me first!"

"Quite unintentionally, I assure you. Rosie is very friendly. She would never have hurt you."

"Of course! How silly of me. I should have known. I imagine it's an everyday occurrence to have a monkey sitting on one's face!"

"She often plays in this room. Her stuffed animal is underneath your pillow."

Great. She was sleeping in the monkey's playroom. What was next? A turtle in the bathtub? "Look, buster. You better get out of here before I call the earl."

"That's not necessary."

"Oh?" She folded her arms across her chest, but couldn't still the sense of dread fluttering in her stomach. "And why is that?"

"Because I'm the earl."

Bad to worse, Mallory thought with a groan, tossing the bedcovers over her head.

"Mal? Are you all right? I heard screaming and—Well, hello."

Mallory eased down a corner of the covers to see Freddie framed in the doorway wearing her jogging outfit—a skimpy, red sports bra and matching bike shorts—showing off her perfectly toned body. What happened to jet lag? The girl seemed immune to external forces.

Cummings appeared in the doorway next, sparing Freddie only a cursory glance, which earned him an immediate jibe. "Oh, look. Bigfoot does exist."

"Still our bright and sunny self, I see," Cummings drawled before he turned his attention to Mallory. "I trust you slept well, Ms. Ginelli?"

"Yes, I did." *Until a few minutes ago,* she silently added. "And please call me Mallory."

Cummings nodded and then zeroed in on Freddie. "If you'll come with me, I'll be happy to draw you a map so you can find your way back here once you're finished . . ." His gaze took in her scantily clad figure without a flicker of interest. "Well, once you're done with whatever it is you plan to do in that outfit."

Freddie's back snapped into a rigid line. "You can take your map and shove it up—"

"Freddie!" Mallory warned.

Cummings quirked a brow at Freddie, a hint of amusement in his dark eyes. Then he pivoted on his heel. "Come along." He headed out into the hallway, obviously expecting Freddie to follow.

Freddie flashed a flabbergasted expression at

Mallory. "Come along! Who does he . . . how dare . . . if he thinks . . . Oh, now that tears it!" She stormed out of the room, hot on Cummings's heels.

Leaving Mallory alone with the nutty professor.

She found herself being scrutinized by a pair of round black eyeballs as the monkey peered at her over the earl's all too broad shoulders, its gaze tentative yet curious.

Mallory's own tentative yet curious gaze moved from the monkey's face down the length of the earl's back. She wrinkled her nose at the ugly brown tweed jacket he wore, which covered what she suspected to be fabulous buttocks.

She silently harumphed. He was all right, if one liked the Greek god type. Not her. She preferred men who didn't have the shoulders of a linebacker.

"Intriguing," the man muttered, turning to face her, something whirring behind those unusual blue-gray eyes.

Instead of demanding he remove his person from her room, Mallory said tersely, "What's intriguing?"

"Hmm?" His gaze centered on her, a slight frown creasing his forehead as if he had just been reminded of her presence.

"I asked what was so intriguing."

"Your friend."

Mallory was not surprised. Men could not resist Freddie. Obviously the sex professor had succumbed in the mere minute he had been in her presence. Why Mallory felt upended by that discovery, she couldn't say.

Well, at least she had nothing to worry about. She would not be subjected to any untoward sexual advances or lustful innuendoes or being chased around a desk. And that was exactly how she wanted it. Strictly business. Right?

"What about her?" Mallory asked, expecting him to begin extolling the beauty of Freddie's eyes, the lush fullness of her lips.

Instead, he replied, "It appears your friend is enamored with Cummings."

Mallory's eyebrows rose into her hairline. "Freddie? Enamored with . . . my Freddie . . . the one who just . . . and Cummings?"

"Do you and Ms. Feldman have some sort of speech difficulties? I could help you with that if you'd like. It's merely a matter of—"

"I have no speech difficulties!" Mallory yanked the covers so hard she pulled them out at the end of the bed. "I'm simply amazed at your ridiculous observation." *You big, beautiful buffoon.* "It is so absolutely preposterous it defies comment." But she commented anyway. "If anyone is enamored, it's Cummings. Every man falls in love with Freddie as soon as she flashes those baby blues."

With his forefinger, her host pushed up his sliding eyeglasses and then adjusted his monkey. "Nonsense, madam. As you may have noticed, I have not succumbed. Perhaps if you understood the psychological make-up behind that emotion referred to as 'love,' you might recognize the peculiarities and nuances of body language."

That emotion referred to as love? If that wasn't pleasantly cold and impersonal.

"I suspect your reaction correlates with a more fundamental, linear-style thinking," he went on. "And perhaps not viewing the scene as a cohesive whole."

A cohesive whole? Oh, she would give him a cohesive whole all right—one he would not soon forget! "If Freddie had an ax, Cummings would be minus a head right now."

The earl regarded her with a bland expression. "If you would but let me conclude my analogy."

"How rude of me to interrupt. It isn't as if I've been abruptly awakened, doused with a glass of cold water, or had anyone imply I'm stupid or that I don't know my own best friend—and all before breakfast, no less."

"I was merely trying to say that I believe the passive-aggressive tendency your friend displays cloaks her insecurity, which most likely stems from long held feelings of inadequacy."

Feelings of inadequacy? Freddie?

Mallory gritted her teeth. "Are you quite finished?"

"Quite."

"Good. Now I have a rebuttal."

"A rebuttal?" A single dark eyebrow slowly rose above the rim of his glasses, his look one of disbelief, as if any opinion other than his own could not possibly have merit. "And what is that, madam?"

"This!" Mallory yanked the pillow from behind her head and flung it at him, satisfied when it smacked him squarely in the face. The monkey squawked and climbed on top of his head.

The man blinked, his gaze moving between her and the pillow at his feet. His silky brown hair was mussed, his glasses tilted to the side, and his already askew bow tie was now even more crooked.

"If one didn't know better," he said in a measured tone, "one might believe you were displeased with my conclusion, madam."

Displeased? How dense was this guy? "Call me madam one more time and I swear by all that's holy I'll slug you!"

"Violence is not necessary, ma—" He paused when he caught her look. "Ms. Ginelli."

He plucked the monkey from his head and stroked her, soothing her jittery nerves. Mallory couldn't help but notice his hands as they moved over the monkey's back. They were large yet lean, strong yet oddly gentle. Hands Paganini would envy. Hands that could make a woman wonder how they would caress her body.

Good Lord, what was she thinking! Dexter Harrington was a first-class dweeb and an inconsiderate lout. She suspected his idea of fun was playing astrophysics charades. Books on the theory of relativity and quantum mechanics and the entire, unabridged history of the woolly mammoth probably got his blood pumping. How a man so utterly starched could be an expert in human sexuality, Mallory couldn't begin to fathom.

"Why do you have a monkey in your house?" she asked when the monkey in question started rifling through his hair.

"I am currently researching Rosie as she goes through the process of choosing a mate. Monkeys are, in many aspects, like human beings in their pair-bonding methods. And the tamarin, like its cousin the marmoset, generally chooses a single mate for life."

That was what she got for asking. She could only be glad he hadn't elaborated.

"But I digress. We have business to discuss." He checked his watch. "I shall have my butler, Quick, bring you a breakfast tray and then return for you in approximately an hour.''

"Gee, a whole hour? How kind of you.''

"Think nothing of it,'' he said, obviously missing her sarcasm. Monkey and master then headed toward the door. As the earl opened it, he tossed over his shoulder, "And don't worry about the test. I'm sure you'll do well enough. Cummings has a great deal of faith in you, and I, in turn, have a great deal of faith in Cummings.''

Test? "What test?''

"It's more a survey, actually.''

Had she come all the way to England for a survey? "And what exactly is this test-survey about?''

On the threshold, he turned, and with a straight face replied, "Why, sex, of course.''

CHAPTER FOUR

"The girl will not suit," Dexter told Cummings as he searched for his notes on frigidity and impotence hidden somewhere among the neatly disorganized stacks that seemed to clone themselves every few days. Each time he entered his office, he had to steer himself through a maze to find his desk. "I don't know what you could have been thinking. She looks like a child. How could she possibly help me with my"—he cleared his throat—"problem."

"She's not a child, Dex. She's twenty-six years old. And you're only thirty-two. Not Methuselah."

Dexter snorted. "I have a pair of loafers that look older than her. Damn it all! Where the hell are those papers?"

Cummings rose from his seat in front of Dexter's massive, cluttered desk and retrieved a folder from the middle of a haphazard pile of papers and article

clippings. "Here. Now, about Ms. Ginelli ..."
Cummings prompted, returning to his chair.

Dexter thumbed through the file. "What about
her? As I said, I don't see how we could possibly
function well as a team—considering the project.
I expected a mature woman. Not some child that
looks as if she should be in one of my freshman
classes."

"Why does it matter how she looks or her age?
If she can help you with your, er, problem, then I
don't see an issue."

Dexter frowned, thinking about the sprite-sized
woman who had challenged him as she lay propped
in the middle of a bed that nearly swallowed her.

He hadn't meant to invade her privacy, but Rosie
had leapt from his arms and darted into the room
before he could stop her. His pacing in front of
his guest's bedroom door for a half hour had had
nothing to do with Rosie's antsy behavior, he
assured himself.

Perhaps he had been mildly curious to see her
in the light of day, if only to assure himself that
his mind had exaggerated what his hands had felt
as he had carried her sleeping form to one of the
spare bedrooms the night before. A silky mass of
inky black tresses had veiled her face as she nestled
against his chest, rubbing her cheek back and forth
over his shirt and purring like a contented cat.

He told himself it was merely the dynamics of
the male species and the inherent need to be the
protector that had caused his heart to step up a
beat as he held her. Such jolts were no more than
a biological reaction and a component of thousands of years of conditioned male behavior.

Yet his conscience prodded him, saying it was

more than that. Something about Mallory Ginelli scared the hell out of him—and from that fear the ridiculous idea of making her take a sex quiz had been born. That was the only thing his befuddled mind could produce on short notice.

Perhaps he thought his request would offend her and she would leave. Perhaps she was calling the airport at that very moment? Part of him felt relieved by the prospect. But a bigger part of him was frustrated, warning him that he was once again taking the easy way out and not facing his problem.

"Did you read the book I left for you?" Cummings queried. "I marked specific chapters."

Dexter's gaze drifted to the paperback book entitled *Now and Forever*, by Zoe Wilde. He had reached for it a few times, but could not justify reading something that had no basis in theoretical fact, and which was, for all intents and purposes, *fiction.*

Fiction! What could he possibly learn from such a thing? The idea of gleaning anything even remotely useful from a publication that pulled supposition out of the air seemed patently ridiculous.

And he was a professor. A man known for speaking knowledgeably about those things steeped in fact. If it could not be weighed or measured, it simply did not exist.

Yet, much to his dismay, romance novels were creeping into the study of sexuality so that in a roundabout way, he and Mallory Ginelli had something in common. They both dealt with the mysteries of human behavior.

Case in point was the file he held in his hand, an in-depth study of *Madame Bovary.* Emma Bovary would have been an avid romance reader. She lived from assignation to assignation, yearning for the excitement of a secret touch, a forbidden embrace.

Yet her obsession would ultimately be her downfall. She loved to love and was therefore blinded by that dark need, allowing verbal innuendo and calculated deceit to break her resistance, make her surrender to the primal hunger within.

" 'In my soul, you are like a Madonna on a pedestal, revered, pure, and immaculate.' "

Dexter didn't realize he had recited the words aloud until Cummings murmured dryly, "Why, Dex, I'm flattered."

Dexter scowled. "Don't be an ass."

"But it's what I live for. Why deny me?"

"Don't you have something to sort?"

"You know, Dex, if you'd wax poetic like that to a woman, you might find yourself called the sex doctor for more than one reason."

Dexter's scowl deepened, but he made no remark. What could he say? Cummings was right.

Talking. That was part of the problem. It wasn't as if he hadn't tried to speak his thoughts to a person of the female persuasion, but whenever he opened his mouth to tell a woman she was pretty, what came out was, "Why do some women endow men with the power to dominate them?"

Needless to say, the conversation ended quickly after that.

He just didn't know what to say or do with females. Hard to believe considering his field of study. Yet the cold truth was, he was monumentally average and grippingly dull, which was why it always surprised him when a woman approached him in a purely hormonal way. And they did. A goodly number, in fact.

Quite a few remarked that he looked like some chap named Kevin Sorbo, whoever he may be. Yet, whenever Dexter attempted to dazzle a female with his sparkling repartee and Ernest Rutherford charm, all that came out was clinical commentary.

He could speak for hours on the phenomenon of the "soft" male syndrome caused by estrangement from a father figure and the prevailing role of an overprotective mother. But women, he had discovered, didn't want to hear about science—and science was all he knew.

They expected Casanova in a lab coat.

They got Elmer "Dud" in suspenders.

"If you concentrated on wooing a female with the same vigor you put into your studies," Cummings continued, "you could overcome that enigma-wrapped-in-a-riddle label that clings to you with a stench that could offend b.o."

"How eloquently put," Dexter murmured dryly.

"It's all in the delivery."

"Need I remind you what I have a Ph.D. in? I know every possible way to pleasure a woman." Trouble was, he hadn't gotten many chances to practice what he preached.

"Wooing and pleasuring are two different things, old boy. And, *need I remind you*, it is necessary to get close to a woman in order to pleasure her?"

"Why do I tell you anything?"

"Because you're a reclusive prick, and reclusive pricks don't have a plethora of friends."

Cummings said the words so straight faced that Dexter couldn't help a begrudging smile. "A prick, am I? That sounds remarkably unlike you—and remarkably like the waspish-tongued Ms. Feldman."

That wiped the smile from Cummings's face. "And how would you know?"

"Your voices carried quite clearly down the hallway, making me privy to some interesting exposition."

"Welcome to my nightmare," Cummings muttered, his lips compressing into a grim line. "Apparently, the girl was never taught the value of using an inside voice when one is—How shall I put it?"

"Inside, perhaps?"

"Quite. Ms. Whimsy she's not."

"But you must admit, she is somewhat fetching." Although not his type.

A vision of Mallory Ginelli rose in Dexter's mind. Light hazel eyes with flecks of gold, a pert nose, and lush lips with a bedeviling tiny black mole in the top right corner, which had, much to his annoyance, captured his gaze time and again during their less-than-amicable first encounter.

"Do you see the outfits the girl wears?" Cummings asked, sounding disgusted. "A sausage casing would fit looser. You can see—Never mind. And what do you mean she's fetching? Why are you looking? Ah, I mean, she's all right. Now, if you want fetching, then Ms. Ginelli is the one. She may not be a knockout in the classic sense, I admit, but—"

"What do you mean she's not a knockout? Ah, I mean, you're letting Ms. Feldman rattle your usual unflappable demeanor."

"God, man, can you blame my unflappable demeanor?" Cummings returned, clearly disgruntled. "Now I know how Superman felt in the presence of Kryptonite, how the Egyptians felt when

Moses sent the plagues down upon them. I might just prefer locusts, frogs, and boils to that woman.''

"I'm sure that could be arranged."

Cummings shot him a look that could have disintegrated stone. "Just imagine, I could be relaxing in the soothing baths of Bath had it not been for having to baby-sit some forked-tongue she-cat that makes my scalp burn like it's being massaged by Lucifer. Do you know what the woman said to me when I foolishly—and never again, mind you—tried to compliment her?"

"I'm all aquiver with wonder."

"She said she'd puke, but it would be a waste of good vomit. The bloody things I do in the name of science!"

Dexter silently chuckled, enjoying his friend's discomfit, especially since little ruffled Cummings. "Hmm. I seem to recall some intriguing pet name she gave you. Now, what was it?"

Cummings glowered. "Chief Black Cloud?"

"No, not that one."

"The missing link?"

"No."

"Yenta?"

"No."

"Caligula?"

"No."

"A big bag of duh?"

Dexter shook his head and then scratched his chin, thinking. "Ah yes! I remember now. Huckleberry Dumbbell. Rather amusing, wouldn't you say?"

"No, I damn well wouldn't say," Cummings bit out. "And I wouldn't laugh so quickly, my good man. She said you looked like an overinflated gas bag and that you were probably as much fun as swimming naked in a barrel full of live jellyfish."

"The hell you say!"

"Ha! It isn't so pleasant on the receiving end, now, is it?"

No, Dexter thought, but it probably wouldn't sting so much if it wasn't true. "Clearly the girl has not turned out to be a delightful conundrum."

"A masterpiece of understatement if I ever heard one. But enough with trying to change the subject. Did you read Ms. Ginelli's book or not?"

"Or not," Dexter returned gruffly, not feeling inclined to discuss that topic. "I didn't have time. I had a lecture to prepare on *Madame Bovary*, defining the dynamics of aberrant sexual and social behavior manifesting in female dsyfunction."

With an aggrieved sigh, Cummings rose from the chair. "You're running out of time, Dex. You have to stop avoiding the issue. The girl is here. And your future is at stake." That said, his friend turned and left the room.

Dexter lowered the folder in his hand and stared at the door, mulling over Cummings's words.

You're running out of time.

Damn the man, why did he have to be right?

He shot a glance at Mallory's book, his hand clenching and unclenching at his side. "Hell," he muttered and snatched it up. Sinking down into the chair behind his desk, he flipped the book open to the chapter Cummings had marked and began to read.

He touched her gently, almost reverently, his thumb sweeping lightly over her nipple, eliciting a moan of pure aching need that sprung from the very depths of her.

"You humble me, lady," he said, his voice husky with promise as he slowly lowered her to the bed, his body enveloping hers, heat consuming them, dragging them into a sweet conflagration.

Her back arched as he took a straining peak into his mouth, drawing it higher and higher with each pull, his tongue circling and flicking without releasing his hold.

His fingers teased the other tight bud. She writhed against him, fanning the flames of his desire, pushing his passion to the brink and his control to the edge of his endurance.

Willingly, she separated her thighs, and he moved between them. His fingers sought the engorged pulse point and found her hot, wet, and ready.

He groaned deep in his throat as he stroked her, fast then slow, back and forth, bringing her to a fevered pitch. She cried out when he slipped a finger inside.

His head dropped to her shoulder, his moan mingling with hers as she convulsed around his finger. He had never felt so alive, so powerful as he did at that moment. She completed him. Strengthened him.

Taught him the true meaning of being a man.

She wriggled her hips in silent plea, perhaps sensing there was more, wanting the consummation as much as he did, seeking surcease in the joining.

He positioned his hard length where his finger had been, sinking into her warmth only a little bit, death and rebirth clashing as her inner lips clenched around him.

"Are you sure?" he asked, his control hard won.

She smiled. It devastated him, broke him down, and built him up again. His heart hammered against his ribs as something he had never felt before awoke inside him, rousing like a long-dormant dragon.

She cupped his cheeks. "Yes," she breathed. "I'm sure." Heady emerald eyes gazed up at him as she said the words he knew were reflected in his eyes. "I love you—only you. Now and forever."

Slowly, Dexter closed the book, dragged in a lungful of air, and made his first observation.

He was sweating.

CHAPTER FIVE

Mallory stared unblinkingly at the two sheets of paper set out before her that made up the all-important survey, the purpose of which she had yet to discover but which she suspected had nothing to do with her opinions on sex—especially any preconceived notions she might have about the average length of a man's penis, per the first question—and more to do with testing her mettle. She shouldn't be angered by the earl's childish attempt to fluster her.

But she was. Most definitely.

"You can't actually want me to answer these questions?" she asked, pleased that her tone had achieved the perfect balance of outrage, umbrage, and censure.

Eyes that appeared silvery blue in the muted light leisurely elevated to meet hers. "I can't?" His face was set in its usual mask of seriousness. "Oh, but

I assure you, Ms. Ginelli, I can—and I do." As though the matter was settled, he dropped his gaze back to his papers.

"What for?"

He regarded her over the rim of his glasses. "Excuse me?"

"What do you need my answers for?"

"Our project."

"Which is?"

"I shall explain in due time."

At this rate he might be nursing the wounds she inflicted before he got the chance.

Mallory sighed inwardly. What was the point of arguing? Wasn't it a bit too late for protests? The six-foot-four, bespectacled Adonis had been secretive from the word go. So why should she expect more now? Besides, she had, in a way, sold her soul to Dexter Harrington, Ph.D.

The asking price: a mere twenty thousand dollars.

However, Mallory thought with a slowly spreading grin, that didn't mean she had to do things his way. Thankfully, the Good Lord had blessed her with a creative mind.

Using that imagination, she took pen and paper in hand and breezed through the survey in record time. "Finished," she chirped, slapping the test down on top of the material the earl was perusing.

He quirked that childish-antics-are-not-necessary eyebrow and then sat back in his chair. Mallory waited for his first reaction. It didn't take long. Slowly, he levered his gaze over the top of the papers, looking none too pleased.

"Is something the matter?" she inquired with feigned innocence.

"Of course not. Why should anything be the matter?"

I don't know. Perhaps because I said the average length of an erect penis is twenty-two inches? He never said she couldn't write in her own answers.

"Your responses are most original."

She treated him to a bright smile. "Why, thank you. I try to be different."

"And you do a commendable job, I assure you." Sarcasm fairly dripped from his words. "However, if we are to proceed, I need you to circle one of the answers provided."

Mallory folded her arms across her chest. "And if I don't?" she asked in a challenging tone.

He shrugged. "That is your prerogative, of course. But I will then have no choice but to void our contract. That will be *my* prerogative. I'm sure you understand."

Oh, she understood all right. Either she did it his way or the deal was off. Mallory shot him a glare she hoped conveyed what she thought of his backhanded tactics even as she grudgingly gave him a point for holding his own.

Stiffly, she held her hand out. He laid the sheets of paper down gently on top of her palm. Once more, she swiped up her pen and set to answering the questions. Then, reluctantly, she slid the papers over to him and scowled at his bent head.

For five solid minutes her host *hmm*ed and *aah*ed over her answers, each syllable he uttered twanging Mallory's last nerve. "Well?" she demanded when he said nothing.

He steepled his fingers beneath his chin. "Well, what?"

"How did I do?"

"Do?"

"On the test!"

He regarded her with those implacable blue eyes. "It wasn't so much a test as it was a survey."

"And the survey says?" Never had she expected to utter that coined phrase, no matter how fitting the occasion.

"Well, if you're sure you want to know . . . ?"

That didn't sound promising. Mallory wondered if she really wanted to find out. But it was too late. She had demanded answers, and she was one Ginelli who never backed away from the truth.

"Of course I want to know. Now, what did that thing"—she waved a finger at the paper— "tell you?"

"I must confess, it was rather intriguing. Had you not been seated in front of me, I would have thought I was reading the responses of a sixty-year-old unmarried female from the Midwest with religious affiliations. One more wrong answer and I would have believed you to be British, as we have a tendency toward prudishness."

Prudish! Her? The scalding kettle of passion?

What would her legions of fans think if they heard Zoe Wilde was a prude?

No, not Zoe Wilde, she corrected. Mallory Ginelli.

She sprung from the suffocating embrace of the high-backed chair. "You must have read it wrong!"

"A rare occurrence, I assure you. I've been doing this for quite some time."

Mallory stomped toward the window. "Sixty-year-old female my behind," she muttered. "I was just nervous. I've never been good at taking tests. I tense up—and why am I explaining this to you?"

"I understand your chagrin—"

"I'm not chagrined!"

"Nevertheless," he continued in a disbelieving tone, "your answers make one wonder how you . . ." He paused.

She whirled around to face him, hands on hips. "How I what?" she demanded.

If Mallory didn't know better, she might think he looked uneasy. "How you write such heated"—he cleared his throat—"love scenes."

Curiosity overrode Mallory's pique. "You've read my books?" That greatly surprised her. She wouldn't have imagined it in a million years.

"No, I haven't read your books—exactly."

"What does that mean?"

Now the man definitely appeared uncomfortable. He shifted in his chair. "I read a few pages a short while ago." He opened his top drawer and pulled out her book *Now and Forever*, one of her steamiest novels. Also one of her favorites.

Every time Mallory saw the book, she smiled—a small, secret smile of joy that she and probably many other writers possessed. And the joy was not because of the lovely cover or the challenge the story had posed or just being thankful another book was finally completed.

No, the smile was for the love of the story, for uniting two people who had so desperately been meant for each other. Though the names may change and the settings differ, the message remained the same.

Love conquered all.

Here was where she put forth her passion, her desire, her longing, her despair. Every emotion flowed from a place she tapped only for her books, a part of her she had never given to anyone.

Slowly, she moved back to the chair, placing her hands on top. "You . . . read one of the love scenes?"

He nodded.

The knowledge felt intimate, even though she knew thousands of people had read the same thing. But she had never thought about it, never pictured a man's gaze sweeping over her words.

And never had she thought it would be a man who looked as this one did—or who had the capacity to see what others may not, to recognize the passion between the pages was not pretend, but real and existing inside her.

Get a grip! This is the nerd sex doctor, for goodness sake!

The sex doctor . . . who chose that moment to remind her of his profession by saying, "I'm interested to know how you feel about copulation."

Mallory choked.

He rose from his chair, probably with the intention of slapping her on the back with one of those Paul Bunyon hands.

"I'm fine!" she practically shrieked, relieved when he shrugged and retook his seat, his words replaying in her head like a scratched record.

I'm interested to know how you feel about copulation . . . copulation . . . copulation.

He sounded as if he were speaking about the weather. *Lovely morning, isn't it? Would you like some milk in your tea? Lemon? Sugar?*

Copulation?

Was he asking her opinion on the subject or inviting her to indulge in a little afternoon delight?

And why was she just sitting there blinking instead of telling him to mind his own damn business?

She swallowed. "Copulation?" The word came out a squeak.

He stuck a finger in the collar of his shirt, as if it suddenly fit too tightly around his neck. "It is just that you write so . . . with such . . . quite . . ." He frowned and then cleared his throat. "One can't help but compare your responses on the survey to the heated passages in your book. If one didn't know better, one might think you were two different people."

And one might be right, Mallory silently replied. In many ways, she was two different people. Zoe wrote the burning passion, the longing.

The hot, sweaty lust.

Mallory, on the other hand, made sure the manuscript got to Karen on time, took care of the bills, and kept her family out of jail.

She decided to turn the tables on him, asking, "How do you feel about copulation?"

His brows drew together in a heavy frown. "The question is moot. We were discussing you."

"No, *you* were discussing me. Now I'm asking the questions."

Those linebacker shoulders flinched under today's tweed jacket. "I'm the scientist and you're the subject."

"Let's get something clear right now. I'm not your subject. And while we're discussing who's playing what role, I think now is a good time to tell me what I'm doing here. My editor said you were a fan."

"A fan?" he scoffed. "In my rare recreational time, I have enjoyed the offerings of such notables as John Locke and Bertrand Russell, whose work in epistemology, the how-do-we-know-what-we-know philosophy, also referred to as the origin of knowledge, is most thought provoking. If I'm feeling particularly cerebral, I indulge in Plato and the Sanskrit. As you can well see, romance novels would not be high on the list of my chosen reading material. Cummings, for reasons unknown, seems to enjoy such senseless frivolity.''

Senseless frivolity! Oh, how she would like to sic the entire institution of the Romance Writers of America on him. They would pound his bones into mulch and spread his desecrated remains around his bushes to keep the dandelions away.

"Sometimes," he went on, "I think Cummings fancies himself a Viking named Thor the Mighty, alone on a ship full of voluptuous wenches who throw themselves at his feet. They tell him they can no longer resist his overwhelming virility and he simply must show them the delights of the flesh." His lordship darted an embarrassed glance in her direction. "Uh, or at least I think so."

"I see. And was it some weird fantasy you had that brought me here? If so, you can just forget it. I'm no man's sex toy."

He quirked a brow. "Sex toy?"

For the first time, Mallory saw something besides bland inquiry in his eyes.

It had been replaced by amusement! He was laughing at her!

"Madam, I have no intention of ravaging you. I give you my word as a scholar and a gentleman that making love to you is the last thing on my mind—the very last."

The very last, she silently mimicked. He had made

his point. Had it been necessary to bring it home with a full frontal thrust?

"Good! Because I'm taken anyway." That lie spiraled out of nowhere. But she had to salvage her pride. Besides, she was glad she had cleared up that issue. Let this guy know there would be no hanky-panky—even if she did wonder if his chest was as solid as it looked beneath the light blue twill shirt he wore.

"Taken, are you?"

Why did he have to sound so incredulous? Was it that hard to picture her with a boyfriend? Perhaps even a fiancé?

She was pretty. She was perky. She had a lot to offer.

So why are you alone?

"That's right, I'm taken! So keep your mitts to yourself."

He leaned back in his chair and regarded her. "I knew nothing about this."

"And why would you know anything about it? It's not as if my life is any of your business. You have your secrets. Well, I have mine!"

His humor fled at that remark. "That will be all for now," he muttered, bowing his head over his papers again.

Was he actually dismissing her? Like some servant? "You may be through with me, but I'm not through with you. I want some answers. I've had enough of this cloak-and-dagger bit. I want to know what this 'job' is."

"You will. All in—"

"Due time. I'm getting tired of hearing that. Just because you paid for my services doesn't mean I'll tolerate being treated like the hired help."

"Certainly that is not my intention."

"What is your intention?"

"All—"

"Do not say it," she warned through gritted teeth. "Every time I hear those four words, I feel like the people in that Abbott and Costello skit who go berserk when Costello mentions the Susquehanna Hat Company."

"Abbott and Costello?"

"Don't tell me you—Never mind. Look, I want to know why I'm here. My time is very valuable."

Dexter regarded his fiery-tempered guest, a muscle working in his jaw. He knew that had it not been for his money, Mallory Ginelli would not be standing before him now.

Under normal circumstances, he couldn't have attracted the attention of someone like her, a woman who wrote of exciting men. Men with charm and endless wit who could melt a woman's heart with a single boyish smile. The type of man he had never been. He could see it in her eyes that she knew it, too. For some reason, the knowledge angered him.

"I believe you have been well compensated for your time. But, by all means, feel free to leave if you are so inclined."

She eyed him warily. "Just like that?"

"Just like that. You're not being held prisoner. Simply return the money I advanced you, and we can go our separate ways."

Dexter watched her face cloud over at the mention of the money. He knew all about her misguided sister. He did not step into a venture unprepared. He had researched the woman now standing in front of him and concluded that money and a fully stocked library would be his best chance to get her to come to England.

She worried her bottom lip, which drew his attention to its fullness—and lower, to where the swell of her breasts teased the eye beneath the large lavender T-shirt she wore. He imagined she had lovely breasts, pert, perfectly proportioned to her slim frame, but enough to fill a man's hands. Her skin would be smooth, warm, her body firm . . .

Dear God, what was the matter with him? He was not some randy schoolboy who couldn't control himself. Even in Lady Sarah's presence, with her striking violet eyes, auburn hair, and model figure, his animalistic stirrings were minimal at best. He had experienced nothing like what he felt at that moment staring at the pony-tailed girl from New York.

Dexter remembered what he had said to Cummings earlier, that he and this hellion would not suit, but it was not for any of the reasons he had given.

The truth was, when Mallory had laid her head against his chest in sleep, he had felt something, like a rusty door creaking open. If he peeled back the layers, he would recognize that he was attracted to her. Certainly not an odd reaction.

Had it been any other man but him.

With his line of work, he came in contact with a lot of women, but he had begun to believe himself immune to them, as if he had been vaccinated from feeling the things a man usually experienced in the presence of a beautiful woman.

But Mallory was not a beautiful woman. Not in the classic sense at least. She was petite, her features soft yet average, no one thing standing out . . .

except her eyes. They were riveting, the light color a marked contrast against her dark, thick hair. The ends of her eyes were slightly tipped, giving them a hint of the exotic.

He wondered at his motivation for not telling her the reason he had brought her to England. He had no cause to delay any longer. So why, then, did he want to wait a few more days before revealing the truth?

"So, Ms. Ginelli, what will it be? Shall I have Cummings make plane reservations?" Dexter disliked his heavyhanded tactics even though he knew he would do the same thing if presented with the problem again.

Vulnerability flashed in her eyes for a brief moment before she tilted her chin up, exhibiting a great deal of pride to go along with her hot-blooded temperament. "I've come all this way. I might as well stay a few more days."

Dexter nodded, wondering at his relief. "We will be heading to Braden Manor, my country home in Wales, come the morning. Please be ready to leave by nine A.M."

"Leave?"

"Yes. Is that a problem?" He hoped she wouldn't make another fuss. As Cummings had so eloquently pointed out, he was running out of time. He had to be alone with the girl, away from London and Lady Sarah. Secluded. And Braden Manor was as secluded as it got, nothing around for miles. No tongues to wag. He could carry out his project in complete secrecy. And should the girl decide she wanted to leave again, it wouldn't be quite so easy.

He wondered at his reasoning for not wanting her to run away and told himself that his actions had nothing to do with attraction and everything to do with simple logic.

A man whose days were numbered had no time to waste.

"Fine," she said in a clipped tone. "Until the morning, then."

Dexter inclined his head. "Until the morning." He watched her leave, perplexed as to why he felt a need to call her back. "Women," he muttered, swiping up his papers, ready to banish Ms. Ginelli from his mind—which he managed to do for all of five seconds.

Slowly his gaze lifted and slid to his closed office door, the words he had spoken earlier coming back to him.

Making love to you is the last thing on my mind.

That should be the truth.

But it wasn't.

The words she had spoken haunted him next.

You have your secrets.

He did.

The question was, how had they suddenly multiplied?

CHAPTER SIX

"Men are like dogs. You can either neuter them or let them hump your leg. I prefer neutering; lets them know who's boss."

Mallory sighed as Freddie lobbed yet another gratuitous slam at Cummings, as she had been doing for over an hour.

They were on their way to Dexter's estate in Wales, and for the entire trip Freddie had been relentless in her attempts to get a rise out of Cummings—all to no avail. The man merely smiled at her like a benevolent father with an unruly daughter or ignored her altogether—even after Freddie asked him if he bought his cologne at the slaughterhouse. Mallory had to admire Cummings. He possessed great stamina and willpower to deflect Freddie Feldman at her worst.

Having spent time with Cummings the day before, Mallory had discovered Dexter's secretary had other good qualities as well, among them charm, wit, and a great deal of loyalty to his friend.

Since Dexter had holed up in his office the previous day in what Mallory suspected was an attempt to ignore her so that she wouldn't pepper him with any more questions, which she had almost done on a number of occasions, Cummings had acted as gracious host.

In fact, had it not been for Cummings, Mallory probably would have given in to her overactive imagination and her rising anger at being put off by the professor and told Dexter to stuff his "project" down his jockey shorts.

"Dex is not a bad guy once you get to know him," Cummings had said to her the day before as he studied the chessboard in front of him while they sat at a wrought-iron table nestled under an ancient oak tree with far-reaching limbs.

She had beaten Cummings twice, and had thought that he was either a truly rotten player or it was his way of being a gentleman or, and more likely, he was attempting to mollify her irritation at his employer by letting her win.

She captured his knight with her pawn. "I don't know if I'll be around long enough to get to know him."

He retaliated by taking her rook. "He has a lot on his mind right now."

"Oh? Like what?"

"It's not my place to tell you."

What was it with these men? Were they playing some elaborate version of I'll give you fifty guesses? "Well, I wish someone would tell me something."

He must have heard the frustration in her voice because he sat back, regarding her for a moment as if weighing what he was going to say. "Dex is a complex man. He doesn't let too many people get close."

Mallory didn't have to be a member of a think tank to realize Dexter rarely opened himself up for scrutiny. He wore his aloofness like a badge of honor. She wondered what a person had to do to gain admittance to his inner sanctum.

"If I stay, I'll remember to keep my distance."

Cummings gave a nearly imperceptible shake of his head. "That's what everyone does," he said, a somber note to his voice. "If people would just get to know him, they'd discover a man who would walk through fire to help them, who'd give the shirt off his back if they needed it, and who would risk being mocked by his colleagues to save one small monkey from death."

"Rosie?"

He nodded.

Mallory remembered the way the monkey had clung to Dexter the morning in her bedroom. She had been too angry at the time to see that Rosie was more than simply a research project to Dexter.

"Why are you telling me this?" she asked.

"I don't know. Maybe I sense you two are kindred spirits."

"Kindred spirits?" Mallory scoffed. "We are like night and day. Two people couldn't be any more different."

"Perhaps." He shrugged. "Then again, you might be surprised what you discover if you take a closer look."

The Rolls hit a rut in the road then, jolting Mallory back to the present. Her gaze slid to the man who had so recently occupied her thoughts.

Take a closer look. Could there be more to Dexter than what she saw?

She studied him covertly. He sat across from her, attired in brown loafers with tassels, dress socks, linen-colored khakis with a perfect pleat, white button-down shirt, and navy blue suspenders peeking from beneath a tweed jacket of speckled blue and green.

A little old-fashioned, but the outfit suited him. The color accentuated his olive complexion and a rugged jaw that looked as if it had never seen a day's stubble.

Instead of enjoying the lovely scenery, he held a musty old tome in his hands, obviously not one to miss an opportunity to study.

Mallory's gaze was drawn to the view outside her window, watching the ever-changing landscape slide by, little hamlets and rolling green hills, horses and sheep grazing.

Life seemed to move backward, as if they were driving into the past, a different era, a time of kings and ladies-in-waiting and legends.

The land was beautiful in a rugged, unsophisticated way, but one that lent it charm. Uplands interrupted by sudden, irregular crags and peaks. Hills barring the horizon. Rocks of every dimension and variety: knotted, gnarled, gray, green, purple-spotted. A place that seemed at once tragic, yet heroic and decisive.

This was the land of King Arthur and the Knights of the Round Table. Excalibur. Home to the Celts, Normans, Saxons, new Christianity, pagan Rome, and Druid lore. Mallory felt the magic of this place stir her. Something about it seeped into her bones.

"Oh, my," she gasped.

"What is it?" Freddie asked, sounding brusque now that she had lost game, set, and match to Cummings.

"That castle. It's . . . beautiful."

Freddie hung over her shoulder, and together they gaped at the castle atop the high crag in the distance. The structure seemed to rise out of the earth, conforming to its surroundings, one with the land. Neither town nor village crouched before it. It stood a solitary figure.

"The precipice must be at least five hundred feet high," Freddie mused, a hint of awe in her been-there-done-that New York voice.

"Nine hundred feet to be precise," the earl corrected.

Mallory glanced over at Dexter to find his gaze not on the view outside but locked on her. He appeared angry, though why he would be, she couldn't fathom. This was the first time she had seen him since she had glimpsed his hulking figure standing at an upper-floor window while she and Cummings had played chess the day before.

Freddie plopped back against the seat. "It's probably owned by some poor old geezer just aching for a little excitement in his declining years."

Cummings appeared ready to make a retort, but Mallory noted the nudge Dexter gave him. The combination of that gesture and the fact that something Freddie had said had stirred Cummings from the restraint he had shown all day told Mallory all she needed to know.

"That's your home, isn't it?" she asked Dexter.

Dexter had returned his attention to his book and only lifted his head nominally to meet her incredulous gaze. "How astute, Ms. Ginelli."

His brusque manner stilled any further questions she had thought to ask. If possible, he seemed to have grown even more aloof. Why?

Ten minutes later, in silence, they pulled up in front of the massive double-door entranceway to Braden Manor. To Mallory's surprise, Dexter held out his hand to help her from the car. She bumped into him when she momentarily lost her balance. Large hands gripped her upper arms, holding her firm. Dark, unreadable blue eyes searched her face.

Then, as if she had suddenly morphed into Medusa, he abruptly released her. Scooping up Rosie's cage sitting in the front seat of the Rolls, he disappeared inside the house. Mallory stared after him, her arms still tingling where he had held her.

"Don't mind him."

Mallory looked up to find Cummings standing at her shoulder, his gaze on the door Dexter had just disappeared through. Then he turned and gave her a reassuring smile.

Freddie came to stand on the other side of her. "Could we be any more isolated out here?" she griped.

"There's always Siberia," Cummings muttered under his breath, unable to hold his tongue any longer. Before Freddie could make a stinging comeback, he pointed to the large Gucci make-up case she rarely let out of her sight. "What did you pack in there? The Rock of Gibraltar?"

"Rock of—Oh, you're asking to be punted into the moat, Kato."

With a look that said, *I've heard that before,* Cummings plucked the suitcase from Freddie's hand

and marched toward the front door with a curt, "Follow me."

Freddie's furious glare drilled holes through Cummings's back. "Three words. Dead man walking." With that promise on her lips, Freddie stormed after the person who had taken the one thing she held most dear in the world.

Her cosmetics.

Mallory chuckled and pulled up the rear, taking her time to admire the architecture of the castle, awed at the history it represented.

She could almost see knights in chain mail sitting around a long trestle table in the enormous room she spied as she climbed the stone stairs. She pictured trenchers piled high with legs of mutton, goblets filled with dark, rich wine, a fire blazing brightly in the hearth, and two or three hounds waiting eagerly on the rush-strewn floor for a scrap of food.

Mallory caught up to Cummings as he was closing the door on an irate Freddie. "A man could bleed to death cutting himself on that girl's tongue," he muttered, wearing the only expression he seemed to sport in Freddie's presence: irritation.

Mallory muffled her smile and followed Cummings. They headed down a side corridor. Huge, ancient tapestries hung from the walls, their colors still remarkably vivid. She knew from her research that such tapestries had been used as more than decoration. They also had the practical purpose of keeping out the chill that seeped through the stones.

Gawking, Mallory nearly collided into Cummings's back when he halted in front of one of the numerous doorways lining the hall.

"This is your bedroom."

Embarrassed, Mallory skirted around him and stepped inside. She had barely taken three steps before stopping in her tracks to stare at the loveliness spread out in front of her.

A huge four-poster bed sat in the middle of the room, swathed in rich burgundy damask. On the beside table sat a tall glass vase filled with roses, pennyroyal, and sweet fennel, their sweet fragrance filling the air.

A lancet arch graced a deep window seat embrasure, giving a spectacular view for miles, and a fire already crackled in the belly of an arched stone fireplace.

"Will this room suit?" Cummings asked.

"Oh, yes," she murmured.

Cummings chuckled softly. "Good. Then I'll leave you to get settled. I have some work to do for Dex. I'll check on you in a little while."

The mention of Dexter reminded Mallory of the question she meant to ask Cummings, which she blurted out as he turned to leave. "Why do you stay?"

"What do you mean?"

She hadn't meant to be so abrupt, but it was too late to retract her words. "You're obviously well educated and could get employment anywhere. So why do you work for your best friend?"

An odd, almost painful expression briefly crossed Cummings's face. "Perhaps because he *is* my best friend." He shrugged. "And perhaps because I owe it to him."

His response struck her as strange. "Owe it to him?"

"Dex has done a lot for me."

"Like what?" she couldn't help asking.

He looked as if he would say no more, but then he shoved his hands in his pockets and leaned a shoulder against the doorjamb. "For years, Dex thought the only way he would ever have any friends was to buy them. He learned from example. His parents were too busy to give him the love and attention he craved, so they gave him material possessions instead."

"So you befriended him?"

Cummings couldn't quite meet her eyes as he replied, "I was one of the 'friends' Dex bought."

"Oh," she murmured, feeling an unexpected pang of sadness for Dexter, to think he would have to buy anyone's friendship, least of all Cummings, who had seemed so genuine.

As though discerning her disappointment in him, he said, "I grew up poor on a farm not far from here. Many nights I listened to my baby sister crying because she was hungry. We were all hungry, always tired and dirty. I vowed someday I'd find a way out. Then I met Dex and knew he was my ticket to a better life."

"Oxford?" she quietly said.

Cummings nodded, his expression grim. "He paid for it, all four years out of his trust fund. God, I was such an ass. I almost walked away from the truest friend I ever had. But my biggest regret will always be that I didn't realize until it was too late how much my family loved me . . . and how much my defection hurt them." He shook his head and swept a hand through his hair. "I'm sorry. I have to go."

Mallory stared at the empty doorway, Cummings's words hanging in the air, leaving her to think about a lonely boy who had wanted a friend so desperately he had had to buy one. It made her wonder if Dexter had bought her.

And if she had been bought, what did that make her? Mallory didn't want to know. Only one thing was clear at that moment. Before the day was through, she would know what it was Dexter wanted from her.

CHAPTER SEVEN

"Shall we retire to my study for a nightcap?"

Dexter's deep voice brought Mallory out of the trance she had dwelled in all through dinner. She had been replaying Cummings's words while she covertly stole glances at Dexter, looking for signs that might confirm he was not the stiff-necked brainiac he appeared to be.

She hadn't been the only person at the table consumed by their own thoughts. Her three dinner companions had been strangely quiet as well; conversation kept to a minimum.

"Ms. Ginelli?" Dexter prompted.

To her mortification, Mallory realized she was staring at him. "I'm sorry. What did you say?"

"I asked if you'd like a nightcap."

Mallory wondered why the thought of having a drink with Dexter made her nervous. He had yet to do anything even remotely untoward.

"Unless you're too tired," he said, studying her.

She couldn't quite make out the expression in his eyes. Anxiousness, perhaps? Was it possible he was as leery as she? "No, I'm not too tired." Even if she was, she needed answers, and she intended to get them.

He held his hand out to her and reluctantly Mallory took it. For the second time that day, neither of them moved once she stood in front of him.

Mallory didn't understand why she felt so strange when those blue eyes locked on her, or why it was suddenly hard to catch her breath. He came to his senses first, dropping her hand as if he held a red-hot poker.

No words passed between them as they headed down a network of mazelike corridors, passing suits of armor, crossed swords, old battle shields, and portraits of dead relatives whose eyes followed Mallory as if asking her if she knew what she was doing—which she had some doubts about at that moment.

She had found out that afternoon from one of the servants that the castle consisted of forty-two rooms in all, and at least fifteen generations of Harringtons had occupied Braden Manor at one time or the other.

Dexter came to a stop in front of a set of ornately carved double doors that looked thick and heavy. Yet, surprisingly, they opened with a quick twist of the knob.

Mallory stepped into the room and gasped. A vaulted ceiling soared above her head. Figures she couldn't quite make out were carved into the corner molding. She craned her neck back to admire the fresco and made contact with the solid wall of a man's chest. Namely, the professor.

Their gazes connected, and Mallory thought, *He's got the most incredible face.* High, chiseled cheekbones, a perfect aquiline nose, dark, slashing eyebrows showcasing those bluer than blue eyes, a strong jaw with an interesting dent in its center, and full lips that looked surprisingly soft for such a masculine countenance. She knew a strange urge to touch those lips and see if they felt as soft as they looked.

Enough of that! she scolded herself, straightening and quickly moving away from him.

In the center of the room, she made a slow circle. Row upon row of books lined the walls, floor to ceiling, long, sliding ladders giving access to the uppermost shelves.

"So many books," she murmured in awe.

As a child, she had always loved the smell of books, feeling like some strange addict as she stood in a secluded corner and held a book to her nose, as if by doing so she could breathe in the words it contained, absorb the knowledge, find forgetfulness within the pages. Books had become her solace; writing her outlet.

Dexter came up behind her, and the tiny hairs on the back of her neck stood up like static electricity. "Do you like it?" he asked, gesturing to the books. His voice was a low, vibrating hum, deep and very male. Nothing remotely nerdy. Why hadn't she noticed before?

"I think it's wonderful."

A tentative smile curved up the corner of his mouth, wavering slightly as if he did not smile often and had become rusty. "You may use any of the books you like. They are at your disposal."

The endearing, boyish quality of his smile made Mallory think about the young child who had lived in a castle with no siblings and forty-two rooms, who had led a lonely existence, a boy who quite possibly still dwelled inside the towering scientist now regarding her so intently.

"So did you grow up here?" She asked, wanting to know more about him.

The smile slowly slipped from his face. "For the most part. We owned several estates besides this one."

Several estates? Mallory was finally starting to see the extent of his wealth. But his money was the least important thing to her at that moment. It was the man who intrigued her more.

"I imagine you and your friends spent hours playing hide-and-seek." She wanted to hear the truth about his childhood from his lips instead of relying solely on Cummings's version. "With all the rooms, I bet the game could have gone on for days."

He averted his gaze. "My parents didn't like disruptions."

How could anyone consider a child's play disruptive? Especially a parent? To Mallory, kids were wonderful. Uninhibited and free.

She loved to watch them play, even if the joyful giggles and exuberant faces often made her wistful, wondering if she would ever have any children of her own or if she was doomed to forever take care of her family.

"I didn't enjoy such games anyway," he added,

as though an afterthought. "They were rather pointless."

"But that's the fun of it. The pleasure of not having anything more to do than be silly."

"We Harringtons are not known for our silliness." His words were crisp, yet a hint of pain passed fleetingly through his eyes.

"I can't imagine a child not being even a little silly." And she hated to think of anyone squashing that natural tendency, tamping it down until it no longer existed.

"Things are a bit different here in England, Ms. Ginelli. We believe in maintaining a certain decorum, keeping a tight rein on our behavior."

"Baloney."

A single dark brow rose at her remark. "Excuse me?"

"I said baloney. I don't believe that one bit. I saw children playing in a stream we passed on our way here. They didn't seem too concerned with decorum."

"They're different."

"Different? How so?"

"They are commoners."

Mallory's back went up at his snobbish attitude. "If that isn't the most elitist thing I've ever heard! Those children and their families are no different than you and I."

"You mistook my meaning. What I should have said is that those children can act differently. Their families aren't titled. They don't have the same strictures on them." A grimace touched the corners of his mouth. "They don't have hundreds of years of tradition to dictate their every move. They can create their own path."

If she didn't know better, she might think he sounded bitter about the life to which he had been born. "And you can't?"

"No," he murmured. "I can't."

Mallory couldn't understand that kind of logic, couldn't fathom being locked into a life she hadn't chosen for herself, forced to walk a path that wasn't of her own making.

"What were your parents like?" she asked, surprised to discover a rather strong desire to understand the forces that had molded Dexter.

A frown creased his brow, the question clearly making him uncomfortable. "Why do you want to know about my parents?"

Mallory shrugged, not wanting her curiosity to make him close up on her. "I am a writer after all, and we like to probe."

He sunk his hands into his pockets. "What do you want to know?"

She thought for a moment, a multitude of questions tumbling through her mind. She picked an innocuous topic, hoping to draw him out. "Did your parents work?"

He nodded. "My mother was an anthropologist specializing in the study of Egyptian mummies, and my father was a nuclear physicist and Nobel Prize recipient." All of this was said without inflection.

An anthropologist and a Nobel Prize–winning physicist. That explained the mystery behind the man. Dexter was no anomaly, but rather a product of his upbringing.

"Where are your parents now?"

"They were killed a year and a half ago in a plane crash."

"I'm sorry."

He shrugged and averted his gaze, staring out the large, multipaned window overlooking the magnificent garden Mallory had spied that afternoon—a bright, beautiful place that seemed incongruous to the somber atmosphere that pervaded the inside of Braden Manor.

But the garden was not half as compelling as Dexter himself, who showed one thing on the outside but something entirely different on the inside. A man who saved a monkey from certain death, who put a farmer's son through Oxford, who hid his masculine beauty behind bow ties and tweed instead of flaunting it. Amazing.

Even more amazing was the fact that Dexter didn't seem to know or care that women would pay good money to see him naked.

Mallory could picture him adorning the cover of one of her romance novels, brandishing a glittering sword and wearing a short kilt sans shirt.

Or perhaps he would wear a pair of snug black trousers and a white shirt, open wide and billowing in the wind, one arm stretched above his head grasping a length of rope, his other arm entwined around some willowy blonde.

Who looked an awful lot like Freddie.

Mallory frowned.

"Are you feeling all right, Ms. Ginelli?"

"What?" An embarrassed flush heated Mallory's cheeks as she realized her gaze had been riveted to Dexter's torso—her thoughts less than pure. "Yes, I'm fine. I was just . . ." *Wondering what you look like beneath all those buttons.* "You can call me Mallory, you know. It's not necessary to be so formal."

"Thank you, but I'd prefer Ms. Ginelli for now.

We don't know each other well enough to be so casual."

He preferred Ms. Ginelli? They didn't know each other well enough? Incredible. Another man like Dexter could not possibly exist on the face of the earth, which made him entirely unique—and perhaps more than a little special.

"Fine," she said. "Call me what you want, but I refuse to go around referring to you as your lordship." Or Dr. Lovejoy as Freddie called him. "And Dexter, well . . ." He didn't look like a Dexter. He looked like Eros, the god of love. "I'll just call you Professor."

"As you wish. Would you like that drink now?"

"Yes."

"I have a well-stocked wine cellar," he said, "but I imagine you aren't a connoisseur, so let me offer some suggestions."

How was it that the man made her want to comfort him one minute and slap him the next? Not a connoisseur! How did he know she wasn't a connoisseur? She wasn't, of course. She rarely even drank. But he didn't know that.

"I can offer you a '62 Cantermerle or a full-bodied '53 Gruaud Larose or a '78 Bourgogne, which is deuced hard to come by but well worth the effort to acquire. Ah, and there is a '96 Marquis de la Cases, powerful in its complexity with a hint of blackberry and—"

"How about a beer?" That effectively cut him off at the pass.

"Beer?"

She nodded. "A Corona with a wedge of lime, if you have it." Mallory had never drunk a beer in her life and wouldn't know a Corona from a coconut.

"I don't believe I have any . . . beer." He said the word as though it was some highly contagious disease. Beer translated to the bubonic plague or the Ebola virus or a fatal case of the trots.

"All right, then, I'll take a glass of Scotch." As if she had ever drunk Scotch. It just sounded good and mollified her need to tweak his arrogant, perfect nose. What did he think? That just because she was from New York she had no class? Or was it anyone who didn't possess a Ph.D.?

"Scotch? Isn't that rather strong?"

"No," she lied.

"All right." He shrugged. "Scotch it is."

She watched him stride toward the sideboard, trying not to admire the way he moved or wonder why just looking at him twisted her stomach into a knot. Her reaction to the professor was completely illogical.

Yet . . . she couldn't deny that his old-fashioned ways intrigued her. Perhaps it was because she wrote about men like Dexter in her novels. Men who were gallant, refined.

Something about that cockeyed bow tie, his slightly mussed hair and thin-rimmed eyeglasses, made her want to touch him, rifle her hands through those silky, shoulder-length locks and toss his glasses to the four winds.

The man was a centerfold waiting to happen.

"Here you go."

Mallory shook her head and realized he stood in front of her—and she was gaping. Again.

She plucked the glass from his hand and headed

for the nearest wall of books, grabbing a fat volume off the shelf and clasping it like a lifeline.

Unfortunately, when she turned around, she found Dexter closing rank. She tried to move back, but discovered escape was futile as the bookshelf pressed into her shoulder blades.

When he stood before her, even his shadow dwarfed her. "Do you like Molière?" he asked.

"Molière?" she repeated, sounding like a rusty hinge. The name sounded familiar, but her usually acute memory was suddenly failing.

Gently, he slid the book from her grasp, his large fingers sweeping lightly over hers, sending an unexpected frisson of electricity sizzling up her arm.

He held up the book she had just been clutching. "Molière."

Her gaze darted to the title of the book. *The Misanthrope.* "Oh, that Molière." She groaned inwardly. That Molière! She sounded like a dolt! "Yes, I like him."

He smiled, and she noticed that with a little practice, his efforts toward having an utterly disarming grin had much improved. Her heart would attest to that.

She searched for her voice and found it halfway down her throat. "I think it's time you tell me why I'm here."

His gaze flicked to her lips, studying them closely, curiously, before his eyes slowly lifted to hers. Instead of answering, he said, "You know we're very isolated out here, don't you?"

Isolated? What did he mean by that?

A spurt of panic shot through her. Had she been correct in her assumptions? Did he intend to use

her in some weird experiment? Was she to become
the subject of his next research paper?

*The Effects of Isolation on a Virgin Romance Writer
Secluded with a Male Model in Disguise.*

"Yes." She took a breath. "I know we're isolated."

"It is necessary for privacy, you see. I need to
carry out my research without disruptions."

His research? Good Lord, she had been right!

"Research?" she squeaked, and then cleared her
throat. "And what research is that?"

"It's really rather simple," he murmured, moving closer to her. "I need to learn what women
desire . . . and I need you to teach me."

CHAPTER EIGHT

Mallory blinked three times before coherent thought returned, and when it did, she was glad the bookshelves braced her in an upright position.

"Did you just say you wanted me to teach you what women desire?"

He shifted slightly and put a finger to his buttoned collar. "Among other things."

Among other things? *Among other things!* He had managed to stun her again with another how-do-you-feel-about-copulation type remark.

He regarded her with an expression that hadn't changed one bit from the moment he made his request. The man really looked upon this . . . this preposterous notion as research! Why hadn't she listened to her common sense and stayed home where she belonged?

I'll give you twenty thousand little reasons.

"W-what . . . 'other things' are you referring to?"

she stammered out. As if he could possibly say anything else that might measure up to his first shocking declaration.

And why was she just standing there instead of storming out of the room in the best exit scene of her entire life?

Curiosity.

And far too much wild imagination.

He slid the book that he had taken from her hands back into its spot on the shelf. Then he swirled the brandy in his snifter, regarding her over the rim as he replied, "Pitching woo, for one. That seems the logical place to start."

"Pitching woo?" Of all the self-indulgent, scheming, insane requests . . . As if she might pitch woo with him *or* do the other thing with him for that matter.

And who on God's green earth said pitching woo anymore?

"If you think for one minute that I'll be your . . . your plaything or sex toy or . . . or love kitten or whatever you people call it, you're d-e-a-d wrong!"

"Love kitten?"

"You know what I mean!"

"There is no need for hysteria, Ms. Ginelli."

"I am not hysterical!"

A single quirked eyebrow articulated his doubt. Then he took her glass, and as if she were a toddler, he held the drink to her lips. Her mind otherwise occupied with the remnants of her pique, Mallory took a healthy swig . . .

And gagged as the Scotch cauterized a hole in her esophagus. One large, impersonal hand thwacked her on the back and nearly sent her flying.

"Now," he said crisply, "I understand you're a

bit high-strung, and this may contribute to these bouts of needless drama you seem prone to; but I haven't a clue what it is you're going on about. Enlighten me, if you will."

Oh, she would enlighten him all right. Straight to Uranus! "I will not make love to you—or pitch *woo* as you call it. So you can just get that out of your head right now."

An odd sound, like choking or gurgling, came from him. "Make love . . . You and I? We?" He waved a finger between them. "The two of us?" He tipped back his head and roared with unrestrained mirth. When his seemingly endless humor finally abated, he said, "Don't be absurd, madam. I have no intention of making love to you. I was speaking metaphorically—and in the broadest sense of the term, I might add. I thought I made my position on this subject clear previously."

He shook his head, amusement still lurking in his eyes. "Really, what is it with you and this preoccupation you have with jumping in bed? If one didn't know better, one might think you never had sex before."

And one might be right! Mallory silently retorted, her face suffusing with color. "My sex life is none of your concern!"

"Nor do I want it to be, thank you. I doubt I could keep up with the tales of your bedroom escapades." Before Mallory could dredge up her indignation, he went on briskly. "Now, to clarify my position. In this one instance, I will be the pupil, and you the teacher."

"And just what am I supposed to teach you?"

"I believe I already answered that."

Mallory gritted her teeth. "I was sputtering incoherently at the time. If you would be so kind as to lay out your . . . er . . ."

"Desires?"

Did he have to put it that way? *"Plan,"* she corrected with some emphasis.

He set his shoulders back, his expression businesslike. "Well, I want to learn how to please a woman, to find out what it is a female really craves from a man. As you may have noticed, I am not possessed of the urbane charm of Francis Crick."

Francis Crick? Who the heck was Francis Crick?

Mallory searched her mind, pulled back to the days of Mr. Prescott's science class in PS 92. She had been his best student. He hadn't known she had a secret crush on him. That was the only reason she had learned anything about life science, which might be the reason she could recall anyone with the dubious name of Francis Crick.

"Are you referring to the guy who discovered DNA?"

Her host cocked an eyebrow, obviously surprised she possessed a brain. Had he been testing her, perhaps? "The double helix of DNA, to be precise."

Mallory shook her head. Only this Mensa lummox would make an analogy using Francis Crick instead of Brad Pitt—even if Mr. Pitt didn't measure up to the raw masculine beauty of the man standing before her.

"Excuse me for being dense, but I still don't understand how I can help you." Why was she even listening to him anymore?

He gave her a look of impatience. "I would like you to tutor me on how to speak to women and, er, other things women related."

Tutor the professor? "I see." She didn't. And there was that mysterious "other things" again. "May I ask *why?*"

He hesitated and then replied, "Research." It seemed as if he had intended to say something more, but clamped his lips together instead.

"Let's see if I have this right. You want me to tutor you."

"Yes."

"About women."

"Yes."

"And 'other things' women related."

"At last, we are getting somewhere."

"Just one question."

"Yes?"

"*Are you crazy? Completely mad? Bonkers? Touched in the head? Hearing bells? INSANE?* What makes you think for one tiny itsy-bitsy miniscule fraction of a second that I would consider such an outrageous request? I am a writer! I have things to do with my life. Serious things. Writer things."

Writer things? Oh, that sounds intelligent!

He looked not the least bit moved by her vehement denunciation. "Well, actually this was Cummings's idea. He seemed to believe a man could learn a great deal about what it is women want by reading romance novels." The last three words made his lips purse in distaste.

Finally, some logic! It had certainly taken men long enough to deduce the obvious! Since the days of ancient drawings in caves, women had been trying to map out what they desired from their male counterparts. And for that entire time, men have scratched their heads and stared at each other in stupefaction.

Mallory drew a steadying breath. "So why not read a romance novel, then? I just write them. I don't live them." Which was not to say she didn't wish she could sometimes.

"I believe I made my point on that issue."

"Ah, yes. You're a fan of Bertrand Russell and the Sanskrit, not romance novels." She nodded. "And how do you feel about the Bible?"

He stared at her quizzically. "What does the Bible have to do with anything?"

"It's a book, right?"

"Of course, but—"

"Well, there was romance in the Bible. Or pitching woo, as some people refer to it." Her look clearly stated what "people" she meant.

"Are you mocking me, Ms. Ginelli?"

Yes! "I am merely stating a fact."

He folded those lumberjack arms over that massive chest and regarded her with disbelief. "Which is?"

"That some parts of the Bible could be considered romance."

"And what part would that be?"

"Solomon."

"That's not the same."

"Have you read any of the Song of Solomon?"

"I have."

"Well, let me pose this question to you . . . Why do you think the man was singing all the time? Hmm? It wasn't merely because the wine and fruit were plentiful."

His lips pressed together. "You've made your point."

"Good. Now let me make another one. I am

not your girl Friday or your girl anything. I am a respected romance writer and—"

"I respect you."

That cut Mallory off mid-diatribe, even as her mind clamored that far too many women had foolishly fallen for those three little words coming from a man's lips.

Virgin she may be. But she was a New York virgin, which automatically put her three steps ahead of her counterparts—five steps ahead of those in the Midwest and undeveloped countries.

"I'm glad to hear that," she said, "but it still doesn't change my position on this matter."

In the back of her mind, she realized one other reason she couldn't oblige him—were she crazy enough to consider his request.

Odd as it may be, even with all his arrogance and bow ties, he moved her in some indefinable way. Her internal warning bells clanged whenever he came near, and that kooky robot from "Lost in Space" blared, *Danger, Mallory Ginelli! Danger!* Not a particularly warming revelation nor one she wanted to explore.

Casually, he sipped his drink. "Are you saying your answer is no?"

Mallory hesitated, wondering what his reaction would be to her response, which was to tell him that he was correct and that she had no intention of obliging his absurd request.

Teach him about what women want. Ridiculous!

But would he expect his money returned for non-compliance, as he had when she had put her proverbial foot down regarding his highly inaccurate sex survey?

So instead of answering him, she said, "Can't

you see how cork-brained it seems that you need *my* help considering *your* line of work?"

He scratched his chin and she waited for him to make a pithy remark or some long-winded commentary on his background and credentials.

She got none of that.

Instead he replied, "Yes."

"Yes? That's it?"

"What else do you want me to say?"

"Well, perhaps explaining why you need me to teach you anything about women would be a start. I would think someone like you knows everything there is to know about the subject."

"And, viewed clinically, that would be correct. I understand a woman's physical needs. I know the erogenous zones, where to touch and for how long, how to build desire, what things to do to bring the greatest pleasure"—he shrugged—"which would, of course, culminate in multiple orgasms."

Multiple—she swallowed—orgasms?

Mallory's palms grew uncomfortably clammy and her knees felt remarkably like aspic. If she survived the conversation, she was writing an ode to the bookshelf. Had it not been at her back, she would currently be on the floor.

Dexyer cleared his throat and stepped away—at last! His nearness combined with words like *erogenous* and *orgasm* made Mallory go all wobbly.

She studied his profile as his gaze moved aimlessly over the books, which denied her the opportunity to see much of his expression.

"Anyway," he went on, "I've been told that I . . . well, that I lack passion and that I don't feel things here." He pointed to his heart. "As well, I don't . . ." He mumbled the rest of his words.

"Could you repeat that last part?"

"I said that I don't . . ."

"You have to speak up. I can't hear you."

"I said that I don't know how to speak love words to a woman!" he practically shouted, clearly disgruntled. "There. Are you happy now that the whole house knows my private business?"

Mallory tried to repress a smile. With forty-two rooms, she suspected the only thing that heard his confession besides her were the suits of armor down the hall.

"Love words? Do you mean tender words that tell a woman how beautiful she is and how she makes you feel? Those kinds of words?"

"Yes, yes," he replied gruffly, looking utterly miserable and endearingly vulnerable.

Her heart went out to him. She realized his admission had to have been a hard one for a man like him to make. But oddly enough, now that the initial shock of hearing the sex doctor confess he didn't know how to act with a woman had worn off, she couldn't say she was surprised.

On topics he understood, she imagined he could expound for hours. As well, he had the arrogance associated with a man of high intelligence who also happened to be a scientist, a combination that could repel women who wanted candlelit dinners that didn't consist of having to listen to their date detail the sexual revolution and counterrevolution.

Highlighted by case histories.

"Why me?" she asked.

He shrugged, still not looking at her. "As I said, it was Cummings's idea. He felt you were the perfect choice to help me with my"—he cleared his throat and mumbled—"problem." He clasped his hands behind his back and then nervously shoved them into his pants pockets. "He said that with the way you write, you had to be a scalding kettle—"

"Of passion?"

He nodded.

Incredible. If people believed everything she wrote, she would also be five inches taller with waist-length blonde hair and big . . . blue eyes. Like Freddie.

"And you believed him?"

He turned to look at her, a puzzled expression on his face. "Of course. He is my best friend, after all. Whom can one trust if not their closest friend?"

Whom indeed, Mallory thought.

Cummings's words came back to her all too clearly.

For years, Dexter thought the only way he would ever have any friends was to buy them.

I was one of the 'friends' Dex bought.

Did Dexter know how Cummings felt? she wondered. Or what he had done? And did Cummings remain in Dexter's employ out of a sense of guilt over his actions or because he had become a friend to Dexter in the true sense of the word?

Once more, Mallory found her emotions sliding back down the scale, seeing another piece of the man inside the scientist and fitting that piece into the puzzle. When she created her characters for her stories, she had to understand their histories, what made them tick.

She wanted to understand what made Dexter tick.

Or perhaps it was just that strange deficiency inside her that tended to fix what was broken, to right what was wrong.

I sense you two are kindred spirits, Cummings had said.

Kindred spirits. Doubtful. They had nothing in common nor did they really like each other. At least, Dexter had given her that impression.

Mallory wondered if he noticed the contradictions that resided within her. The difference between the scalding kettle of passion and the sixty-year-old woman with religious affiliations.

What did it matter if he saw the truth or not? She was just another one of his projects. Conversely, he had been an unwitting benefactor in the Genie Ginelli Betting Fund. Besides, who could like him anyway? He was too uptight. Too strident. Too arrogant.

Research. That was all she was to him. The question was, what would he be to her? And how far did research go before real life began?

"I have to think about this," she finally told him. But she knew what her answer would be. No. And it wasn't just for the obvious reasons, that the whole plan was nuts.

There was also the fact that she didn't know the first thing about teaching a man how to behave with a woman. She only knew what *she* wanted in a man and what *she* wanted from love. She couldn't speak for all womankind.

"I understand," he said, regarding her intently, and she knew heavy thoughts were happening behind those intense eyes. Now, whether he was calculating the Fermat equation or wondering how she would look naked, Mallory couldn't tell—although she suspected the former rather than the latter.

"And when might you have an answer for me?" he then asked.

The twenty-seventh of never? she almost replied. "In the morning," she said instead.

"Until then." He held up his glass in acknowledgment and then downed the remaining contents, leaving Mallory to admire the sleek line of his muscular neck and strong contour of his jaw.

She took a small sip of her drink and tried to keep the grimace from her face. Then she put the glass down on the table beside her. "If you'll excuse me. I find I'm very tired."

"You've had a long day."

If that wasn't the truth. "There is no need to walk me back to my room. I can find it." Or so she hoped. She could just imagine getting lost and drifting through the endless hallways and forty-two rooms until she died of hunger. Doomed to forever haunt this place. She shivered. "Good night."

"Good night," he murmured. She had made it to the door when he said, "Ms. Ginelli . . . ?"

She turned halfway, knob in hand. "Yes?"

"Whatever your decision tomorrow, I will abide by it."

"Thank you."

"And don't worry about repaying the twenty thousand dollars."

Mallory breathed a sigh of relief. She had been wondering what his stand would be on the money, and now without that added concern, her decision would be much easier to make.

Her relief, however, was short lived when he said, "Just fifteen thousand of it will suffice. Consider the other five thousand my way of thanking you for your time."

Unblinkingly, Mallory stared at him. "You want me to return fifteen thousand?"

"Why, yes. Certainly you didn't intend to keep it, did you? It was payment for services not yet rendered. I would have paid you per diem, but you requested the advance. If you leave . . . Well, I'm sure you see what I mean."

She saw. All too well.

Too numb to do anything but nod, Mallory headed out the door, but not before she heard Dexter add, "Sleep well, Ms. Ginelli."

Dexter watched the door click shut after Mallory and grimaced in self-disgust as he thought about his less than gentlemanly tactics, and that because of him, she would probably not sleep well at all, conflicted between wanting to leave and having to stay. Tonight, he had done something he couldn't recall having ever done before.

Manipulate someone.

He had more money than he knew what to do with. He certainly didn't need that fifteen thousand dollars back. But he knew she *did* need it.

There was always the chance she would tell him to bugger off or perhaps confess she couldn't pay him back right away and expect him to act honorably. Yet, she had a great deal of pride, and something told him she wasn't the type to shirk a responsibility, a fact he had well counted on to get what he wanted.

Dexter moved to the sideboard and refilled his glass, trying to take the edge off his disquiet, to settle thoughts that whispered his reasons for not letting her leave weren't entirely pure.

While it was true he needed her help, it was also true that she intrigued him—in a purely scientific way, of course. Definitely not in a man attracted to a vivacious, opinionated, strong-willed, exciting woman kind of way. For that way madness lay. But he had gone this far and he had to see this thing through. His future might very well depend on the outcome.

His future. Now there was the rub.

He had everything going for him. A successful career, wealth, a well-stocked library, an impressive wine collection, the original version of Bach's Bradenburg concertos. There was really only one hurdle left to jump.

So why did the prospect of that hurdle weigh him down like an exceptionally heavy millstone?

And why hadn't he told Mallory the complete truth about why he needed her help? He had had every intention of doing so, but when the moment arrived, he had remained oddly mute.

He tried to console himself with the fact that he hadn't really lied. All he was truly guilty of was not being entirely forthcoming. Besides, it wasn't as if he owed her any explanations. She was only his employee.

What business was it of hers if he was getting married?

CHAPTER NINE

"I tell you now that man is going to get a swift kick in his pompous British backside if he doesn't quit baiting me," Freddie fumed, shimmying into a pair of body-hugging jeans. "He's so damn superior. Thinks he knows everything." She jammed the top button of her jeans into the buttonhole and zipped them up with a furious tug.

"He is such a *man* that he cannot accept the fact that maybe I know more than he does—which it is patently obvious I do. And I'm far more worldly, too. I live in New York, after all. I know things. But does he see that? No. He thinks all I do is go shopping and get my hair and nails done." She swung around. "Do you believe that, Mal? Me? As if I'm that shallow and superficial!" She pointed at the bedside table. "Can you hand me my nail polish? No, not that one. The Drop Dead Red next to it."

Mallory handed the polish to Freddie, who promptly plunked down in a cushioned seat in front of the vanity and began applying the bright red nail polish to her toe nails, still muttering about *that man*, who could be none other than Cummings. Mallory listened with half an ear, her mind occupied with thoughts of Dexter.

She had been handed a reprieve from giving him a response about whether she would be staying or going. He had been called away for the day and wouldn't be back until late. That gave her time to consider a plausible excuse.

She had contemplated showing him a tough front and telling him he wasn't going to intimidate a Ginelli, that if he wanted his money, he could take her to court.

All well and good, of course, except she didn't particularly relish the idea of being subjected to the whims of the justice system. She had had enough of that with Genie to last her a lifetime.

"What's the matter with you?" Freddie asked, eyeing her. "You're being awfully quiet. What happened? Did Dr. Lovejoy make a pass at you?"

"A pass?" From the man who told her he didn't know her well enough to call her by her given name? Mallory almost laughed.

"No, he didn't make a pass at me."

"What a shame. If I didn't have an aversion to tweed, I'd wrap myself around him like a big venus fly trap."

Mallory doubted Dexter would mind being wrapped in Freddie's trap. "Do you really think he's good-looking?"

"Do I think . . . ? Have you seen that build? Who knew lifting books could produce muscles like those?'' Freddie leaned forward, treating Mallory to her X-ray vision stare. "Don't *you* think he's attractive?"

Mallory shrugged. "He's all right, I suppose."

"All right?" Freddie stared at her as though she had lost her mind. "Looking at him is like drinking a glass of Tequila. Both have a boomerang effect."

"I just don't think looks are all that matter in a man."

"You act as if he's eye slaughter or something. So what else is important? Brains?"

"To a certain—"

"And I imagine it is important he be employed— or financially independent at least."

"Well, I think—"

"And he would have to be an animal lover?"

"Certainly, but—"

"Uh-huh. And someone who relished the inside of a house as much as you do?"

"Now that's—"

"Far as I see it, you and the professor are perfectly suited."

Mallory frowned at her friend. "Thank you for your advice, Dear Abby, but I think I can choose a man on my own."

Freddie shrugged. "I'm Jewish. Matchmaking is in my blood."

"Then use your skills on yourself."

"No, thank you. I'm not ready to submit myself to that hallowed institution erroneously termed 'domestic bliss.' "

"But don't you want one man to come home to every night? Someone to plan your future with? To dream with? Who you know loves only you?" That was why Mallory had held out. She wanted her soulmate. Her other half. Just anybody would not do.

Freddie shrugged and stared down at her painted toe nails. "I don't know. Maybe I do want those things. But marriage isn't all it's cracked up to be."

Mallory understood Freddie's lingering pain. Her friend had married her college sweetheart and had been devastated when the marriage fell apart barely a year later. Freddie had never known failure.

Since that time, Freddie had erected barriers, using her cutting wit and haughty demeanor to keep an emotional distance, never allowing any one man to get too close.

"Love will find you again, Freddie—if you let it."

Not surprisingly, Freddie returned to form. "Geez, Mal, don't go getting maudlin on me." She shook her head. "Must be all this isolation that's making us loco—and the fact that the men here are either frigid or big-mouthed, arrogant secretaries who are asking to be flattened."

"Cummings isn't so bad." And Mallory highly doubted Dexter was frigid.

"Ha! The man shouldn't be allowed to speak on any day that has an *a* in it." Then in usual Freddie-style, she reverted to her favorite topic: other people's business. "You know, I'm coming to believe that if you don't get laid by a certain age, you become gender neutral. Better watch out, Mal. Last thing I heard, there wasn't a pill to cure numbness below the waist."

"Must you be so crude?"

"Must you be so medieval? Virginity might have been the rage back in the day of Rapunzel, but these are modern times; women are liberated and enjoy sexual freedom. If we want to wear spurs and ride the wild pony, shouting, 'Giddyup, Cowboy,' we can.''

"I'm not ready for spurs, thank you." Yet Mallory knew in many ways Freddie was right. She did live in a fantasy world, waiting for that gallant knight to come and whisk her away, expecting Prince Charming to find her and transform her from a commoner to his princess.

"So what's the matter? Irked that the love doctor hasn't made any untoward advances? I can do a little Tae Bo on him. I guarantee he won't stand erect for a week."

"Eye gouges and groin kicks are not necessary. He's just a little ... reserved. There's nothing wrong with that. In fact, it's rather refreshing."

"Refreshing, huh?"

"Yes," Mallory said with emphasis, surprised to find herself defending Dexter.

"Well I for one expected more from him. From what that bloated jerk Cummings says, the women are all agog over the professor. His classes are always packed, and he leaves his female students panting in the aisles."

Mallory wondered if any of his female students had come to his house to do "research." She pictured Dexter and how he had acted toward her since she had arrived and decided the possibility that he was Don Juan in disguise was highly unlikely.

"Dexter is an old-fashioned guy," she said. "I don't think he recognizes his effect on the female population."

"Old-fashioned, hmm? Well, there's another reason he would be perfect for you. You both live in the sexual Stone Age."

"Perfect? For me?" Mallory snorted. "I have no interest in him. I'm merely here to ... er, help him with some research."

"Research?" Freddie lifted a perfectly tweezed brow. "The plot thickens. Spill, my girl—and no half-truths. I know you too well to be fooled."

Mallory heaved a sigh. Freddie was right. She couldn't hide anything from her. She wondered why she had wanted to do so. The nature of the subject probably—and nothing to do with the feeling she was violating Dexter's trust by confiding in Freddie.

Mallory rose from her chair and moved to the window, knowing she was purposely avoiding looking Freddie in the eye. "He wants me to teach him some things."

"Teach him things? What could you possibly know that he doesn't? How to write a romance novel?"

"Not writing them exactly," Mallory said, feeling remarkably like Genie at that moment as she nibbled a nail, waiting for the other shoe to drop.

"Not exactly? Boy, you are being evasive." Freddie came to stand next to her at the window. "How do you 'not exactly' write a romance?"

Mallory slid a glance at her friend. "By living it instead."

"How does one live—Oh, Good Lord, you're kidding me! You don't mean to say that he ... and you ..." She laughed. "This is priceless! He wants you to play house with him? His Hansel to your Gretel? His Jack to your Jill? Like some weirdo fantasy?"

"No! He wants me to teach him how to be romantic."

Freddie's chuckling only increased. "You? Teach him how to be romantic? Your idea of romance is sitting alone on a Saturday night with a box of Kleenex watching *Casablanca* and weeping piteously. You get glassy eyed if you hear someone say 'Here's lookin' at you, kid.' "

"I do not."

"You forget, I've seen you break down watching *Bambi*."

"Anyone with a heart would feel sorry for Bambi."

"I have a heart," Freddie returned defensively, no longer laughing. "But I'm not crying over some fictitious deer. And let's not change the topic. What I want to know is why the man would possibly pick you to teach him about romance out of all the millions of women on this planet. First, he could have just asked one of the eager Barbies in his class—and second, you are the least likely candidate."

Freddie's attitude rubbed Mallory the wrong way. "I happen to know plenty about romance!"

"Just because you write it doesn't mean you live it."

Mallory recalled saying nearly the identical words to Dexter the day before. "That doesn't mean I can't," Mallory retorted. "I've just been busy." Busy, yes. Writing about romance.

Writing it instead of living it.

Freddie waved a dismissive hand. "You are so repressed in your personal life that I would bet my bottom dollar just hearing the word orgasm makes you cringe."

Mallory frowned, remembering another person who had recently used that word.

"See?"

"I'm not cringing! And I'm not repressed!"

"If you say so." Freddie shrugged. "Now, what do you intend to tell the professor? To book us a flight home on the earliest departing Concorde?"

"No. Yes. I don't know!"

"I see. Well, I guess you have a lot to think about." Freddie moved back to the chair in front of the vanity and put on her low pumps. "I'm going into town. Need a mental health day away from this place. Are you sure you don't want to come into town with me?"

Mallory knew Freddie was having people withdrawal. They were both used to the hustle and bustle of New York, a mass of humanity everywhere, things to see and do. Smells assaulting the senses. A completely different lifestyle than the one they now found themselves in, where the loudest noise was the occasional bleating of the sheep that roamed the hillside and the evening wind buffeting the castle.

"I wish I could, but I have a lot of work to catch up on. I'm falling behind on my writing." Which was the truth, but not the reason Mallory didn't want to go. She needed some time alone to think. "Have a good time."

"I'll try. But I doubt these people know the meaning of fun. Probably the most excitement they have is picking lint from their navels."

Mallory shook her head, knowing the Lord had broken the mold when he made Freddie.

Thank heavens.

* * *

Alone in the cavernous library Mallory felt utterly dwarfed.

Her laptop was placed in front of her on the round mahogany table where she had been thoroughly engrossed in staring at the blinking cursor for a quarter hour, having written not a single word since entering the room.

She paged back to reread what she had typed the day that Genie had infiltrated her apartment and Karen had told her about a Ph.D wielding peer of the British realm with a unbelievable request. The words *jutting manhood* jumped out at her.

Ironic. What did she really know about jutting manhoods? She had to be the only twenty-five-year-old virgin in New York—if one believed any virgins yet existed in New York.

But that didn't mean she was repressed! Or a prude! Or a sixty-year-old woman with religious affiliations!

Antsy, Mallory rose from her chair, needing to stretch her legs, hoping for a burst of inspiration. She walked the perimeter of the library, a single finger rolling over the books, feeling more at ease with each passing minute.

The room possessed a lived-in feeling the rest of the house didn't. Chunky high-back chairs in a variety of colors were strewn about, with little side tables placed next to them. Old tomes teetered in every conceivable spot.

In front of a large bay window sat a massive burl wood desk, a heavy piece that from the quality, she suspected hadn't come from a modern-day craftsman or warehouse.

She imagined Dexter sitting in the giant black leather chair situated behind the desk reading some book or working on one of his papers, head bent forward, silky hair tumbling over his forehead, looking very scholarly.

Mallory frowned, wondering about her thoughts regarding the professor and why she couldn't seem to shake them. "Perhaps because you're in his house." Lovely. Now she was talking to herself. She hoped the walls didn't have ears.

A book caught her eye and she slid it off the shelf. *Sex: An Oral History.* Heat flushed her cheeks and Mallory could hear Freddie saying, "You are so repressed."

She was not repressed.

Was she?

Staring at the book, an idea began to take shape in Mallory's brain—an idea that just might be the answer to how to deal with Dexter and his request.

He wanted to look at their time together as research. Well, so could she. She did research all the time for her books, though she rarely got the chance to do her research in real time—or using real people. Now she could.

She could have an actual, honest-to-God, get-her-hands-dirty experience and use this unique opportunity to her advantage, take what she learned and put that extra spark in her books.

Now the only question was, where to begin?

CHAPTER TEN

"You want me to do *what?*"

Mallory frowned at Dexter because he was frowning at her. "I want you to stop fighting me; that's what I want. Let's just get down to business. All right?"

He shook his head, looking mulish. "I have a reputation to protect. My good name could get besmirched should anyone find out what happened behind closed doors."

"Besmirched . . . ? You're joking, right?" Mallory put her hand up to forestall the reply she knew was coming. "I know. You don't joke. But you're making a big deal out of nothing. People do it every day."

"Well, I don't."

"Don't be a prude."

"I'm British. Prudery is in our blood."

Mallory resisted the urge to laugh. She remembered Freddie categorizing her with a similar stereotype.

"Just whip it out, put it in, and let's get started."

"Whip it out, indeed," he grumbled. "Why are you Americans always in a rush? Can't anything be leisurely? Anticipation is a sensory delight, need I remind you."

"Stop balking and give it to me."

"Good Lord, woman, you are impatient!" he huffed. "Now, let's see." He fumbled around for a minute, touching everything, adjusting his glasses and pressing his face close to get a better look.

Mallory heaved an impatient sigh. "Slip it in the opening. There's only one."

He glowered. "The patently obvious is not necessary, madam. The merely obvious will suffice."

Clearly, he didn't take well to directions. A man trait. But the sooner the lessons began, the better for both of them.

She had woken up that morning surprised to find her resolve still intact. In fact, she had been somewhat eager to start their research.

"Oh, bloody hell," he groused. "It's stuck."

"Push harder."

"I am pushing!"

"When was the last time you used it?"

"I don't know. A year ago, maybe. My schedule doesn't allow for such frivolity."

"Maybe if you relaxed, we could get it to work."

He ignored her and fumbled some more. Then he shook his head. "It's too big. It won't fit."

"Don't be ridiculous. I've never heard of one not fitting."

"I'm going to take it out. It might break."

"It won't break for goodness sake! Just give it a good shove."

He gave her a doubtful look. Then, with a grunt, he shoved, and it went in all the way.

Mallory smiled with satisfaction. "See? I told you it would fit."

"Gloating is very unbecoming in a woman, Ms. Ginelli."

"And grumpiness is very unbecoming in a man, Professor."

He harumphed and repositioned his big body, folding his arms over his chest.

She harumphed and folded her arms across her chest.

Together, they turned their eyes to the television set. Black-and-white film rolled by until the title screen came up on the video they had just put into the VCR.

"*Casablanca?*" Dexter said in a disparaging tone Mallory didn't appreciate. "What kind of quality viewing is this?"

"The very best kind."

When Freddie had come home earlier, she had told Mallory how surprised she was to have found not only a decent restaurant in this "backwater molehill of a English town," but, she had added with some degree of glee, there was also a video store. *Imagine that,* her expression had said.

Dexter snorted. "I've never heard of this movie."

Mallory gaped at him. "You've never heard of *Casablanca?*" Who hadn't heard of *Casablanca?* It was a classic.

"Should I have?" he asked in a bored tone.

"Bogie and Bergman, does that ring a bell?"

"Not even a tinkle."

"Unbelievable."

"Why must we watch this? There is a good documentary on the History Channel."

"You wanted to learn about romance, what women want in a man. Right? Well, this is how we are going to start."

"How this could possibly help, I can't begin to imagine."

"Well, if you don't want my help . . ." She started to get up to press stop. A large, warm hand wrapped around her wrist, pulling her back down on the couch—practically into her student's lap.

Her free hand fell across his chest. Muscles flexed and bunched beneath her palm, and her heart lurched. She glanced up to find Dexter's gaze pinned on her face, and she couldn't help but stare.

She had always been fascinated by eyes, and his were so unusual. She truly believed the eyes were windows to the soul. And looking into his warmed her from the toes up.

When she noted the questioning lift of his eyebrow, she realized, to her mortification, that she was lying across his lap like a clinging vine. As though on fire, she scrambled away and resumed her former position, staring straight at the TV screen, her palms still tingling from the contact with hard muscle.

"We'll watch *A Streetcar Named Desire* next," she said a bit breathlessly. He made no reply, and she didn't care to look at him to see his expression. "Then we will watch *Bambi.*" A good cry might unstiffen his rigid bearing.

"*Bambi?* That's a children's movie."

Forgetting her vow to stare straight ahead, Mallory turned to look at him.

Mistake.

Why did he seem closer than he had only a moment before? And why did those eyes, focused so intently on her face, do strange things to her insides?

It had to be a stomach bug. Perhaps something she had eaten hadn't agreed with her. Probably the duck l'orange they had been served for dinner or maybe the eggs benedict they had eaten for breakfast or perhaps the poached salmon in dill sauce they had consumed for lunch.

Whatever happened to a bagel with cream cheese? A bowl of Cheerios? Or even a good old-fashion New York deli turkey sandwich, light on the mayo, extra tomato, lettuce, and no onion with a kosher pickle on the side?

It wasn't that she didn't like eating fancy food—since normally the closest she got to such fare was sniffing the air as she passed the French restaurant around the corner from where she lived—but did everything have to be dilled, sautéed or l'oranged?

"Why are you staring at me like that?" he asked, his expression wary.

Because I was picturing you as a Whopper with cheese, Mallory almost replied. That answer certainly wouldn't do, and who knew what Freudian type of message it might send. "Perhaps because I'm dumbfounded that you know about *Bambi* but don't know about *Casablanca.*"

"Contrary to popular belief, I was a child once, too."

"I just find it unusual. That's all."

"That I've watched *Bambi* or that I was a child?"

Both, she wanted to say.

How had he gone from being a *Bambi* lover to ... what? A monkey lover? A tweed and bow tie lover? A John Locke and Plato lover? The connection seemed to have gotten lost somewhere along the line—which only made Mallory more curious to figure out exactly when things had changed.

"You can't fault me for being surprised someone like you watched *Bambi,*" she said. "You don't exactly seem the type."

He quirked an eyebrow. "And what type is that, Ms. Ginelli?"

Oh, great. Now he was getting that offended expression. Either the man was stone-faced or he was prickly. "Let's just say I can more easily picture you studying Einstein's Theory of Relativity than plunked down in front of a TV enjoying the antics of Thumper the rabbit and Flower the skunk."

"Well, you'd be wrong, then. I thought *Bambi* rather enlightening, if you must know."

Enlightening? Mallory had never heard it referred to as such, but then again, this was the professor she was dealing with. Unusual was the man's middle name.

Still, she found it hard to believe Dexter liked *Bambi* and had watched it as a child. It was a whimsical tale. And with his sculpted cheekbones, firm jaw, high forehead, piercing eyes, and books with titles like *The Lives of A Cell, The Double Helix* and *The Chaos Theory,* he looked far from the whimsical type.

"Shall we get on with it?" he asked impatiently.

Mallory refrained from sticking her tongue out at him. Instead, she pushed play. Bogie and Bergman lit up the screen.

By the time Rick and Ilsa parted ways at the airport, Mallory had a box of Kleenex in her lap. How they got there, she didn't know.

We'll always have Paris, she mouthed, sniffling pathetically as she reached for another tissue to find she didn't have any left.

A handkerchief appeared in her tear-blurred line of vision. She plucked it from Dexter's hand with a weak, "Thank you." Then she blew her nose.

Once she had her emotions under control, she turned to face him, eager to discover if he had learned anything from his first class in Romance 101. His look of bland inquiry didn't bode well for her.

"So tell me, what did you think of Rick? I want to know the first thing that pops into your head."

He gave her a sideways glance and shrugged. "He seemed rather insipid and foolhardy."

Mallory blinked. Bogie? Insipid and foolhardy? "You're joking, right?"

"I'm not sure what drives you to ask me that question time and again. But no, I'm not joking. I'm completely serious."

"Why do you think he's insipid and foolhardy?" This she couldn't wait to hear.

"Well, look at him. Clearly, he's tortured, completely miserable, and it all seems to be over a woman. It's irrational if you ask me."

Mallory was agog. "They're in love!"

"I see. So that equates with being in hell? They make illogical choices. For example, why does Rick twist the knife by asking Sam, the piano man, to play that song? It's obvious the song causes Rick pain."

"He wants to remember the woman he loves."

"Which brings me to another point. Were he intelligent, he would not have pursued her in the first place when he knew she could never be his."

"So you mean to say you wouldn't do whatever it takes to be with the woman you love? To not lose the person you know in your soul is the one for you? You wouldn't be willing to risk anything and everything to cherish bliss, no matter how fleeting, because you know you are one of the lucky, one of the blessed who will find a rare kind of love in their lifetime?"

Mallory took a breath, surprised at her impassioned declaration. Yet she meant every word.

She expected Dexter to give her a blunt "no" in response to all her questions or tell her that she was spouting female nonsense or that her comments stemmed from the romance writer side of her.

Instead, he regarded her as if just seeing her, a hint of sadness in his eyes. Yet his answer reflected nothing of what she sensed lay behind that mask of indifference he wore so well. "Sometimes," he murmured, "you have to play the hand life deals you."

Could he be any more cryptic? Mallory wondered, frustrated. The man held on to every morsel tighter than Scrooge. What hand had he been dealt? He had money, fame, incredible good looks, a house the size of lower Manhattan. What was missing from that picture?

Love, her inner voice replied. *Love is what's missing.*

Mallory stole a sidelong glance at those chiseled, implacable features. Was that what the professor wanted? Love? It seemed improbable . . . yet somehow not so improbable.

He was a puzzle—one, for reasons beyond her comprehension, she wanted to solve.

She intended to question him, but he rose from the couch, slid *Casablanca* out of the VCR and put in *A Streetcar Named Desire*, effectively cutting off any questions, which she was sure had been his intention.

And as Brando and his tormented cries of *Stella!* filled the room, Mallory wondered if there had ever been an Ilsa in Dexter's life.

"I can't believe you gave him the *Casablanca/ Bambi* treatment," Freddie said, shaking Mallory from her musings. "That couldn't be any less romantic."

"I'm not trying to be romantic," Mallory returned defensively. "I'm trying to be sensible. This is the best way I know how to teach him."

"I've always preferred the hands-on method myself." Freddie winked.

"This is a business arrangement. There will be no 'hands-on.' " Mallory only wished the idea Freddie had just presented hadn't already crossed her mind. The more time she spent with Dexter, the more she came to understand his nuances, his subtle boyish charm.

How well formed his thigh muscles were.

He could be positively distracting. Each time he had bent over to switch the movies in the VCR, Mallory had received an unimpeded view of his buttocks—and what a buttocks it was.

She couldn't believe how strong her reaction to

him was. If she didn't know better, she might think she was attracted to the professor.

Ludicrous.

She was no more attracted to him than he was to her—and he wasn't attracted at all, that much was clear.

She frowned. Why wasn't he attracted to her? She wasn't ugly or fat. In fact, a few men had said she was pretty. One even told her she had beautiful eyes—not that Dexter ever noticed.

His gaze never stroked over her the way a man's gaze stroked over a woman he found desirable, his look caressing, lingering. Heated. She just didn't evoke passion, not like Freddie, and not like the female characters in her books.

"If you are set on making him watch movies," Freddie said, primping in front of the mirror, "then why not show him something worthwhile like *The Big Easy* or *9 1/2 Weeks* or *She's Gotta Have It*."

She's Gotta Have It? Mallory could just imagine what that movie entailed.

"That'll get his motor running," Freddie added.

"I don't want to get his motor running," Mallory replied a bit too vehemently.

She caught Freddie's expression in the mirror; it said, *You poor, poor girl. You do need help, don't you?*

Mallory wanted to change the subject. "May I ask why you are in my room in your underwear?"

"This is my sleeping attire," Freddie returned, sporting a clingy heather gray tank top and matching bikini underwear.

"Forgive me. Why are you in my room in your *sleeping attire?*"

Freddie glanced at the clock on top of the mantel. "You'll find out in just a moment."

A minute later, a knock sounded at the door.

Freddie grinned. "Right on time." She sauntered to the door and opened it, posing on the threshold like a cover model for Victoria's Secret.

Cummings stood on the other side.

Utter silence reigned.

For about one second.

Then Cummings inclined his head at Freddie and whisked past her with barely a second glance. "Good morning, Mallory."

"Good morning, Cummings." At least one person in Dexter's household called her by her first name. Since she had arrived, she had been Ms. Ginellied to death.

"I've brought you today's newspaper."

Mallory smiled. "Thank you."

"You're welcome. And may I say you are looking positively fetching this morning."

Fetching? Unlike Freddie—who, Mallory noticed, glared at Cummings's back as if wondering how it would look with a sharp object protruding from it—she was still in her terry robe adorned with tiny red rose buds, her hair in disarray, and the bags under her eyes screaming for concealer.

"I think you need to get your eyes checked, Cummings," Mallory told him with a chuckle.

"Do not underestimate your immeasurable charm, my girl. You are as refreshing as a spring day."

"Oh, please," Freddie muttered, rolling her eyes. "I haven't seen this much crap since the circus left town."

If Mallory didn't know better, she might think

Cummings was purposely goading Freddie—and that Freddie's goat had been gotten.

On his way out the door, Cummings stopped next to Freddie, who glared at him as if contemplating how his head would look on a pike. "You might want to cover up," he remarked dryly. "You could catch a chill." Hands clasped behind his back, he strolled from the room.

Hands clenched at her sides, Freddie whirled around, eyes blazing fire, and marched toward the adjoining door to their bedrooms, mumbling something about lacing Cummings's tea with hemlock, before closing the door after her with a resounding slam.

CHAPTER ELEVEN

A week later, Mallory stood staring out a window in one of the tower rooms, absently twirling the blood red rose she had plucked from the garden that morning.

She did not see the view before her; the lush green valley sweeping out in all directions or the silver-limned waters of a meandering stream or the group of ducklings waddling after their mother. Her mind was too preoccupied with other things.

She was frustrated with the good doctor. The same type of frustration she felt when she got hung up in the middle of a manuscript and wanted to toss the thing off the roof of her apartment building, chortling with psychotic glee as the papers rained down like confetti in Times Square.

Her plan of using the visual approach with Dexter was not working as she had expected. In fact, her idea was beginning to look as insipid and foolhardy as Dexter's view of Bogie—and she had hit the professor with both barrels.

They had watched *Wuthering Heights*, *An Affair to Remember*, *Love Story*, *The Other Side of the Mountain*, and *Gone With the Wind*. The last movie baffled him entirely. He told her that it seemed Scarlet loved Tara more than her husband—and where was the romance in that? No man wanted a woman who valued a house more than him.

Mallory had tried to explain to Dexter that both Scarlet and Rhett were stubborn people, prideful, seeming so very different but really very much alike. But the discussion had been a study in point-counterpoint.

Yet, thinking back, Mallory couldn't say she hadn't made some progress. She had. Dexter had cracked a genuine smile a few times, albeit wobbly, and she had overheard him whistling "As Time Goes By." They had even had pizza for dinner one night, although he had insisted on anchovies. Mallory made a face, remembering.

But the biggest breakthrough had been when he came to the table sans bow tie. If that wasn't a miracle, then neither were the multimillion-dollar sales of a two-cent piece of speckled gray foam that toy makers ingeniously labeled the Pet Rock. Mallory was beginning to think Dexter slept in those ties.

She wondered what else he slept in, then she frowned at the thought—something she found herself doing often recently. She had not sought a place to be alone so she could dwell on her increasing fascination with Dexter. No, she had other pressing matters to consider.

Like Genie.

Her sister had begun calling more with each passing day, never really having much to say and never admitting that she just wanted to talk. Her reason was always something silly like, *By the way, your microwave imploded.*

Of course, the microwave hadn't broken on its own. Genie had put an entire lasagna wrapped in aluminum foil in the unit. Mallory imagined the resulting destruction had left her kitchen looking like the Valentine's Day Massacre. Somehow she doubted the rest of her apartment was in better shape.

Mallory realized that her being away was hard on her sister. Genie might act tough and sound tough, but she was neither. Perhaps that was why Mallory continued to do whatever she could to help her sister, because she felt Genie was silently crying out for help. Yet the more Mallory tried to do, the farther away her sister pushed her.

Mallory thought about the phone call she had received from her mother an hour earlier to tell her that Genie had been spotted with Bruno. The news had not only been unexpected, but unbelievable.

Her sister wouldn't dare fall back into trouble with Bruno after Mallory had just gotten her out of it, would she? Mallory was too afraid of the question to look too closely at the answer.

"Ah, there you are, Ms. Ginelli."

Mallory started at the sound of Dexter's voice. She glanced over her shoulder to see him striding toward her, devastatingly handsome as usual. Her stomach did a strange little flip.

"I've been looking all over for you," he said.

She craned her head back as he came to a stop

next to her, feeling slightly overwhelmed by the height and breadth of him. "Oh, really? And why is that?"

"Well, you missed our daily meeting."

Their meeting. That was what Dexter called the time they spent together delving into the mysteries of wooing. With a sigh, Mallory returned her gaze to the view outside. "Sorry. I forgot."

"We were to discuss the merits and pitfalls of *Romeo and Juliet,*" he went on as if she hadn't spoken. "I read the play last night, and while there were some appealing elements, I found the death scene bothersome. Romeo's actions seemed rash and highly irregular for a man possessed of a fair amount of common sense."

"He thought the woman he loved was dead, so he wanted to die himself. He was bereft without Juliet."

"We all have disappointments in our lives, things we wish we had done differently, things we wish we could change." The sober tone of his voice made her turn and look at him. He gazed out the window, appearing as if he had gone someplace inside himself, perhaps remembering one of his own disappointments? Something he wanted to change? He must have sensed her regard because he then added somewhat brusquely, "Nevertheless, we don't go around killing ourselves."

"Romeo was Juliet's soulmate," she endeavored to explain, "her other half and vice versa. One without the other was like . . . a chocolate chip cookie without the chocolate chips. Something's missing."

"A chocolate chip cookie?" He treated her to a rare grin.

"What can I say? I like chocolate chip cookies."

He chuckled softly, but stopped abruptly as if remembering he had been in the middle of a serious conversation, even if he was the only one being serious. "The point I'm making is that Romeo and Juliet came from families that had a system of duty, honor, and respect, a system many families still have today. They knew their actions might affect a number of people and cause a great deal of heartache."

"I don't think they cared. They wanted to be together, and nothing else mattered."

He frowned at her, as if she were speaking in a foreign tongue. "What good did all these machinations do them in the end? They both died."

"It's love, Dexter, and love often doesn't make a lot of sense, like who we choose to bestow our love upon and why. It just . . . is."

He seemed endearingly perplexed, over thinking the whole thing, as usual. Then he shrugged, either dismissing her explanation as female romanticism or reminding himself that *Romeo and Juliet* was fictional and, therefore, not worth additional comment.

"Well, at least *A Midsummer Night's Dream* was enjoyable," he said. "The whole 'love juice' idea was rather comedic and a very modern day idea." His expression turned contemplative. "If only making someone love you were that easy."

If only, Mallory thought. "Love can be the most wonderful experience you could ever have or it can be the most heartbreaking." It had been a long time since she had felt the wonderful part of love, in any aspect of her life. She had loved her father, and from that love irreconcilable wounds had resulted. She loved Genie, but her sister was slipping from her grasp a little more each day.

"Is something the matter, Ms. Ginelli? You don't seem quite yourself today."

"I have a lot on my mind."

"Do you want to tell me about it?"

Oddly enough, she did want to tell him, but she had kept silent about her family for so long that her reticence now seemed a natural part of her. "Thank you . . . but no."

She thought that would end it, but he moved closer, leaning a shoulder against the wall. She could feel his gaze on her face, yet she didn't want to look at him. "Does your upset have anything to do with your sister?"

Why Mallory was surprised at his astuteness, she wasn't sure. They had been together during a number of Genie's calls. And while Mallory had never divulged anything about her sister, Dexter clearly didn't miss much.

She hesitated and then said, "I love my sister, but sometimes she can be . . ." Mallory searched for the right word.

"A handful?" Dexter supplied.

That was putting it mildly. "For someone who doesn't have any siblings, you seem to understand how they can act."

"You are not the only one possessed of a vivid imagination, Ms. Ginelli. When you are an only child in a house with forty-two rooms, you end up creating siblings."

His admission was so forthright, so honest, it was almost painful for her to hear. Nevertheless, Mallory didn't want to get into a discussion about her sister.

"I believe I owe you a lesson in romance, Professor." She thought for a moment he might call her on the switch in subjects. He didn't.

"It's not necessary."

"The day is too nice to waste. So I suggest we head to the garden and I can teach you the proper way to present a woman with flowers. It requires a certain delicate execution that most men haven't mastered."

"Flowers?" The self-possessed man of a moment earlier suddenly looked ready to bolt. "Isn't it too soon for that?"

Mallory hid her grin and patted his hand. "Don't worry. We'll take baby steps."

"You have lovely eyes. They remind me of chips of . . . er . . . sea glass. Yes. Green sea glass, most definitely." Dexter glanced at her, looking pleased with the compliment he had produced.

Mallory gave him a reassuring smile, fairly certain that no one had ever described her eyes as chips of sea glass. Then again, there was only one Dexter Harrington, and trying to teach him how to be a suave lady killer was a task beginning to look as enormous as Moses leading the Hebrews out of Egypt.

Three days had passed since their conversation in the tower room, and things had subtly changed between them. While Dexter still grumbled and enjoyed the occasional balk and sometimes uttered a remark that made Mallory want to put an *X* on his forehead and use him as a bull's-eye for archery practice, in some ways, he had mellowed. She was actually coming to enjoy spending time with him.

Cummings had told her to take a closer look, that she might see something she hadn't expected. That was turning out to be true.

"That's very good, Professor. What else can you think of?"

His pleasure wilted, as she knew it would when she pushed, and he muttered, "Learning how to be bloody romantic is harder than quantifying the half-life of radioactive nuclei."

Mallory bit the inside of her mouth to keep from laughing. "I'm sure you're right, Professor. Perhaps we should stop for the night." She couldn't take much more anyway. The man had something like three educational degrees, and yet he got completely flummoxed when he had to think of sweet words to say to a woman. "It's after ten anyway."

Dexter glanced at his watch. "So it is." He gave her an uncertain look. "I don't think I'm quite getting it, Ms. Ginelli. Do you think we could practice a little while longer?"

The man was a perfectionist. There was no doubt about it. Clearly he enjoyed torture as well. "All right. A little while longer."

That earned her a smile. "Let's see now. Where was I? We did the eyes."

"Yes, they were sea glass."

"And we did the eyebrows."

"They were like two arching brown stalks."

"No, no. Not stalks, Ms. Ginelli. Two slender brown penduncles—the botanist variety. There is a difference, you know."

"Thank you for clarifying that." Mallory refrained from rolling her eyes. "What else?"

"Well, your hair color reminded me of the same deep black found in premium driveway sealer.

Although, I must say, the driveway sealer does not sparkle with hints of red highlights when the sun hits it just so.''

Mallory tried to keep the pained expression off her face. "That's very sweet. Anything else?" She hoped not.

"Hmm." He scrutinized her as though she were a particularly interesting fossil whose origins were unknown. "Your skin is like ... dough, perfect, lump-free dough, not too pasty and not too dry. Dough that has been rolled out into thin, manageable strips and molded over your skull by the finest ... the finest ..." He laid his chin in the palm of his hand, a frown marring his brow as he searched for the right word.

"Chef, perhaps?"

He wagged a finger at her. "That would work. Although a forensic criminologist came to mind as well. Since they see a lot of skulls, I imagine they are adept at facial reconstruction."

"How ... interesting." Some day when she was ninety, she would look back and remember the man who had described her skin as dough. "Give me a little cherry pie filling and some whip cream and I'd make a fabulous dessert." Oops. Did she say that out loud?

From the sulking expression on Dexter's face, she obviously had. "If you are going to mock my endeavors, Ms. Ginelli, I don't think I want to do this anymore."

"I was only joking. You're doing very well." If he would just relax, they might get somewhere. An idea suddenly came to her. "Close your eyes."

"Why?"

"Indulge me."

He hesitated, then shrugged and closed his eyes.

"Now, picture a woman you've seen and thought was beautiful, someone you have wanted to say something to but the words got jumbled in your throat. You walk up to her. She smiles at you. What do you say?"

"Nice weather we're having?"

Mallory's shoulders sagged. "I mean, give her a compliment. Which of her features draws your eye the most."

A moment passed before he murmured, "Her lips."

"And what about her lips?" Mallory's gaze was drawn to Dexter's lips now that she could scrutinize him unobserved. She watched his mouth a lot when he spoke, the way he shaped his words, finding his accent to be one more thing that added to his appeal.

"She has a beautiful mouth," he said.

"Good. And?"

"Her lips are full, lush." Dexter's fingers stroked over his thumb as if he itched to touch the lips he envisioned. Perhaps she was getting somewhere.

"Anything else?"

"They are lips that are meant to be kissed."

Mallory blinked, not expecting that kind of admission. "Kissed?"

Dexter nodded, a silky lock of hair tumbling across his forehead. "Often, and thoroughly—very thoroughly."

Mallory swallowed. "Well, I think that's en—"

"They look as sweet as rain-dampened strawberries," he went on in a husky voice. "The kind you want to sink your teeth into because they are so plump, so ripe you know they are going to be the best thing you ever tasted. You want to savor that sweetness, explore it with your tongue and lick away every drop."

Mallory pressed a finger to her lips, wondering why they suddenly tingled.

Slowly, Dexter opened his eyes, and Mallory was captured by the drowsy-lidded look on his face. His gaze dropped to her mouth. Certainly he hadn't been referring to her lips. Had he?

Realizing her fingers still lay against her lips, she pretended to yawn. "I guess I'm more tired than I thought. If you'll excuse me?" She rose from the table.

He rose, too. "What did you think of my description?"

The one that caused her palms to sweat? "It was very, er . . . descriptive." Another fabulously witty reply. "We can pick this up tomorrow." If she hadn't thought of a new plan by then, she silently added, something that wouldn't feel so . . . intimate. But what? Considering the nature of their research, it would not prove to be an easy task. "Good night, Professor." She hustled to the door and flew out into the hallway.

"You may want to wait a few more minutes before departing, Ms. Ginelli."

Mallory halted on the bottom step, hesitated, told herself not to look, and then threw logic to the four winds and glanced over her shoulder at Dexter. He stood just outside his office door, his face partially in the shadows, making his expression unreadable.

"And why is that?" she asked, attempting to sound insouciant and failing miserably.

Car headlights flashed through one of the rectangular foyer windows then. "That's why," he replied, walking over to the window to look out.

Curiosity got the better of Mallory, and she moved to the window flanking the other side of the door, opposite Dexter.

She saw Wheatley hop out of the Rolls and promptly open the back car door. A second later, a head emerged, but Mallory did not see the person's face. But she didn't need to see the face to know immediately who it was. She recognized the hair-style.

Her mother had been wearing her hair the same way since Mallory was a child.

Before Mallory could speak, another person emerged from the car, bobbing around with a frenetic energy she well knew. Her sister.

Stunned, she swiveled her head and stared at Dexter. "What is my family doing here?"

He didn't look at her. "I thought they might like to see England."

"You thought—What would make you think they wanted to see England?"

His answer was a shrug.

But Mallory didn't need to hear his reply. She already knew what it would be. "You invited them because of what I told you a few days ago, didn't you?"

"No." Then he shrugged, reluctantly admitting, "Well, perhaps."

Mallory couldn't believe Dexter had brought her family to England just because he had sensed she was worried about her sister.

Cummings's words came back to her.

If people would just get to know him, they'd discover a man who'd give the shirt off his back if they needed it.

Dexter didn't even know why she had been concerned about her sister, nor did he know about Genie's troubles; yet he had invited her into his home.

Mallory chewed her lip, wondering what might happen now that her sister was here. She contemplated telling Dexter about Genie's history, or perhaps "warning" was more apropos.

With some reservations, Mallory decided against it. She could keep an eye on Genie and make sure she didn't get into any trouble. "It was very sweet of you to invite them. Thank you."

Clearly her praise made him uncomfortable. He stuffed his hands in his pockets. "There is no need for gratitude. My actions were precipitated by nothing more than common logic."

Her brow furrowed. "Logic?"

"Yes." His face was a clean slate, giving nothing away. "If your mind was preoccupied with your sister, then I wouldn't have your full attention for our research."

Mallory didn't know why, but his answer hurt. "I see. Certainly we can't have anything getting in the way of the research now, can we?" She thought she saw him flinch, but figured it was only a trick of the light.

"That is why you're here, after all."

"And I promise I won't forget that again," she said tightly. "I assume you paid for their plane tickets?"

"I invited them," he replied, which was his way of saying yes.

Why had she thought for one minute that his action had been prompted by anything other than cold, hard logic? "I will pay you back."

"I don't expect reimbursement. They are my guests and will be treated as such."

"Well, you're getting your money back whether you like it or not."

"I think you're overtired," he said in that oh-so-superior tone of voice that grated on Mallory's nerves. "Why don't we discuss this tomorrow when you're a bit calmer? I believe things will look clearer then."

"Don't you dare treat me like a child!"

"Don't act like one."

"I'm not one of your servants to be dismissed at the wave of a hand."

"I merely said we should have this discussion tomorrow."

"There is nothing to discuss!" His cool, unruffled demeanor angered Mallory. "You can't keep using your money to buy people! If you want something, open your mouth and ask for it and stop taking the easy way out!" She regretted the words as soon as they left her mouth.

His lips compressed into a thin line. "I apologize if my decision upset you."

Mallory felt horrible. She had lashed out at a man whose very nature was to be logical, whom she had expected to act differently merely because that was what she wanted. She had blamed him for being himself—and she had done it in the worst possible way.

"Dexter—" she began, only to be cut off as the front door swung open, admitting her mother and sister, leaving an apology on Mallory's lips . . . and a dull ache in her heart.

CHAPTER TWELVE

Privacy at last.

Mallory allowed herself a moment to revel in the peace now that her mother and sister had gone to the movies, giving her an evening to herself.

For two days she had played tour guide as if she were lady of the manor instead of a guest herself, revisiting the same hallway three times at one point because she had gotten lost. Yet there was method to her madness. Keeping Genie busy being the key objective.

Mallory wanted to make sure her sister stayed out of trouble. Although, she wondered if her worry was unnecessary considering Genie's mind had been thoroughly occupied with other pursuits.

Namely, Dexter. Genie was utterly infatuated with their host.

When Mallory had introduced her sister to Dexter, Genie had gaped in a most unbecoming fashion, to the point where Mallory had to nudge her in the side.

Uncomfortable yet gracious, Dexter had accepted Genie's youthful adoration with aplomb, which only succeeded in making Mallory feel even worse about her horrendous behavior.

When he finally walked away to speak to her mother, who stood across the hallway admiring a huge oil painting, the zombielike trance Genie had been in ended—and the homage to all things Dexter began.

"Oh . . . my . . . God. The man's a hunk! Did you see those eyes?" she asked, as if Mallory had spent all this time looking at Dexter's eyeless head. "I swear he could see right through my clothes." Clearly Genie didn't mind the prospect. "And that bod! The man's muscles have muscles."

On and on it went. Mallory got no reprieve from Genie's living memorial of Dexter even in her own bedroom, since her sister had—with an abundance of bedrooms from which to choose—decided to bunk in with Mallory, believing a castle as old as Braden Manor had to be haunted by the ghosts of the undead.

"She must have met Cummings," had been Freddie's caustic addition to the conversation.

If nothing else, the busy time spent with her sister had given Mallory some space from Dexter. They had not had a "meeting" since her family arrived, but she suspected he was avoiding her. Could she blame him?

Nevertheless, they had research to do. She had promised him she would not be foolish enough to forget that again. Besides, she owed him an apology.

So what was her next move?

She was pondering the answer to that question when she heard a muted noise coming from somewhere in the house. She couldn't figure out exactly what it was. The castle had a tendency to capture sound and distort it.

Mallory opened her bedroom door and peered out. The hallway was deserted, but that was nothing new. She could walk the corridors for a half hour and not run into another soul.

The house was emptier than usual as the few servants had been given the day off, and Freddie had left hours earlier to go into town to become better acquainted with a "luscious hunk of a man" she had spotted the day before.

"I swear there must be something in the water around here," Freddie had remarked, her blue eyes glinting with wicked delight. "You should have seen the arms on this guy. Like two cannons. Bet he has the intellect of a cabbage, though." She smiled. "Dumb and built. Just the way I like 'em."

"Oh, really?" Mallory intoned. "I thought you preferred educated men—like Cummings, for example."

That had wiped the smile from Freddie's face. "The man has the personality of a bedpan," she muttered, and then quickly took her leave.

Shortly thereafter, Dexter had also left the house. Where he had gone, Mallory hadn't a clue. Most likely, he was stocking up on pepper spray to protect himself from another one of her outbursts.

Mallory realized she had been walking aimlessly down the corridors and that the sound that had drawn her from her room was getting dimmer.

She turned around and headed toward the stairs leading to the lower level.

She made it to the second-floor landing, which looked down into a long foyer with highly polished dark-wood flooring, an obviously modern update, when a door flew open and out poured the sound she had been following.

Music.

An oddly clad body came sliding out of the study, stocking feet carrying him to the middle of the floor where he proceeded to hold up a cordless screwdriver turned microphone and sing, *"Just take those old records off the shelf . . ."* Cummings stopped abruptly when he spotted her.

Mallory hid a grin behind her hand as he quickly fixed the upturned collar of his pristine white button-down shirt and tried to pretend he hadn't just been acting out Tom Cruise's role in *Risky Business*.

"Good evening," he said as she met him at the bottom of the steps.

"Good evening," she returned, praying she could keep her laughter behind her teeth. The poor man looked so uncomfortable, she just couldn't embarrass him further.

Mallory couldn't understand why Freddie disliked Cummings so much. He was smart, handsome, funny, and clearly uninhibited, if his musical display was any indication. The kind of man any woman would be proud to call her own. Mallory, however, liked him as a friend.

She glanced into the study and spotted the source of the music; a portable stereo, which sat on top of an expensive sofa table.

"I'll turn that off," Cummings said and started toward the room.

Mallory halted him. "Don't. I like it." She used to listen to music all the time, enjoying the rhythms, feeling the beat seeping into her blood.

For years, she had taken dance classes, but she had stopped when money became tight, having to decide whether to keep going to class or help her family with the steadily mounting bills her father had left them with. She really had only one choice.

"There is something about listening to good music that relieves my tension," Cummings said.

"Mine, too."

He smiled and held his hand out to her, saying with Victorian gallantry, "My lady, would you honor me with a dance?"

Mallory's gaze flicked to his hand and then up to his face. "Here? Now? Like this?"

"Here. Now. Like this."

She made to protest, but a soulful rift of guitar chords filled the air as Santana's song "Maria" began to play, begging someone to sway to its passionate beat.

Mallory returned Cummings's infectious smile and took his hand. "I'd love to, kind sir."

She was swept up into the rhythm, closing her eyes and allowing the music to flow through her and take away her worries.

It was then she found the answer to her question about what to do next with Dexter. If music could soothe the savage beast, it could certainly relax one very uptight professor, and if he was relaxed, perhaps she would be able to teach him what he wanted to know.

When he had closed his eyes while they were in

his office, he had been at ease for a few minutes and had done remarkably well with his description of the mystery woman's lips—too well, in fact.

Now, if she could loosen him up from top to bottom, she might finally get somewhere. She could show him some dance moves—ones that did not require touching, therefore keeping in line with her visual approach.

She was feeling rather pleased with her solution, envisioning scenarios, which might be the reason she didn't realize that she and Cummings had an audience until a familiar voice boomed, "What the hell is going on here?"

Over Cummings's shoulder, Mallory's gaze collided with riveting blue eyes—eyes that had thus far looked at her only with bland inquiry or confusion or questioning her sanity.

Never had she seen those eyes looking as they did now.

With fury.

As the sultry song came to an end, Mallory thought Dexter was one beast who appeared far from soothed.

"Ms. Ginelli, as long as you are in my employ, I expect you to refrain from flirting with my associates."

Mallory glared at Dexter and rubbed her arm where he had gripped it when he high-handedly dragged her into his office, slamming the door so hard she expected one of the four turrets adorning the castle's corners to plummet toward the ground like a rocket re-entering the earth's atmosphere.

But she didn't care at that moment. The stones

could come tumbling down around her like the walls of Jericho and it wouldn't change one simple fact.

She, too, was mad.

When Dexter had stormed toward her, Mallory had gotten a glimpse of the person who had been hidden behind his massive form.

Freddie. Beautiful, wind-blown, Coppertone Freddie.

Had they met up somewhere? Perhaps spent some time together? Gotten better acquainted? Shared a few laughs, even? Or had it simply been coincidence that they arrived home at the same time?

Mallory frowned. Why did it matter if it was coincidence or if they had been together? What Dexter did was none of her concern. She had no claim on him, and he had no claim on her. And that, she told herself, was the real reason she was angry. He had no right to act as if he owned her!

"Are you listening to me, Ms. Ginelli?" he asked curtly. "I won't tolerate being tuned out—or your bewitching Cummings with your feminine wiles. Is that clear?"

Mallory might have taken some pleasure in his assumption she had feminine wiles if he hadn't said the words as if they were a curse.

Bewitching Cummings! Bewitching was Freddie's territory not hers. And besides, who did the man think he was? She certainly wasn't kowtowing to that autocratic, I'm-in-charge tone of voice. He was asking for a fat lip!

"I'll do what I want when I want," she returned tightly, folding her arms over her chest.

They faced off across his desk. She refused to

back down, even though the look he sent her was enough to freeze water. She knew the desk would not be a deterrent should mayhem break out— and with each passing moment, the odds of an eruption steadily rose.

"While you are in my house, you will behave yourself. Save your trysts for your friends in New York."

"My trysts?" Mallory sputtered, a cornucopia of words clogging her throat; choked as it was with blazing indignation.

How dare the man accuse her of something so ... base! To think she would fool around with Cummings—sweet, charming, *gentlemanly* Cummings—was positively preposterous! She had never had a tryst in her life.

Her temper needing a vent, Mallory's gaze swept Dexter's desk, looking for an object to throw at his head in the hopes of knocking some sense into him. She spotted a paperweight. A nice, chunky marble paperweight. She swiped it off his desk and hefted it in her palm.

"What are you doing with that paperweight, Ms. Ginelli? Put it down before someone gets hurt."

Oh, someone was going to get hurt all right. "Are you worried?"

"No, of course not." He looked worried, though. "You wouldn't do anything so childish as to heave that at me. Now, if you would please be so kind—"

"You think so?" Mallory started around the side of his desk. He, in turn, began to walk backward.

"If we could just discuss this like rational adults."

"I was rational. Now I'm enjoying a bout of *irrational.*"

Dexter continued to back away from her. If she

took a moment to think about it, she might realize how utterly ridiculous they must look. A six-foot-four man of some two-hundred-twenty pounds' worth of solidly packed muscle being stalked by a woman half his size.

Mallory stopped in her tracks as a single thought careened to the front of her mind: she was chasing the professor around his desk!

Oh, dear God, she had cracked. Her last hold on reality had just slipped off the edge of a cliff to its untimely death.

She mentally shook herself, unable to believe what she had been about to do, that she had let this man push her buttons so easily. What was the matter with her?

She took a deep breath, intending to put the paperweight back . . . until he said, "If you could learn to subdue your raging impulses, Ms. Ginelli, we would not be having this discussion or subsequent infantile display."

Her raging impulses? Infantile display?

She would show him infantile!

She lifted her arm, wound up the pitch, aimed . . . and in the next instant, found herself on the floor. How she ended up on top of the professor, she couldn't quite fathom. But the how and why of her current predicament took a backseat to the almost sinful enjoyment she felt having the upper hand.

Dexter's glasses had flown to parts unknown, and for the first time, Mallory could look directly into those blue eyes. He, in turn, studied her, his gaze skimming over her brow, down her nose, along the contour of her lips, over her jaw . . . and then returning to her lips; each sweep of his gaze like a heated caress.

His hair looked so soft and cool, and she knew a strong desire to comb her fingers through the silky strands and discover the truth for herself.

"Am I hurting you?" she asked, wondering at the breathless quality of her voice.

"No," he replied, his voice equally low and husky, the sound washing over her like a warm wind.

"Would you . . . like me to move?" Mallory didn't know what possessed her to ask that question instead of simply getting off him. But there it was. The truth. She didn't want to move. Not yet.

Not yet.

He hesitated, then slowly shook his head. "No."

That lone word shot a thrill all the way down to her toes. She affected him. And for that, she was most grateful, because Lord knows he affected her. Rather ardently, in fact.

So much so that she knew the strongest urge to kiss him, softly, tenderly, to taste his lips with her tongue and brush the sensitive skin of her mouth over his. The need thrummed so forcefully inside her that she felt herself succumbing to the temptation.

"I'm going to kiss you, Professor," she murmured, the words leaving from her lips before she could stop them, before she could think of what she was saying.

Before her senses returned and ruined the moment.

He swallowed. "You are?"

"Umm-hmm."

"Do you think that's prudent?"

His question made her want to laugh and cry at the same time. No, of course it wasn't prudent. It was completely mad, foolhardy, and so very, very irresponsible, especially for a girl who had never been anything *but* responsible.

Perhaps that was why she said, "Yes, it's entirely prudent."

Although his expression seemed to hold no more than curiosity, his eyes had subtly darkened. "What purpose will kissing me serve?"

What purpose? Mallory had to tamp down her female pique at his question. "To further our research," she replied.

"This is research?"

She nodded and wished he would stop talking. "Kissing is part of wooing, a very important part." All too important at that moment.

"It seems rather forward to kiss someone whose family I've just recently met."

Amazing. When was the last time a man had felt it necessary to meet the kinfolk before kissing a woman?

"I don't even know your favorite color," he added.

Mallory couldn't help a slight smile. "It's turquoise."

"Turquoise?" His brow furrowed. "I haven't seen you wear one thing in that color."

"Perhaps because I don't look good in it."

"I find that hard to believe."

"Why, Professor, was that a compliment?"

He frowned, clearly not appreciating her amusement at his expense. "Merely an observation, Ms. Ginelli," he returned gruffly.

"Do you think you could call me Mallory this

once? I've told you my favorite color after all—and you have met my family."

He looked at her as if she had just asked him if he had any last words before the firing squad riddled his body with bullets.

Then, hesitantly, he said, "Fine . . . *Mallory.*"

Her name on his lips sounded so sweet, so deep and perfect, that she swept her mouth gently over his before she knew what she was doing.

"Was that it, then?" he asked when she pulled back.

It took a moment for Mallory to realize what he was asking. "The kiss, you mean?"

He nodded.

"No." No, no, no. "That was a different kind of kiss. Kind of a thank-you kiss."

"What are you thanking me for?"

"It's complicated," she evaded. But one thing was clear: the kiss had been more than just a thank-you. What else, precisely, she wasn't sure.

"So are going to kiss me again?"

Did he want her to kiss him again? She couldn't tell. His face could be utterly implacable.

But what about her? Did she want to kiss him again?

"Yes," she replied to both him and herself. "Now just relax and think of this as a test."

"A test?"

"More of a survey, actually," she said, teasing him with his own words. "For purely scientific purposes, of course."

He regarded her for a long moment and then shrugged. "All right. Go ahead. I, for one, know the value of research." He closed his eyes and said, as though being martyred at the stake, "I'm ready."

If that wasn't the most unromantic, impersonal invitation to share a kiss that she had ever heard. Mallory almost expected him to add, *I regret that I only have one life to give for my country.*

Mallory hesitated, then closed her eyes and lowered her head, pressing her lips to Dexter's in a tentative exploration. A sensation so heady, so exquisite, coursed through her, she knew no words could ever describe it.

His lips were warm, pliant, and he tasted like the brandy he had after he had dragged her into his office to accuse her of corrupting Cummings with her feminine wiles. What these supposed 'feminine wiles' were—as she had yet to witness them Mallory hadn't the foggiest, but at the moment, she wasn't inclined to care as Dexter tilted his head to deepen the kiss, and her tongue tentatively swept inside his mouth.

A jolt rocked her as his lips wrapped around her tongue and sucked gently on it, his mouth slanting across hers, causing a maelstrom of liquid heat to burgeon forth and spread. Only one solitary thought ran through her mind.

The professor was a superb kisser.

He certainly needed no instruction. Did his flawless technique come naturally? Or had he honed his skills with lots of practice? Mallory preferred to think it was natural ability.

She gave in to her earlier urge and combed her fingers through his hair, reveling in its texture, the silky strands caressing her palms.

He, in turn, reached up and removed the band that secured her hair in its ponytail, causing a mass of dark tresses to cascad forward, wrapping them in seclusion and building desire.

His fingers twined through her hair, one hand slipping toward the back to cup her head, bringing her mouth in tighter against his.

Mallory moved restlessly against him, her body pressing closer to cradle the hardness at the juncture of his thighs. A low moan rumbled from deep inside his chest, the sound a combination of pleasure-pain.

She thought he murmured her name, but whatever he said was drowned out by a rapping sound, which her hazy mind recognized a moment too late as someone knocking on his office door.

Catapulted into a guilt-ridden frenzy, Mallory scrambled off Dexter, but fate conspired against them that day, tangling their limbs so that he was half on top of her when the door suddenly opened.

CHAPTER THIRTEEN

That kiss.

Dexter couldn't stop thinking about it. The memory had plagued his sleep and lingered still, seeming even more haunting in the early morning light drifting through his office window as he stared at the spot in front of his desk where Mallory's body had been pressed to his ... until they had been caught red-handed, like two youths necking behind the barn.

Cummings. The bloody rotter. Him and his lousy timing. Dexter wasn't generally prone to violence, but he had felt very much like smashing his fist into his friend's face as Cummings stood in the doorway looking too smug by half.

But what might have happened had Cummings not interrupted them when he had? Dexter wanted to believe nothing would have transpired between himself and Mallory, that he would have put her away from him and done the right thing. Yet with all good conscience, he couldn't say he would have been able to let her go.

Good Christ, he had lost control, and he was a man known for his control, for his steely determination and clear-headed thinking. And yet, with Mallory in his arms, he had been anything *but* clear-headed.

"I'll have to remember to walk in on you more often, Dex," Cummings remarked, his posture cocky as he sat in a chair in front of Dexter's desk, a satyr's grin running from ear to ear—and his chin asking for a punch. Clearly he was a man on a mission. "God only knows what I might see next time."

"Are you here for a purpose?" Dexter asked as calmly as humanly possible, knowing better than to feed into Cummings's need to goad.

"Just thought I'd set the record straight and tell you it was your fault I barged in on you and Mallory last night."

"My fault, was it? Well, this should prove enlightening."

"You must admit that you were not acting like yourself. Good Lord, man, you looked like a thundercloud, veins were actually standing out on your neck. Thought you were going to rearrange my vital organs."

"Try not to be asinine. I wasn't angry with you."

"Could have fooled me. But it wasn't myself I was worried about. When everything got quiet shortly after you hauled Mallory away—and keep in mind that you slammed your office door so hard the reverberations are still being felt—I figured something dire must have happened."

"You know I would never have hurt a woman." Hurting Mallory had been the last thing on his mind, but it bothered Dexter that his friend would think he might.

Cummings waved a dismissive hand. "I had no doubt she'd be fine. It was you I was worried about. I figured I'd come in and find you doubled over from the knee to the groin I was sure she would give you—which you richly deserved, by the by."

Dexter didn't need the reminder of his highly irregular and borderline raving behavior of the previous evening. He had yet to stop thinking about it.

"You know," Cummings went on in a tone that didn't bode well for Dexter's peace of mind, "I don't think this room has seen that much action since those two mummies your mother brought home from the museum fell on top of each other."

Dexter's ire was beginning to unravel from its closely monitored confines. "Nothing was going on," he growled. "Ms. Ginelli was just—"

"Seeing how far her tongue would go down your throat?"

"Look, leave Ms. Ginelli out of this!"

"Don't you think you could call her Mallory at this point?"

Dexter scowled, remembering how Mallory had asked him the same thing. And he remembered quite clearly what her response had been when he had said her name. A sweet brushing of her lips across his—followed by a good morning tonsillectomy he would not soon forget.

Dexter pointed. "The door is that way. Use it."

Cummings ignored him. "Since you're obviously feeling testy, I will expedite this process by asking the following question ... Did you tell Mallory about Lady Sarah? Knowing what a noble fellow you are, shall I assume the answer is yes?"

Cummings, the sod, would have to bring up the one topic Dexter did not want to talk about. His thought processes were still too muddled for any sort of rational discourse on the subject.

"No," he replied tersely. "I didn't tell her. But I will."

"You didn't tell her?" Cummings sat up straighter in his chair. "And may I ask why?"

"No, you bloody well may not."

"So I assume you'll tell her now?" Cummings went on as if Dexter had not spoken. "Considering the passion you've shared, it's only right."

Dexter picked up the paperweight Mallory had intended to launch at his head last night. He could see how such an item could prove useful. "We were doing research."

"So that's what people are calling it these days?" Cummings said, his grin unrepentant.

"There is nothing between Ms. Ginelli and myself."

Cummings looked unconvinced. "So when do you plan to tell Mallory that you are sacrificing yourself, ah, I mean, getting married?"

"Soon." Never sounded better.

"Soon, hmm? Well, that's a shining monument to vagueness if I ever heard one." Cummings eyed him closely. "You do intend to tell her?"

"Of course." He had to, more so after the kiss they had shared. So why was he reluctant to do what he knew he should? He had no plausible excuse not to tell Mallory the entire reason behind his request for her services. No excuse not to explain to her why he wanted to learn how to be more passionate and charming.

The reason was simple, really. He needed to learn how to be the type of man who would make his future wife happy, and that man was not the stuffy scientist. That man was a disaster when it came to women.

His marriage to Lady Sarah Benton had been planned since he was fifteen and Sarah a child a five, following a two-hundred-year Harrington tradition of arranged marriages.

To some people, it seemed an antiquated custom. And there had been a time when Dexter had felt the same way, when he had revolted against the invisible chains that bound him to a woman he had not chosen for himself.

But with his parents' death and being the only son, he felt obligated to fulfill their wishes. It had taken him nearly two years to get to this point, and he thought he had finally resigned himself to the idea.

"So you haven't changed your mind, then, and decided not to go through with this farce, I mean, this fiasco, er, I mean this marriage?" Cummings asked, though not for the first time since learning of Dexter's decision.

"No, I have not changed my mind." But he wanted to change the subject. He didn't want to think about Sarah. And he sure as hell didn't want to think about marriage.

He turned and glanced out the window, spotting Mallory meandering through the garden. His gaze followed her. He was drawn to her, there was no denying it. She had a brightness about her that lit up whatever room she entered, alleviating the gray pall that had haunted Dexter for too many years.

Her spirit was indomitable; the strength of her will, a sheer yet palpable force. Quite frankly, he admired her. Nevertheless, he couldn't allow his admiration to lead him astray as it did today.

"You know, Dex, no one would fault you for not going through with this marriage."

"I know that," he murmured, dragging his gaze from Mallory and dropping into the chair behind his desk.

For most of his life, he had not measured up to the standards set for an heir and a Harrington. He cared too much about things his parents cared too little for, and cared too little about things his parents cared too much for.

He had been searching for his place since he was old enough to understand why he didn't quite fit in. He had begun to believe that with his marriage to Lady Sarah, he would at last be at peace.

"If you know you don't have to propose to Sarah," Cummings said, "then why the hell are you doing it? You look bloody miserable."

"I don't want to get into this again with you. Just accept the fact and let's both try to move on."

"Have you given any consideration to how Sarah feels?"

"Feels about what?"

Cummings shook his head. "About having a husband who doesn't care about her?"

"I do care for her."

"As a friend."

Dexter couldn't deny that truth. He had known Sarah since she was a child and still pictured her with her long auburn pigtails. She had looked up to him as her protector, and he had treated her like the sister he never had.

He had thought his feelings for her might mature as he got older, but they never had. Nevertheless, he couldn't hurt her. She had never cried off on their childhood betrothal, and that became one more reason he had to go through with it. Perhaps in time they would grow to care for each other the way a husband and wife should.

"You seem to forget why I invited Mallory here," Dexter said. "I'm doing all this for Sarah, to try to be a better husband to her."

"Do you think Sarah loves you, Dex?" Cummings asked, posing the one question Dexter had never asked himself, though he suspected the only kind of feeling Sarah had for him was misplaced admiration.

"Like me, Sarah understands duty and tradition."

"Tradition be damned, man!" Cummings said with a vehemence that surprised Dexter. "There was a time when you used to listen to your heart, not bloody duty. What happened to that man?"

Dexter felt the old frustration and pain boil up inside him—and yes, the anger. What he wouldn't give to be as free as Cummings. To live his own life and not be bogged down by the burden of his birth.

"You don't understand," he bit out. "You've never been—" Dexter stopped, realizing what he had been about to say, how it would sound.

"I've never what, Dex? Spit it out. Been privileged like you? You're damn right I haven't. I had a lot less."

Dexter had always known that deep down Cummings resented his own poverty and Dexter's wealth, though he doubted Cummings harbored those feelings on a conscious level.

Dexter didn't hold that resentment against his friend, because he knew that Cummings could not change the origins of his birth any more than Dexter could change his.

"I just meant that I sometimes wish my life could have been simpler," he replied.

"Like mine, for example?" Cummings's voice hinted at bitterness. "Don't wish for something you wouldn't want. I once lived in a way that you couldn't comprehend, that your kind would abhor."

"My kind?" Dexter shot forward in his chair. "What the hell does that mean? *My kind?* Since when have I ever drawn a line between the two of us?"

Cummings's gaze slid away from him. "Never. But maybe you should have."

"Damn it, man! What are you talking about? You're my best friend. You always have been."

"I know," Cummings murmured. Slowly, he turned back to look at Dexter, his gaze shuttered, his expression unfathomable. "I may not know about the privileged life, but I know a hell of a lot about mistakes and even more about guilt. And I'm telling you to think about what you're doing, what you may be giving up—and what you could ultimately be throwing away in your quest to be the perfect son."

Dexter's jaw clenched hearing those last two words. "I advise that we end this conversation now before we both say something we're going to regret."

Looking world-weary, Cummings pushed himself to his feet and stood staring down at Dexter. "You'll never know how many things I already regret, things I wish I could change. What I wouldn't give to go back and make those things right." A muscle worked in his jaw. "Stop being a goddamn martyr, Dex. Tell Mallory the truth or let her go—before the chance to set things right slips away." And with that denouncement, Cummings turned on his heel and quit the room, leaving his words to echo in his wake.

Tell Mallory the truth or let her go.

Dexter shoved himself from the chair, hoping to shut out the words. He wouldn't have any regrets with Mallory because he wouldn't allow his emotions to get involved. He would remain neutral. He excelled at being neutral, never letting anything affect him, touch him. Hurt him.

Cummings's concerns were unnecessary. Dexter knew what he was doing. He was determined to see this thing through and carry on with tradition.

Only one thing stood in the way.

How would he ever forget that kiss?

Mallory wandered through the garden, searching for the peace of mind she had not found in sleep.

All night she had tried to block out the memory of Dexter's kiss, tossing and turning in bed until another day had crept upon the horizon, sunlight washing through the room, prodding her with its rays, asking her if she intended to hide out like a chicken or toss her shoulders back and face the world like a woman.

She was behaving ridiculously, she knew. Her reaction to Dexter was completely normal. She was a woman after all—one who was currently cooped up in an isolated castle with a man who could pass for a *Playgirl* pinup.

She slipped behind a fat oak tree and glanced heavenward. "Dear God, why are you punishing me like this?" she lamented, enjoying a rousing bout of self-pity. "The man was supposed to look like Horshack from "Welcome Back, Kotter," not a modern-day Adonis from a J. Crew catalogue! Ph.D. is not supposed to stand for perfectly honed delts."

Mallory shook off her pathetic display, reminding herself that she was a confident, successful woman who could control her baser instincts. And that was why she had every intention of following through on the plan she had come up with last night.

No matter how daunting the task may be.

CHAPTER
FOURTEEN

"You want me to do *what*?"

Mallory watched Dexter's eyebrows escalate with each word he spoke, rising along with the volume of his voice, so that the last word ricocheted through the room like a cannon blast, sending the blackbirds resting in a tree outside his office window into a jumbled mass exodus that looked eerily reminiscent of a scene from Hitchcock's movie, *The Birds*.

Clearly the professor didn't relish her idea. But being the teacher did have some advantages. He either did it her way or not at all. And if he didn't cooperate, well then, she couldn't be expected to stay now, could she?

Surreptitiously, Mallory regarded his mulish countenance. Would he let her go this time should she fail at her mission? Or would he insist she keep trying, therefore prolonging her time with him, dooming her to remain under the shadow of his hulking presence, forcing her to look into those eyes . . . day in and day out?

Did she still want to leave?

Mallory frowned. Where had that thought come from? Of course she wanted to leave, to be done with this odd, vexing research and this odd, vexing scientist. She had a book to finish.

So what else is new?

And a deadline to meet.

The world will stop rotating if you're late this once?

And a life to lead.

You need to have a life to lead one.

Mallory forced the thoughts from her mind, yet one question remained.

Was Dexter still thinking about their kiss?

Probably not. So why was she? It wasn't as if she had never been kissed before. True, it had been an infrequent occurrence. And true, those kisses hadn't been quite so sensual or affected her so deeply. But really, it had only been a kiss—a simple, sweet, earth-moving kiss.

Lord, she had to stop this!

Mallory shook herself and slipped a cassette in the tape player. Then, she turned to face Dexter, who stood like a wax effigy, staring mutinously at her. This wasn't going to be easy.

"Don't act like I've just sentenced you to execution."

"I'd prefer execution," he muttered. "And what the hell is a bon-bon anyway?"

All right, so telling him she was going to teach him how to shake his bon-bon like Ricky Martin had not been the best approach, considering El Professor only seemed to grasp those things that were framed in the most clinical of ways, but she had been feeling rather whimsical at the time. Her mistake.

But she had no intention of explaining to this big, beautiful Ph. doofus what a bon-bon was, even if he did have the most spectacular one she had ever been privileged to see.

"Never mind," she evaded. "Now, can you feel the rhythm of the music?"

He snorted. "You call this music? If you want music, we can listen to Mozart or Beethoven or Haydn. Or my favorite. Bach. I'm a particular fan of his concertos. His Toccata and Fugue in D Minor are most arresting."

"You need less fugue and more funk. Now, let me see you swivel your hips."

He folded his indecently large arms across his indecently large chest and glared at her. "I will not swivel my hips, madam."

The man personified stubbornness. "If you don't swivel your hips, you'll go without dessert for supper." Lame, certainly. But it worked with children. This particular child just happened to be extremely tall and well built.

"I shall survive without dessert, I assure you."

"I don't know. You look a little frail to me."

He frowned and then looked down at himself. "You think so?"

Dear Lord, did the man actually think she believed him to be frail? His chest alone looked like forty-eight inches of solid titanium. He really didn't know how attractive he was. And darn it all, it only made him that much more attractive.

"I'm joking. You know, ha-ha." But clearly he

didn't. Humor was lost on this man. Completely
lost.

"I don't understand this propensity you have for
senseless tomfoolery."

Mallory intended to give him the will-you-loosen-
up speech, but paused to wonder at the extra dose
of mulishness coming from him this morning.

If it was possible, he seemed even stiffer and more
shuttered than usual. If she didn't know better, she
might think he was angry. But what did he have
to be angry about?

Could he possibly still be upset over the innocent dance she had shared with Cummings? He
shouldn't be. Clearly nothing had transpired
between herself and his friend.

And anyway, what right did he have to be upset?
He had been out with Freddie. Freddie had con-
firmed it. She claimed they had met by accident
in town and had gone to the video store together.
Freddie said she had picked out a few movies for
Dexter. Mallory could just imagine what they were.

She frowned at her assumption, chiding herself
for letting her imagination run away with her. What
was the matter with her? Freddie was her best
friend!

And yet, she felt compelled to say, "You're not
still miffed about my dancing with Cummings, are
you?"

"I was never miffed," he rejoined, sounding,
well, miffed. "I was merely delineating the acceptable boundaries."

Delineating the acceptable boundaries, was he?
"I'm a grown woman. I can delineate my own
boundaries, thank you."

He said nothing, but his look was patently skeptical. She decided to let the matter rest. For the moment. "Are you going to cooperate or act like a willful child?"

He scowled at her and muttered, "I'll cooperate—but no shaking any bon-bons."

"Fine." It was too early for heart palpitations anyway. "Let's start with a little hip swiveling."

He looked as if he was about to comply, albeit grudgingly, when he asked, "Why are we doing this? What does hip swiveling have to do with wooing?"

"If you want to woo, you have to loosen up."

He took umbrage to that remark, every vertebra in his spine snapping to attention. "I'm loose."

A bubble of that's-the-funniest-thing-I've-heard-since-I-found-out-kinky-perms-were-back-in-style laughter centered in Mallory's chest. "Rigor mortis is looser than you. An animal carcass frozen for three thousand years is looser than you. A polar ice cap in the Alaskan tundra—"

He held up his hand, his displeasure obvious. "I deduce your point."

With the look of a man who had just been asked to go shoe shopping with his wife, the professor reluctantly began to rotate his hips—either that or he was doing his imitation of a long-forgotten jungle mating ritual.

The man may have been blessed with a five-star pelvis, but clearly swiveling was not in his genes. He looked like a life-size version of a gyrating dashboard figurine.

"Do you think you could put a little more swing into it?" Mallory asked, hoping her expression said *You're doing fine* instead of *I believe that move has been banned in forty-eight states and Canada.*

He stopped. "I can't do this."

"You can."

"Have you any statistical data that supports this highly irregular form of teaching?"

"Does everything have to be when, why, how, and the reasons thereof with you?"

He adjusted his eyeglasses and she wished he would take them off. Better yet, throw them to the ground and stomp them to bits. "Yes," he replied, straight-faced. Then he nodded in her direction. "I want to see you swivel your hips."

"Oh, no. This lesson is for you, not me."

"If you don't do it, then I don't do it." Yes, sir. A big willful child.

Mallory thought to balk, but figured that was exactly what he expected. "Fine. Have it your way." She moved to the portable stereo, removed Madonna, who was grating on her nerves anyway, and picked up the first tape within her reach.

She was sliding the tape into the cassette player when he said, "I want you to dance to the same song you danced to last night."

Mallory's hand stilled, but she did not turn around. "Why?"

"Because."

Because? What kind of answer was that?

Either way, she didn't want to dance to Santana's song, not in front of him. The music took her inhibitions away, made her feel the rhythm in her blood.

"I don't want to."

"Why not?"

"I just don't."

"Because you danced with Cummings to that song?" he asked, sounding disgruntled.

Mallory swung around. "Aha! I knew you were still angry over that! Why·didn't you just admit it?"

"I told you, I'm not angry." His fierce scowl warned her not to push. "I ... I just liked ... I mean, I think you ..." His frown deepened as he searched for the words. "You dance well," he finally said with all the emotion of a dry dishcloth.

Mallory couldn't help a slight smile. "You think so?"

He looked flustered. "I just said so, didn't I?"

She decided not to push. Compliments didn't come easy to the professor. Perhaps that was why she felt so flattered. "All right. I'll dance. But I want you to pay close attention to my hips."

"I will," he promised, a husky edge to his voice.

Mallory glanced up and noticed his gaze fastened to her hips. In that moment, she was suddenly, acutely aware that all this man's attention was going to be focused on her.

She forced down the jangle of nerves that threatened her resolve, remembering something Mrs. Feldman always said when Freddie had vexed her, a sentiment both simple and apropos to Mallory's current situation.

Oy vey!

With a slight tremble in her hands, Mallory slipped in the Santana CD, and for the second time in as many days, she heard the low beat of drums and the sweet strum of the guitar filter into the air.

She took a deep breath and closed her eyes, allowing the music to overcome her nervousness as it worked its way up her calves and down her spine.

Slowly, she began to move, losing her inhibitions

to the sensuous rhythm and, for the moment, giving her the freedom to forget she was being watched so intently.

Had he been on fire, Dexter couldn't have looked away as Mallory began to sway to the music, her movements keeping perfect tempo with the seductive beat of the song. He had only glimpsed this side of her last night. . . .

Last night when she had been in the arms of his best friend, a man who had looked as though he enjoyed having here there. In the few minutes Dexter had stood silent and angry on the threshold watching them, he wished his friend to hell.

Damn it! Why couldn't he have the suave charm Cummings possessed? Throughout college, Cummings had had all the women while Dexter had his textbooks and the science lab to occupy his nights, seeing his own failure through the eyes of those around him.

Well, by Christ, this time he would win! He had learned everything else in his life without any problems, mastered each thing he had set out to do. He would master this or die trying! He wanted Mallory, and Cummings could bloody well go hang!

That thought brought Dexter up short. He wanted Mallory? No, that had to have been a mental slip. It was Lady Sarah he wanted. She would be his wife after all. Mallory was just the instrument to make him the man he needed to be so Lady Sarah would be happy. That was what all this was about, the reason he needed Mallory's help.

He tried to keep that thought in mind even as his gaze traveled slowly over Mallory's body. The glimmering rays of the sun slanting through the many windows caught in her hair, streaking the dark tresses with red and gold and emphasizing her flawless complexion and the hint of freckles dotting the bridge of her nose.

Her lips were slightly parted, her expression enraptured, and he knew the strongest desire to pull her into his arms, to taste her lips again, to discover if he had imagined the heated sensation that had sluiced through him as that sweet mouth slanted over his.

His gut clenched, heat washing over him in waves. He hadn't felt this alive in a long time or enjoyed the power of being a man—or yearned to possess something fleeting and deeply beautiful as much as he did at that moment.

The light moved with her, accentuating her small waist, one he could span with both hands. Golden rays skimmed along the contours of slim legs and under the curve of a perfectly formed, taut buttocks.

Her body undulated full circle, the swell of her breasts tormenting him, sweet globes that would fill his palms, that he imagined were pert and tipped with lush, pink nipples . . . nipples he ached to taste.

The image made him groan aloud.

Abruptly, Mallory stopped moving. Her eyes snapped open and locked with his. Too late. He couldn't hide the desire he knew raged in his eyes.

How did he look to her at that moment? Like some besotted schoolboy? Anger roiled up inside him. Anger . . . and that old despair he had never completely locked away, a despair as illogical as it was a part of him, an ache that had dogged him from the time he realized he wasn't worth loving, that he was different, and scarred, and emotionally bereft.

What did she see . . . ?

Perhaps had he known the answer to that question he would not have felt so unworthy, for Mallory glimpsed vulnerability and desire and the man hidden beneath the stuffy scientist. What she saw made the breath lock in her throat and her stomach tighten. Painfully, joyfully. Wantonly.

The heat in his gaze licked over her, heightening the sensuality she felt inside herself at that moment, heightening the need that had burgeoned forth the day before when they had shared that kiss.

Yet behind the heat and desire lurked the pain she had glimpsed on other occasions. Pain he wanted no one to see. She understood that hurt. On some level she recognized an inexplicable connection between them.

Without conscious thought, she moved toward him. She didn't know what she intended, nor did she want to know. All she understood was the need to be near him, to touch him.

She stopped within an inch of him, her gaze moving slowly over the dark, firm skin of his neck, along the contours of a chiseled jaw, noticing the muscle that worked in his cheek, a palpable tension in the air.

She wanted to rub her thumb over that muscle and take away his worries, lay her lips against that cheek and leisurely work her way to his mouth.

Her gaze levered upward in increments, knowing that looking into Dexter's deep blue eyes would be her downfall, and when she met his gaze . . .

the world tilted. She tried to speak, but words would not come.

Slowly, she lifted onto her toes, letting all the questions and concerns fall away, wanting to know if the electricity she had experienced the day before had been real. . . .

Until he spoke and broke the spell.

"You're sweating, Ms. Ginelli. Shall I have Quick fetch you a moist towelette to wipe your brow?"

Mallory's euphoria evaporated in the space of a heartbeat. *Amor* turned into a raging case of female pique in the face of his obvious disinterest. A moist towelette! The irritating buffoon!

"No," she said through gritted teeth. "I don't want anything for my brow, thank you." She would much rather perspire into an embarrassed puddle on the floor.

She took a step away from him, cursing the magnetic pull that had caused her to move toward him while simultaneously scrambling her brain, sweeping away logic and common sense.

It was those damn eyes! She would have to get him Ray-Bans.

And make him wear a bag over his head.

And roll around in a swine pen.

And cover his body in leeches.

A quick exit would have to suffice for the moment. "I hope you learned something." Lord knows she had. "We can pick this up later or tomorrow." Or never, preferably.

"Oh. That's it?" He sounded almost . . . what? Disappointed? As if he didn't want her to go?

Mallory decided that analyzing Dexter was a feat too enormous to tackle at that moment. "We'll work on your clothes next." That would give her a chance to berate herself for suggesting the man swivel his body parts.

His brows drew together, and he held out his arms. "What's the matter with my clothes? My family has gone to the same tailor for years. Mr. Henry's family has been in business since 1885."

Mallory gave him the once-over. Another mistake. Vivid pictures of the day before flashed through her mind—the look in his eyes and the feel of his body beneath hers.

She mentally shook herself. "Apparently the style of clothing has not changed since then."

He continued to scowl at her, and she wondered if she would ever see a genuine smile on his face. "I'm comfortable in these clothes," he balked.

"And I admit, comfort is important." She knew the value of comfortable clothes. Wasn't Freddie forever haranguing her about her choice of attire? "But if you don't want to look like a scientist—"

"I *am* a scientist."

"And a very good one, I'm sure. But you want to woo, and those are not wooing clothes."

He regarded her for a long moment. "You don't like how I look?"

Why did he have to say such things? Allowing her a moment to glimpse something vulnerable inside him? Something that asked for approval?

"I think you look fine." And she truly meant it. She liked the way Dexter dressed—bow ties, tweed, and all. She couldn't really picture him any other way. "Nevertheless, this isn't about what I like." And that was what she had to remember. To forget could be disastrous. "I told you when we first started this . . . research that I had to remain impartial." Something that proved harder and harder each day. "That being the case, I have to think about what most women want from a man." Women like Freddie, for example.

"I see." He adjusted his bow tie—hunter green with tiny black dots. "I still shall not change the way I dress. You can get me to eat pizza with anchovies, make me swivel my hips, and even drink a bottle of . . . *Bud*. But I refuse to capitulate to every harebrained suggestion you feel compelled to foist upon my person. As God is my witness, I will not change the way I dress!"

THE BENEFITS OF BOOK CLUB MEMBERSHIP

- You'll get your books hot off the press, usually before they appear in bookstores.
- You'll ALWAYS save more than 20% off the cover price.
- You'll get our FREE monthly newsletter filled with author interviews, book previews, special offers, and MORE!
- There's no obligation — you can cancel at any time and you have no minimum number of books to buy.
- And — if you decide you don't like the books you receive, you can return them. (You always have ten days to decide.)

lll..l..l.lll....lll..l.l.l..l.l..l.ll.l..l..l.l..lll..l

Zebra Contemporary Romance Book Club
Zebra Home Subscription Service, Inc.
P.O. Box 5214
Clifton , NJ 07015-5214

CHAPTER FIFTEEN

The next day, Dexter changed his wardrobe.

But he did so under heavy protest, grumbling a lot just to make sure the woman inflicting said torture knew how very little he appreciated this particular measure, which he felt entirely unnecessary.

What did it matter what he wore? He was still the same man underneath, wasn't he? The prospect of believing the clothes made the man was completely and utterly preposterous.

"Ow! Bloody hell, that hurt!" he growled when his tailor accidentally poked him with a pin as he pulled the last one from the hem of Dexter's trousers—pre-made trousers. He had never worn anything pre-made in his entire life.

"Stop griping," Mallory told him, clearly conveying he was acting like a baby.

By God, the woman had the power to make him

feel as if he was behaving worse than a lad who had just been told he had to finish his Brussels sprouts if he wanted chocolate cake for dessert.

"I'm not griping."

"Could have fooled me."

He frowned at her, but damn it all, frowning never worked. She just frowned back. "I told you this is completely unnecessary."

"Hmm. That sounded like a gripe." Mallory looked down at his tailor. "Didn't that sound like a gripe to you, Mr. Henry?"

Mr. Henry raised his balding head only enough to give her a smile that said, *I'm staying out of this.* Wise man that Mr. Henry, Dexter thought. Too bad his hazel-eyed warden didn't take a page from the tailor's book and refrain from these nonsensical methods of tutoring.

What could a change of clothing do?

"Turn around, Professor," the blasted woman requested, which sounded more like an order to his ears. Bossy women. Where had they come from? Not from English soil. That much he was sure.

Grudgingly, Dexter pivoted on his heel with a decided lack of grace, which, had his mother been there, would have had her gasping.

A Harrington, she would say, moved with elegant strides, displaying the utmost decorum at all times. One never swung about. Or stomped. Or ate with his elbows on the table. Or spoke with his mouth full.

Or tackled a woman who aimed a marble paperweight at his head.

And a Harrington never took advantage of a woman.

Like he had taken advantage of Ms. Ginelli.

And he never compounded that sin by enjoying the act of taking advantage.

"Well, what do you think?" Mallory prompted.

Dexter's gaze snapped to her. She had the nerve to smile at him, a smile that transformed her face and had the power to root him to wherever he stood.

What was it about her that affected him so strongly, that made him forget why she was here and what he had to do in a few short weeks?

Why did this gamine-faced romance writer with her freckles and big T-shirts and aggravating opinions make him wish. . . .

Dexter cut himself off. *Wrong road to go down, Harrington,* he told himself. He had to stay focused and remember his goal.

Dexter gave his torturer a final scowl for good measure. Then he turned to regard himself in the mirror . . . and wondered who the hell he was looking at. Certainly that nattily dressed man in black could not be him?

As usual, Mr. Henry outfitted him to perfection, but Dexter had never worn black. He dressed as his father had dressed—and his father's father— and his father's father's father.

He frowned, thinking about what Mallory had said, that his style of clothing was somewhat out of date. Could it be she was right?

"What do you think?"

She came to stand next to him, and he caught a hint of the lilac fragrance she wore, which smelled better than the real thing. The light perfume teased his nostrils and never failed to thicken his blood.

She moved in front of him, brushing imaginary lint off his shoulders, tidying him like a mother hen. He discovered he rather liked it. It felt, well, nice to be fussed over.

She stopped abruptly, perhaps realizing what she was doing, and peered up at him through a fringe of thick black lashes. "Do you like it?" A hint of uncertainty laced her voice.

He smiled, something he had done more often in this girl's presence than he could recall doing in many years. "Yes. I do."

She smiled back, hesitant at first, but then full and warm . . . and damnably enticing.

And Dexter knew in that moment he wanted to kiss her again. He couldn't seem to stop thinking about kissing her. He had woken up in the middle of the night with her name on his lips and his comforter in a heap on the floor. He had grasped for the tendrils of his dream only to have them slip away, leaving him feeling empty and hoping sleep would bring the heated images back.

His gaze moved to her lips, wondering if he was awake at that moment or if perhaps he was still held in the thrall of his dream, for he had never felt so bold before, so reckless and determined. Her tongue swept out, and his gut clenched in reaction.

Then Mr. Henry cleared his throat—and Mallory abruptly stepped away from him.

Damn!

Scowling, Dexter's gaze riveted to the tailor, various scenarios of mayhem that he could inflict upon the man dancing in his head. Dexter didn't realize how fierce he looked until Mr. Henry rose and took a step back.

Sweet Jesus, what was he doing? He was acting like a madman. All because of a woman.

A beautiful, alluring, prodding, vivacious . . .

Forbidden woman.

"All finished, my lord," the man quickly stammered out, packing up his tailoring implements with lightning speed.

Dexter wanted to say something, apologize for his insane behavior, but what words might he use? *I'm sorry for wanting to hammer your slight form into the floor? For wishing you were a mirage? For lusting after a woman in your presence?*

Mr. Henry hustled to the door. "No need to see me out, my lord." He slapped his gray derby cap on his balding head. "I shall forward my bill. Good day to you both." Then he was gone.

And once Dexter was alone with Mallory, he discovered his desire had not diminished.

If anything, the ache seemed to have increased. Could it be the clothes *did* make him feel like a different man? A man who had the power to charm, entice . . .

Seduce?

Mallory stood at arm's length, silky strands of hair escaping the loose knot she had fashioned at the back of her head, framing her face, emphasizing the perfection of her skin, the luminous quality of her eyes . . . and the red fullness of her lips.

"I would like to do more research," he murmured, wondering if she felt what he did. Tingling in hands that longed to touch. Tightness in the chest that bordered on painful. A slow-burning heat seeking an outlet.

"W-what kind of research?" she asked in a breathy voice that had the power to escalate his heartbeat.

"The kissing kind," he murmured.

"Kissing?" The word came out a squeak.

He nodded. "Practice makes perfect."

He reached for her and pulled her toward him, carefully, slowly, afraid she might bolt. Afraid he might lose his nerve should she do so.

Her palms seared his chest. The short breaths she took matched his own. He bent his head, every fiber of his body thrumming to life. She watched his descent, and he watched her, seeing her hazel eyes darken, knowing as a man instinctively does that he was affecting her. The knowledge was powerful.

When his lips touched hers, it felt as if a lightning bolt had struck him between the shoulder blades. He had never experienced such a sensation, a fire that burned but did not consume.

And as coherent thought deserted Dexter, he wondered how this Yankee romance writer could bring out the man he was inside, the man buried beneath statistical data.

The man he had always wanted to be.

His tongue swept into her mouth to duel with hers. He felt conquering and conquered at the same time. She made a soft sound low in her throat, and heat spiraled to his groin, heat that seemed to have settled there since the night he carried Mallory into his house, her head cradled against his shoulder, silky strands of her hair caressing his arm.

His hands encircled her waist, wanting to bring her closer, needing to see if she fit against him as well as he remembered. God help him, she did.

Abruptly, she pulled away, a look of shock stamped on her face, making Dexter feel like the worst kind of degenerate, especially since he had savored every moment of their contact.

An inner voice, rusty from disuse, told him to pull her back, to finish a kiss made to have a beginning and an end. But the voice wasn't strong enough to eradicate the scientist—or the man who had obligations.

Now he needed to distance himself, to say something he didn't mean in order to put this moment where it belonged. In the past. Better off forgotten.

"Your skills are laudable in this particular area of tutoring, Ms. Ginelli, and I shall definitely recommend your services to others in need."

Mallory could do no more than stare at Dexter, hurt by his casual words, yet wondering why she should expect any more from him. It wasn't as if he possessed a heart. That was asking too much.

Yes, he was learning. Too fast. And far too well. She had wanted to stay in his arms and revel in that kiss—and that was why she couldn't. She was his employee. He had paid for her time, for her "services," as he had so aptly put it. What would that have made her if she had let the kiss lead to something else?

Worse, why had she wanted it to lead to something else? She had never felt so strongly about taking the next step with a man, to travel to a place she had never been.

But her virginity was the one precious thing she had, and she wouldn't sell it, or barter it, or belittle it. She would give that gift to a man she loved, a man who would appreciate what she had to offer.

That man wasn't Dexter Harrington. No matter how he made her feel. She was research to him, another piece of data to add to his equation.

Distance. She needed distance.

About three thousand miles worth to be exact.

At that moment, the best she could hope for was the opposite side of the room. To leave would look too much like running away. So she walked away instead, trying to appear as though she was simply exploring her surroundings as she searched for something commonplace to talk about.

"I just realized that you've never told me about your research."

Knowing how close to the bone he kept everything, she expected a noncommittal response. Instead, he surprised her, saying, "What do you want to know about it?"

Everything, she thought, realizing she was genuinely interested. She wanted to know more about the very thing that consumed Dexter's life, what she suspected would always be more important to him than anything. Or anyone.

Had it not been for his work, she would not be with him right now. She wondered when she had stopped resenting his intrusion in her life, no matter how well timed that intrusion had been, and had begun to enjoy herself. And him.

"Well, what are you working on, for one?"

"What makes you think I'm working on anything?"

Mallory stopped her aimless wandering and glanced over her shoulder. Dexter stood in the same spot, his regard intense, his hands shoved in the pockets of his perfectly fitted new black trousers.

The white silk knit shirt molded his torso, outlining the muscles of his chest and stomach. He was so handsome he made her teeth ache. She almost wished she hadn't suggested the change. She wanted his tweed jacket and bow tie back.

"Aren't you always working on something?"

"Usually," he replied with a shrug.

Mallory wondered at the look in his eyes, a look that said perhaps he wanted something more besides work in his life. But what? A wife? Children scampering through the forty-two rooms? Or was she once more seeing what she wanted to see rather than what was actually there?

"So what are you working on now?"

"I doubt you'd want to hear about it."

"Why not?"

He averted his gaze, staring down at his new shoes as though something about them suddenly fascinated him. "Science bores most women."

Mallory eased down in the big black leather chair behind his desk, taking pleasure in a stolen intimacy. "I'm not most women."

Slowly, he lifted his gaze to her, studying her for a long moment before murmuring, "No, you're not, are you?"

His words warmed her from the inside out, but she had little time to savor them as he turned his back on her, leaving her to wonder if she mistook his meaning.

He moved to a round table in the corner of the room and picked up a burgundy binder. Then he turned around and headed toward her. She couldn't help admiring the way he moved. She had never noticed the sensual rhythm of his walk, the grace and balance.

For the first time, she realized Dexter didn't need her to teach him what women desired in a man. He encapsulated everything a woman could want.

Certainly she couldn't be the only one who saw that?

He stopped in front of the desk, his eyes unreadable. He hesitated for a hairsbreadth and then placed the binder in front of her. "I don't usually share my work with anyone," he confessed, shoving his hands into his pockets again, showing her that boyish, uncertain side that made her want to lean over the desk, capture his face between her hands, and kiss him as if nothing else in the world mattered.

"Why are you showing me this?"

He shrugged. "Perhaps because you asked. Or perhaps because I know you understand the value of research."

Humbled by his trust, Mallory gave him a grateful smile and then glanced down at the binder entitled: *The Effects of Impotence in Women.*

Opening the cover, she began to read.

For decades, the field of sexual research has been a scientific backwater. The government has closed its eyes to this vital human element, and many professionals consider it career suicide to go into a specialty that lacks financing and evokes snickers from other researchers. But the anticipated renaissance in this arena is long overdue.

Especially for women.

Studies clearly indicate that sexual problems are more prevalent in women than men, and it's time to consider this a very real issue rather than a psychosomatic complaint.

Sexual dysfunction can be devastating.

Mallory read for another ten minutes, engrossed in the subject matter as much as she was taken with the conviction that rang in Dexter's words.

Finally, she looked up at him, wondering about this man who was more concerned about how women suffered through impotence than men, a scientist choosing to no longer overlook or ignore the other half of the equation. A woman's pain.

"This is wonderful."

"You think so?" He seemed so very unsure of himself at that moment, bringing to mind a remark Cummings had once made.

In some ways, Dex is naïve, eager to please.

Mallory had scoffed at that sentiment upon first hearing it. At that moment, however, it didn't seem quite so unbelievable. "Yes, I do. You're on an admirable and worthwhile mission."

"I believe women's issues in this area have been largely ignored, and I want to level the playing field. Researchers seem to be satisfied with having alleviated the male problem of impotence, but have given no in-depth consideration to the female problem."

Dexter's face became animated as he spoke, and Mallory couldn't take her eyes off him.

"Sex is so important in relationships. People need that closeness, that physical contact, and yet in terms of research it has wallowed in obscurity, seeming almost taboo."

Mallory wondered if there was a woman Dexter had shared that kind of closeness with. Had he ever loved someone? Did it matter?

Could she let it matter?

"Viagra," he went on, "was a fluke, discovered

by accident. Scientists were looking for a drug to relieve the chest pain associated with heart disease.''

Mallory knew all this, but listening to Dexter speak about it so passionately made the subject seem entirely new.

''Deuced little is known about sexual function and dysfunction in women, and I want to change that. While I wholeheartedly believe we have to focus our attention on the feelings and components of the male/female relationship, we have to look at mechanics and physiology as well. Therefore, using a series of grants and my own funds, I have been working on a female form of Viagra, believing a combination of therapies is the key to striking the correct balance. Everything is detailed in that binder.''

An elusive memory that had been tickling the back of Mallory's mind hit her then as she realized the importance of the information Dexter was imparting to her, the research she now held in her hands.

Karen's words came back to her.

They say he's developing a new Viagra-type pill, but this one is geared toward women. Just imagine the press you'd receive having that information before anyone else.

Mallory couldn't believe Dexter had just told her about something he had not confided to anyone else, that he had simply handed her material that Karen and many other people would pay handsomely to get their hands on.

Everything is detailed in that binder.

As if the binder had burst into a great ball of fire, Mallory dropped it onto the desk and stared at it as though it had sprouted wings.

"I'm boring you, aren't I?"

Mallory glanced up at Dexter, feeling guilty when she hadn't done anything to feel guilty about. She had no designs on the information contained in the binder.

"No." She managed to shake her head. "You're not boring me."

"I know I'm not the most scintillating conversationalist."

"I find you very scintillating," she said before she had time to think about how her words could be construed. "I mean, I find your research scintillating."

"That's kind of you to say, but hearing myself now, I realize how much I need your help."

"You don't need my help. You're doing just fine on your own."

A hint of a smile turned up the corner of his lips. "Perhaps your tutoring is working?"

What Mallory saw in Dexter had nothing to do with her tutoring. When he allowed himself to relax, he could be charming and sweet—and far too distracting for her peace of mind.

Perhaps that was why she suddenly said, "I think it's time for me to leave."

His smile slowly evaporated. "Leave? But . . . why do you want to leave?"

Sweet heavens, why did he have to make it sound so personal? As if she were deserting him? "I just don't think you need me any longer." But more than that, she didn't know how to handle the feelings he was stirring inside her.

His dark blue gaze held her captive. "You're wrong. I do need you. In fact, I need you quite a bit more than I expected."

A tiny thrill shot through Mallory at his words, but she couldn't allow herself to falter. "I have responsibilities. My book—"

"You can write here. I'll send Wheatley into London for whatever you need."

"My family—"

"Have been no trouble at all. I've discovered I rather like having people around. This house has been quiet for far too long."

Mallory knew she was doling out excuses. She had barely given her book a second thought. Real life consumed her mind. And Dexter was right about her family. They had been no trouble, except for Genie acting a little distant toward her. But her sister could be moody at times. She was still a teenager after all, one whose hormones had been raging since she had stepped foot in Dexter's house.

Genie's adoration had worn Dexter down until he had taken to hiding out behind doors and several massive houseplants to avoid her, peering through the fronds like a hunted animal.

Mallory knew Dexter had been relieved when her sister had found herself a new man to pursue—although how Dexter's butler, Quick, felt about being the current object of Genie's attention was another matter entirely.

As for her mother, she had sparked up a friendship with Adele, the cook. They were about the same age and seemed to have a number of things in common, like a love of gin rummy—and gin without the rummy on occasion.

Mallory was glad things were going so well . . . but what about her? Could she keep things strictly on a business level with Dexter?

"You can't leave me now anyway," he said then, drawing her attention to the fact that he was now standing beside her chair, staring down at her, and what she saw in his eyes nearly took her breath away.

"Why not?" she asked, more than a little shaken by that look.

"Because I've made a breakthrough."

"A breakthrough?"

He nodded, an endearing smile spreading across his face. "Yes. I've decided I want to learn how to shake my bon-bon after all."

CHAPTER SIXTEEN

"Do you have a map? I keep getting lost in your eyes."

Mallory halted outside Dexter's office door the following morning, sure her ears were deceiving her. That wasn't the *professor* who had made that comment? Not the ever proper Ph.D. who needed her name, rank, and serial number to kiss her?

"Your lips are like wine, and I want to get drunk."

Mallory blinked. It *was* Dexter!

"Your body's name must be VISA because it's everywhere I want to be."

A husky female laugh followed that remark. Mallory recognized the voice immediately. Freddie. What was Freddie doing with Dexter? And why was she doing it?

"You remind me of a parking ticket because you have 'fine' written all over you."

Had Dexter invited Freddie into his office? But

why would he do that? He had shown nothing but the most cursory interest in Freddie—and that was simply to discover what form of torture she intended to inflict on Cummings that day.

"There you are with those curves, and here I am with no brakes."

In fact, Dexter was the first man that Mallory could remember who, after being in a room with both she and Freddie, had spent more time looking at her rather than at Freddie.

"Did it hurt when you fell from heaven?"

This was ridiculous. There was nothing going on between Freddie and Dexter. But he certainly didn't need any distractions when there was research to be done—at least no distractions who looked like Freddie.

"You should be glad I'm not a Viking, or you would have been ravaged and plundered by now."

All right! That did it! Mallory had heard enough.

Logic flew away, and anger took over. She stormed into the room, ranting, "Oh, enough already! Why don't you just—"

Her words were aborted as two pairs of eyes glanced in her direction. Innocent eyes. Eyes that asked her if she was feeling well.

Freddie sat on the sofa. Dexter reclined behind his desk. He held a piece of paper in his hands, and Mallory got the sinking feeling she had misjudged the situation.

"Why don't we what?" Freddie asked, eyeing her curiously.

"Ah, why don't you . . ." *Pour some honey over my head and bury me in an anthill?* "Have breakfast with me?"

"We've already eaten," Dexter said. "We didn't want to wake you. I hope you don't mind."

We. Mallory heard that loud and clear. "Of course not."

"Freddie was just keeping me company until you got here."

"How nice of her," Mallory said with a false smile, promptly scolding herself for her less than solicitous thoughts about her best friend.

Just because Freddie was flirtatious, had a gorgeous face and body, had confided to Mallory that she thought Dexter was attractive, didn't mean Freddie had set her sights on him.

Right?

"Dex and I were just laughing over some of the one-liners I found on the Internet last night," Freddie said, flashing Dexter a smile that could only be called conspiratorial. "He, of course, doesn't need such things. He's charming all on his own."

Yes, he was charming, sometimes. So why was Freddie now noticing when she hadn't before? When she hadn't seen the vulnerability and sadness like Mallory had?

Those darn clothes, she thought glumly. He wore one of his new outfits. A pair of slate gray trousers, a matching jacket and a snug-fitting dove gray knit shirt that draped his upper torso like a lover's hands.

He fairly oozed testosterone.

And when did Freddie start referring to him as "Dex," as though they were old, familiar friends?

Freddie rose from the sofa with her usual grace. "Well, I have to go." She came to stand next to Mallory on the threshold and said in a voice only

Mallory could hear, "He's been waiting for you like a lovesick hounddog."

Lovesick hounddog? Mallory scoffed. There was nothing remotely lovesick on Dexter's face.

"I have to meet Simon in town," Freddie went on in a level voice. "He wants me to help him pick out some clothes."

Mallory's brow furrowed. "Who's Simon?"

"I told you about him the other day."

Mallory remembered Freddie mentioning someone. No name, only a brief description of his attributes. "You mean the man with the cannons?"

"The very one." Freddie winked.

"Cannons?" Dexter looked perplexed. "No one around here has cannons."

Freddie's smile would have bested a satyr's. "This one does." With a wave over her shoulder, she breezed out the door, leaving Mallory alone with the professor—a fact which so unnerved her she almost forgot her reason for being there. Then it came to her.

She had to teach the professor how to dance.

Mallory's uncertain gaze met Dexter's confident one. "Are you ready to get started?"

"Yes, teacher." He was clearly in a lighthearted mood. Was that due to Freddie?

Mallory beckoned him over with her finger. "Come here."

He quirked a brow, obviously as surprised as she was at her authoritative tone of voice, and yet he obeyed, rising from behind his desk with a fluidness of motion that was hard not to admire, and heading toward her. She couldn't have looked away even if the grim reaper had just offered her a head start to save herself from certain death.

He stopped in front of her, and the look in his eyes warmed Mallory from the toes up. She swallowed and turned around abruptly, searching for the cassettes she had placed next to the portable stereo the night before.

"Freddie already put a tape in," he told her. "She said you'd like it."

Mallory couldn't think with him standing so close.

Music. Start the music.

She pressed play, and the hot-tempo beat of Donna Summer flooded the room. *"I want some hot stuff, baby, this evening . . ."*

Mallory slammed her hand down on the buttons on top of the stereo. Damn Freddie and her askew sense of humor!

"What's the matter?" Dexter asked.

"That song is . . . too fast." And too filled with blatant sexual messages Mallory didn't want to hear at that moment.

However, it appeared that was the only tape available. All the others had disappeared, and she was fairly sure she knew who had taken them—a certain Jewish girl who was going to get it when Mallory cornered her. This should teach Mallory to keep things to herself.

With a resigned sigh, Mallory pulled out the cassette and looked at the list of songs written on the index in Freddie's flowery handwriting. Every song was as bad as the first.

"Give It To Me, Baby." "Feel Like Making Love." "Rock You Like A Hurricane." "Touch It." "Sexual Healing." "Ring My Bell." "Hold On, I'm Coming." "The Way I Feel Is Sexual." "Jungle Love."

Clearly Freddie had done more than search for one-liners on the Internet last night. She had downloaded songs from Napster, her favorite pastime. That might explain the cackling Mallory had heard coming from Freddie's bedroom.

Mallory decided the radio was her best bet. Static crackled on most of the channels when she turned it on, reminding her that they were out in the middle of nowhere. Only one station came in clearly. A slow, passionate love song filled the room.

She went to shut it off, but Dexter reached out and stopped her; big, warm fingers curling around her wrist. "Leave it," he said, a husky note to his voice.

Mallory stared at his hand. So large, yet so gentle. So capable of inflicting injury, yet more likely to administer aid. Those hands had fascinated her from the first. They fascinated her now.

Taking a deep breath, she glanced over her shoulder. Dexter stood right behind her, so close she could feel his warm breath against her hair, tickling the tendrils escaping her clip.

"I want to dance to this song," he murmured, his deep voice vibrating through her body. "With you. Please," he added when she hesitated.

Mallory acquiesced, powerless to do anything else as his arms wrapped around her waist and pulled her close. She laid a hand on his shoulder, the other on his chest. His heart thudded steadily beneath her palm; making the moment seem that much more real.

Their movements were small, barely perceptible, but it was the physical contact the music required, seeping into her blood, making her feel its seductive heat.

Dexter's arms around her made Mallory feel safe, protected. Never before had she so relished being a woman as she did at that moment.

And never had she understood the meaning of a song more than she did then, in Dexter's arms, with an emotion stirring within her heart—a new, burgeoning sensation that frightened her.

"Have you ever loved someone like that?" he murmured, referring to the romantic lyrics as he stared down at her with eyes of vivid blue, probing and intense. "As though you were consumed by it, no words able to describe how that person makes you feel inside."

The way he spoke, so heartfelt, made Mallory yearn for that kind of love, the kind she had been waiting for all her life. "No . . . I never have."

"What about your boyfriend? Don't you love him?"

Mallory stared at him, confused. "What boyfriend?"

"When we met, you told me . . . How did you put it? Oh, yes. You told me to keep my mitts to myself. That you were 'taken.' "

Mallory groaned inwardly, remembering that convenient but completely untrue remark. She fumbled for a reply. "Well, I—"

"You lied, didn't you?"

"Lied?" Freddie had always told her she was a bad liar, and the look in Dexter's eyes told her that he, too, could see through her. "All right," she confessed with a sigh. "I lied."

He graced her with a beautiful half grin. "You didn't have to do that, you know. I wouldn't have tried anything if that's what you were worried about."

Mallory looked away, recalling all too clearly Dexter's remark about the possibility of anything happening between the two of them.

I have no intention of making love to you.

Did he still feel that way?

"The song has ended," he murmured, the words sounding poignant to Mallory's ears, as if he were telling her that more than just the song had ended.

He released her and moved away, shoving his hands into his pockets. Distancing himself as he always did. Each time his defection hurt a little more.

"What about you?" Mallory quietly asked.

"What about me?"

"Have you ever loved someone like that?"

For a long moment, he looked at her, almost as if memorizing her face. Then he turned and walked to the window, resting a hand against the sill, a solitary word breaking the utter stillness that had descended.

"Yes."

Mallory hadn't expected his response to be a blow. Yet knowing he had loved somebody with all his heart and soul tore at a piece of her.

Go, she told herself. *Leave before your heart is involved.*

Too late, her heart whispered. *Too late.*

CHAPTER
SEVENTEEN

The envelope was propped against her pillow.

Mallory recognized the elegant, bold script immediately.

Dexter.

With trembling hands, she picked up the cream-colored envelope, her heart beginning to pound, wanting to know what it said, but not wanting to know at the same time.

Open it.

Mallory hesitated, and then turned the envelope over. Like a page out of yesteryear, the flap was sealed with a coin-sized dollop of red wax, the Harrington family insignia pressed into it.

Taking a deep breath, she broke the seal and slowly slipped out the vellum nestled within.

Lord Dexter Spencer Harrington, fifth Earl of Braden, requests the company of one Mallory Anne Ginelli for dinner at seven P.M. this evening.

The professor was inviting her to dinner. She couldn't believe it. The gesture seemed out of character—and yet, after their dance, the words he had spoken, it was no longer so hard to imagine.

Something intangible had paved over the inherent sweetness in Dexter, and Mallory felt stronger than ever about chipping away at the surface until she found out what had changed him.

Could it have been this woman he had once loved, whom he might still love, who had hurt him? Had she not loved him in return? Was he the type of man who gave his heart only once? Was that why he withdrew from Mallory whenever she got too close or probed too deeply?

Mallory stared down at the note, telling herself it was best to decline the invitation even as she knew she wouldn't. She wanted to have dinner with Dexter. Just the two of them.

Tonight she would learn what demons haunted the professor.

Dexter paced the length of his room, hearing every tick of the mantel clock, fidgeting like the nervous lad he had been when he had accepted his first award for scientific excellence in the field of Human Sexuality. They had labeled him an expert, but he had never felt like one. God only knew he didn't feel like one at that moment.

Yet he had surprised himself and found the nerve to invite Mallory to dinner. He had never invited any woman to dinner. Not even Lady Sarah.

Dexter frowned. Sarah. He had pushed her to the back of his mind since Mallory had come into his life, allowing himself the luxury of temporary forgetfulness, to put aside the duty looming ever nearer, almost revealing feelings to Mallory that morning that would have been disastrous to both of them.

He had stood at his office window for a long time after Mallory had left, thinking about Sarah, knowing she was hard at work on some charity auction or other social event. Dexter felt guilty for having given her so little of his time. Yet, for as long as he had known Sarah, she had always understood.

The young girl had grown into a beautiful woman. But more importantly, she was beautiful inside, a woman any man would feel proud to call his own. She deserved a loving husband. Could he be that husband? Would he ever feel anything other than brotherly affection toward her?

He had seen the way men looked at her, flirted with her, noticed how she blossomed under the attention. And while he was always protective of her, he had never been angered by the attention given her—not like the anger he had felt seeing Mallory and Cummings dancing together.

Dexter considered himself a nonviolent man, but he had wanted to put his fist through his friend's face until it came out the back of Cummings's head and then throw Mallory over his shoulder like some . . . Neolithic caveman.

That he had even envisioned this scenario, had temporarily reveled in it, was beyond comprehension. Thankfully, he had come to his senses and recaptured a modicum of sanity.

He couldn't allow his emotions to rule his brain, to blot out years of tradition and duty. He had vowed to make every effort to see to Sarah's happiness—and that vow was what had brought the irrepressible Mallory Ginelli into his life.

Every day that he put off telling Mallory about Sarah, it became harder to do. From the beginning, he had convinced himself it was not pertinent that Mallory know about Sarah, that Sarah was part of his personal life and therefore off limits. And he kept on telling himself that until he could no longer believe his own excuses.

Tonight he had to tell Mallory the truth.

Tonight he had to end this strange fascination he had for her.

The mantel clock chimed seven times, alerting Dexter that the appointed hour had arrived.

Taking a deep breath, he checked his appearance in the mirror for the hundredth time. He had donned his new navy blue suit. Mallory had said the color complemented his eyes. But that didn't mean he wore the outfit to please her or that he hoped her gaze would caress him the way it had that morning—until she had asked him if he had ever been in love.

He had thought to lie, tell her no, that he doubted he had the capacity to care that deeply. But when he looked into her eyes, he had wanted her to know the truth.

A noise jarred him, focusing his gaze on the clock. Almost five minutes past seven.

Damn, he was late!

Quickly, he strode from the room and down the long corridor to Mallory's room. Nervous again, he adjusted his jacket, raked his fingers through his hair, and then haltingly lifted his hand to knock on the door. The portal opened before his knuckles had touched the wood.

And there, framed in the doorway, was Mallory. But not the Mallory he knew, wearing her faded jeans and T-shirts with her silky black hair pulled back in a ponytail.

No, this Mallory was one he had never seen before, garbed in a little black dress that sported nearly invisible straps, showing off beautiful shoulders, well-toned arms, and creamy, flawless skin. Sheer black stockings encased slender legs, and black suede, open-backed pumps graced her small feet.

Her hair had been left loose and flowing over her shoulders, delineating her long, supple neck, soft jaw, and high cheekbones.

The light from the lamp on the bureau next to her tinted her hair with gold streaks. Dexter itched to pick up a silken length and fan the smooth, cool strands through his fingers.

She appeared utterly delectable—and completely out of his reach.

"Hello," she murmured, her voice a breathy rasp that never failed to arouse something primitive inside him, something that made him susceptible to the demands of a certain part of his anatomy. Dexter felt he finally understood the theory behind the proverbial "other head," and how its desire to do the thinking could usurp normal brain functioning. At that moment, the appendage seemed most aptly named.

Dexter searched for words, but suddenly found speech difficult. Mallory didn't seem to notice his lack of response, as her gaze stroked over him, seeming to take in every detail.

When her eyes finally met his, she smiled. "You look very handsome."

Dexter jammed a fist against his diaphragm to snap himself out of his stupor. "As do you. Ah, I mean, you look very beautiful."

Faint color rose to her cheeks. "Thank you. I guess I should be grateful Freddie made me buy some new outfits before we came. She said she refused to travel with someone who looked like a fashion reject."

Dexter frowned hearing that. "I like the way you dress." And he meant it. Though Mallory looked magnificent at that moment, he discovered he liked her just as much in her well-worn jeans and big shirts. She could attire herself in a plastic garbage bag and he would probably like that, too.

"I must confess to feeling somewhat uncomfortable," she confided. "I'm not used to getting dressed up."

Dexter understood what she meant. He felt exposed without his usual clothes, like a clam without its shell. Yet, her honest declaration lessened his discomfit, and he started to relax. Mallory had a way of putting him at ease. It was one of the things he liked most about her.

He held out his arm. "Shall we go?"

Mallory nodded and looped her arm through his. "Where are we going?" she asked when they headed in the opposite direction of the dining room.

"You'll see."

Dexter guided her down a series of hallways until it looked as if they had come to a dead end. He could sense Mallory's confusion, but he wanted to keep everything a surprise. He wasn't quite sure why.

Releasing her arm, he positioned her across from him.

Her brow furrowed. "What are—"

"You'll see," he repeated, lifting his hand toward the wall sconce . . . and pulling it down.

A slight scraping noise was heard as the sconce levered forward, revealing a hidden panel in what appeared to be a solid brick wall.

She blinked, clearly stunned. Then she turned excited hazel eyes in his direction. "Is this . . ."

"A hidden passageway?" he finished for her. "Yes, it is."

She moved forward and poked her head into the dim corridor, her eyes alight with the same kind of wonderment he had always felt; the promise of unearthing secrets too strong a lure to ignore.

He had used the passageway often as a boy, disappearing among the musty stones as though entering another realm, where he could become someone else, someone who belonged.

He had allowed no one access to this place. But when he thought about this evening, he knew he wanted to share it with Mallory.

"Where does it go?" she asked, her voice echoing up the stairwell.

"To the battlements. The castle dates back much farther than most people think. It was once a Norman stronghold of noteworthy significance. Knights stood guard at each of the four turrets and men were placed strategically along the wall to defend their home to the end, even if it meant death. Legend has it that King Arthur took refuge here shortly before his last battle with Mordred."

"King Arthur?" With something akin to reverence, she laid a hand against the wall. "What days those must have been, when people united for a cause and believed in something so strongly they'd defend it at all costs."

There was a faraway expression on her face and Dexter wondered if she was envisioning the days of gallant knights who had fought for their home, their honor . . . their lady love.

An odd desire to show her those things still existed stirred to life inside him, a need to prove to her that a once mighty stronghold could still retain that special power, a power that transcended time.

She had allowed him to see things through her eyes, to remember why he had once loved this house—a love that had been gone for many years. It had taken this imaginative, proud slip of a girl to remind him of its magic.

Dexter fought the urge to gather her up in his arms and have her lay her hands upon him instead of the wall. "Shall we go?"

She nodded and then peered into the passage-way. "It's dark."

He came to stand next to her, the small opening leaving only a finger's worth of space between them. "Are you afraid of the dark?"

She turned and glanced up at him. "Not with you guiding me," she murmured, her gaze dropping to his lips, that look fueling a hunger that only seemed to intensify with each encounter.

Dexter knew then that he had made the right choice bringing her here. "Have no fear. I have just the thing to ease our way." He withdrew an engraved, silver lighter from his jacket pocket, the flickering flame illuminating a long staircase lead-ing upward. "After you."

The stairwell was too narrow for them to maneuver side by side, so Dexter was forced to walk behind Mallory, tormented by the seductive sway of her hips, remembering his hands encircling that small waist, and how firm was the flesh beneath, to think about her slight weight on top of him, her breasts pressing against his chest, her lips, warm and wet, moving over his.

Dexter was so caught up in the images that he barely registered Mallory's gasp as they exited at the top of the stairs and stepped out onto the battlements.

"I've never seen anything like it. The view is magnificent!"

"Yes," he murmured, "the view is quite stunning." His gaze skimmed Mallory's profile.

She walked over to the high wall that protected the battlement and laid her hands on top. The sun was just dropping behind the horizon, lighting the sky with a swath of vivid crimson and gold.

Below them, the Crennen River wound its way by, looking like molten fire as the evening rays reflected off its glassy surface. The air was crisp, yet surprisingly warm, and perfumed with a hint of night-blooming jasmine.

Mallory closed her eyes and breathed deeply. "If this was my home, I'd do my work right here just so I could see these beautiful sunsets day after day."

Dexter had to stifle the urge to tell her he would build her an office up here so she could watch those sunsets—and he could watch her. Day after day.

He shoved his hands in his pockets, cursing himself for his lack of control. He wasn't sure what came over him when he was with Mallory, why he forgot what he had to do, what he must do. Yet the emotion got stronger every day.

"Are you hungry?" he asked.

Slowly, she opened her eyes and smiled. "Famished."

"Good. I hope you enjoy what I had the cook prepare." He nodded toward a spot behind her.

Surprised, Mallory turned around, unsure what to expect. Off to the side sat a round table and two chairs. She had been so focused on the view, she had completely missed it.

The table was done up beautifully with a linen damask tablecloth. Matching napkins arranged like swans sat atop fine bone china. Beside the plates lay gold-plated forks and spoons.

Cut crystal goblets graced the front of the plates, and set out on a rolling side cart were several silver salvers with high-domed lids.

And in the middle of the table were two tall white candles in silver holders surrounded by glass globes that reflected the golden shimmer of the dying sun.

She turned to look up at him. "It's lovely. Thank you."

Dexter nodded, not able to look at her. He didn't want to see that soft expression in her eyes. It had nearly been his undoing several times. Instead, he flicked open his lighter and lit the two candles. Then he pulled out Mallory's chair.

She sat down, and he stood transfixed, staring at the creamy smoothness of her neck and shoulders, knowing an urge to press his lips against the pulse fluttering at the base of her throat. Abruptly, he stepped back and made his way to his own chair.

"What are we having?" she asked.

Dexter smiled to himself. In a short amount of time he had come to know the kinds of foods Mallory liked and disliked—sardines and olives topping her list of dislikes. He also discovered something about himself.

He enjoyed surprises.

Lifting the lid from the first salver he watched her face. She blinked and then laughed, delight dancing in her eyes as she looked at him. "Hamburgers?"

"Not just any hamburgers. Whoppers."

"Where did you get Whoppers?"

"I sent Wheatley into London for them."

Mallory gaped at him. "You sent him all the way to London to get Whoppers?"

Dexter nodded, trying to discern if she was pleased or thought he had lost his mind. "Don't you like them?"

"Yes, of course I do, but—"

Damn him for his stupidity. She thought him a fool. "I'm sorry. I made a mistake. He replaced the lid. I'll have the cook get us something else."

He started to rise, but she reached out and took hold of his hand. "Don't," she said softly. "I think it's wonderful."

Did she? Or was she just trying to salvage his pride? "Are you sure?"

"Positive. I was just surprised. That's all. How did you know I liked Whoppers?"

"I overheard you telling Freddie that you'd give your right arm for a Whopper with extra pickles. Apparently you weren't too impressed with the fare served here."

Mallory sent him an apologetic smile. "It wasn't that. I just—"

He held up a hand. "No explanations are necessary as long as you enjoy yourself."

"I am," she murmured, looking so heartbreakingly beautiful in the soft glow of the candlelight that Dexter felt something expand inside his chest, protectiveness, possessiveness, all tangled up in a fierce ache that seared his gut.

"The surprise isn't over yet." He lifted the lid from another server. "You didn't think I'd forget the super-sized French fries, did you?"

"You are too much!"

He smiled, reveling in her obvious joy. "I can't help myself. I'm cursed with perfection."

She tilted her head slightly to the side, the effect devastating as she regarded him with twinkling hazel eyes. "If I didn't know better, I'd think you were joking with me, Professor."

"It seems I possess a modicum of humor after all." He sobered as he added, "I have you to thank you for that."

"Me? What did I do?"

"You made me see that there is more to life than science." He pulled out the carafe chilling in a bucket of melting ice and poured the liquid into her glass, then his. Holding up his glass, he said softly, "May life bring you all your heart desires, Ms. Ginelli."

Mallory felt an unexpected poignancy as she lifted her glass and clinked it against Dexter's over the top of the candle flame. "I wish the same thing for you, Professor." She put the glass to her lips and took a sip of her drink. "Oh ... you are a wicked man," she laughed. "This isn't wine!"

Dexter appeared as wicked in that moment as she had just accused him of being. "Nope. It's

Pepsi. The choice of a new generation—from what I've heard." Then he winked at her! Winked! "I didn't forget dessert, by the way." He raised the lid to the third and final tray. "A slice of apple pie each." He picked up the treat and studied it. "Quite inventive putting a wedge in this box." He shrugged and bent over to fiddle with something on the bottom shelf of the cart.

Mallory straightened in her chair, trying to get a peek at what he was doing. When he glanced up and caught her, he slanted an eyebrow at her. She gave him a sheepish grin, and he laughed, a big, booming rip of sound that warmed her from her toes up.

Finally deigning to end her curiosity, he lifted what he had been hiding. Cummings's portable stereo. "You didn't think I would forget the music, did you?"

"Me? Of course not."

"Somehow this song seemed apropos." He pressed play, and Mallory expected an off-putting fugue or Dexter's favorite Bach concertos.

Instead, the rock-hardened voice of Steve Tyler from Aerosmith belted out, *"She told me to walk this way, talk this way . . ."*

Mallory stared at him for a second, blinked, and then collapsed into a fit of laughter as his reason for choosing this particular tune sank in.

After that, whatever tension might have remained between them flew away, as did the time. Dexter opened up more than he ever had, giving her further insight into his work, telling her about the antics he and Cummings had pulled at the university.

She would have never imagined that Dexter had

even a small wild streak in him or that he would
have participated in stealing a favorite pair of trousers from the vice-chancellor and flying them from
the rigging during the annual boat race between
Oxford and Cambridge.

Yet even with all his candor, there were two topics
he steered away from. Talk about his parents and
his childhood. His reticence only made her that
much more interested in finding out about both.

With the groan of someone who had overin-
dulged, Mallory leaned back in her chair, folding
her arms over her midsection as the Whopper,
extra large fries, and apple pie collided in her
stomach. "I feel like the turkey float in the Macy's
Thanksgiving Day Parade."

"You certainly don't look like it," Dexter murmured, his gaze skimming over her.

His words warmed her and confirmed what Mallory had always thought, that Dexter possessed a
hidden wealth of charm. She almost wished he
didn't. He just made it that much harder to think
straight. And she had to think straight. She
couldn't allow herself to get lost in his eyes, the
curve of a dimple, or the way the light breeze ruffled his hair.

"I'd like to know more about your parents," she
said, aware that her request came out of left field.
She had meant to be more subtle, but the languid
way he looked at her made her want to change the
subject.

"What is there to talk about?" His words had an
edge to them, and his easy-going manner of only
a moment earlier changed into a guarded expression.

Mallory shrugged. "I don't know. Perhaps I'd

just like to find out how you feel about them. Do you miss them very much?''

"They were my parents," he replied cryptically, which told her that he didn't intend to make this easy on her. The subject clearly made him uncomfortable. Why? "They had their lives. I had mine."

"That sounds rather sad."

"Perhaps to someone who doesn't understand the British way of life."

"What exactly is the British way of life?"

His gaze fixed on the star-laden night sky. "Doing things a certain way and never swerving from that course."

"This isn't the nineteenth century, Professor. What you speak of sounds like a scene straight out of Charles Dickens."

His gaze rolled down to meet hers. "Some things don't change, Ms. Ginelli."

What did he mean by that? And why did he refuse to trust her enough with the answer? "My aunt once told me that we can't run from our destiny. Our destiny chooses us."

"And eluding that destiny can be as difficult as dodging rain drops."

Mallory almost asked him what he was dodging, but figured all that would accomplish was to make him stop talking entirely. Instead she reached across the table and placed her hand over his. "I've always believed that there are at least two paths open to us and that we are given a choice of which path to take. Sometimes we make the wrong choices and travel the wrong road."

"And have you ever traveled the wrong road?" he asked, spreading his fingers and intertwining them with hers, making slow circles in her palm with his thumb. She didn't think he knew he was doing it, and she didn't intend to tell him.

"I have some regrets," she replied. Regrets that hadn't gone away even after all these years. "But we have to go on because to do otherwise would be to admit defeat."

He nodded, staring into his glass, looking thoughtful and distant.

"What do you regret, Professor?"

For long moments he remained silent, and she thought she had overstepped the line he had drawn in the sand, the one he allowed no one to cross.

Then he spoke, allowing her to glimpse a part of him that she doubted many people saw. "For months after my parents' deaths, nightmares plagued me, visions of smoke encompassing the cabin like black poison, the plane breaking apart. I wondered if my parents died right away or if they were alive long enough to know that whatever hopes and dreams they still harbored were beyond their reach. We may not have been close, but I couldn't bear to think they suffered."

Mallory hurt for him, understanding his pain. Yet she had no magic words to ease his turmoil, only what she had told herself for years to ease her own. "You can't allow yourself to dwell on it. You have to let the past go and free yourself from the burden."

His thumb stilled against her palm. "Free myself," he said, his voice tinged with self-mockery. "What an interesting choice of words." He looked up at her then, and confessed, "Do you know I've always been afraid to fly?"

"That's nothing to be ashamed of. Lots of people are afraid to fly."

He didn't seem to hear her. "My parents thought my fear was a sign of weakness, and God forbid a Harrington was weak. I used to dread coming home from school for summer holiday. We owned a small villa in the south of France, and even though we could have taken the train or a boat, my father would charter a plane instead. Ironic, isn't it, that my parents died in a plane crash?" He dropped her hand then and rose from his chair, moving to the wall and staring out into the night.

Mallory told herself to leave him alone, but she couldn't. She went to stand next to him, searching for the right words to ease his anguish. But sometimes there were no words. Sometimes there was nothing but a vast, empty silence.

"I don't want or need your pity," he told her, as though that was what compelled her.

"I'm not pitying you."

"Before you start pinning admirable qualities on me, I think you should know I'm not an admirable man."

"You underestimate yourself."

"I'm a scientist, Ms. Ginelli. I try never to underestimate anything, least of all myself. That having been said, I think it's time I got to the point of why I asked you to dine with me this evening."

His remark made Mallory realize how foolish she had been to think that this dinner marked some sort of turning point for her and Dexter, that he had recognized something lay between them. It was the writer in her, searching for meaning where there was none.

"So tell me," she quietly said.

"I feel that it is in both of our best interests if

we conclude our research expeditiously . . . so that you may go home.''

Mallory knew her leaving was inevitable, but why had she not been prepared for it? Perhaps because she had allowed herself to forget why she was there—forget that what was between her and Dexter was business and no more.

"You do want to go home, don't you?" he asked, a flicker of uncertainty—and perhaps regret?—crossing his face. Yet the expression was gone so fast she wondered if she had imagined it.

"Of course I want to go home." But her words lacked conviction. "There's nothing to keep me here . . . is there?"

The fragrance of night-blooming jasmine blew in on the soft breeze, cloaking them in its dark beauty, etching the moment in time, bittersweet and wrenching as he murmured, "No . . . nothing at all."

"Who died?"

Mallory's head snapped up, her gaze slicing through the blanket of darkness to see Freddie, garbed in her silk pajamas, framed in the threshold of the doorway adjoining their bedrooms.

Mallory schooled her features, not wanting Freddie to know she had been crying. "What are you doing up?" She spoke in a whisper to keep from waking her sister, who slept on a cot in the corner of the room.

"I wasn't tired," Freddie replied with a shrug, coming to sit down next to Mallory on the bed. "So, what happened with Dexter tonight?"

"Nothing happened," she lied, in no mood to

discuss the evening's events, not when they were so fresh, the words still ringing in her ears. "We ate dinner. That's all."

Freddie regarded her dubiously. "A man who goes to all the trouble Dexter went to tonight does it for a reason."

"Then why not ask Dexter instead of grilling me?" Mallory immediately regretted her surly tone. She heaved a weary sigh. "We had a lovely business dinner. Satisfied?"

"Hmm, a business dinner. And did you have any onions with your meal?"

"No. Why?"

"Because your eyes are red. I figured you couldn't have been crying, not over a business dinner."

Mallory thought to deny Freddie's all too accurate assessment of the situation. But what was the point? She would never convince Freddie she had not been crying like . . . well, like a girl.

How had it come to this? For years, Mallory had told herself that she would never be one of those foolish, weepy women who fell for a man who didn't return her feelings. Yet she hadn't known until tonight how deep those feelings ran. She wondered when it had happened, how the emotion had crept up on her without warning.

She thought back to the time when she had asked herself what might happen if she let Dexter's "research" become something more. She had scoffed, vowing that wouldn't happen, that she would never feel anything for Dexter.

So what went wrong?

"You're in love with him, aren't you?"

Freddie's words snapped Mallory from her musings. "What?"

"You love Dexter."

"Absolutely not! Don't be ridiculous!"

"I don't think I'm being ridiculous. I think you love him. And more than that, I think he loves you."

Mallory left the bed as if propelled. "I don't love him." She felt something for him, sure. But not love. Not the professor. "And he definitely doesn't love me."

Freddie leaned back on one hand. "Oh, no? What do you call a man who shares his very private research—research he hasn't shared with anyone—with you?"

"I shouldn't have told you about the binder."

"Perhaps not." Freddie shrugged. "But you did. And now I'm curious as to why you're so upset about it."

"Because you're twisting things around!" Mallory returned in a vehement whisper, not wanting to wake her sister.

"What did you do with that binder, by the way?"

"I left it on the table in Dexter's office. Why?"

"Was that before or after you read it?"

"Does it matter?"

"You didn't read it, did you?"

Mallory glared at her friend, and then her emotion-driven anger deflated as if a slowly leaking hole finally burst. "No. I didn't read it."

"Could that be because of what Karen asked you to do?"

Mallory dropped into the chair by the door. "I told her I wouldn't do it, remember? I don't care about the money or supposed fame. I'm not invading someone's private life for a story."

"How noble. But do you want to know why I think you didn't read it?"

"No. But I'm sure you're going to tell me anyway."

Freddie flashed a smile. "Intuitive girl." She leaned forward and said, "I think you didn't read it because you felt that if you did, you'd be violating Dexter's trust—guilt by association sort of thing."

Mallory marveled at how close to the truth Freddie had come. Yet to admit Freddie was right would be to admit she felt more for Dexter than she should. "I put it back because I wasn't interested in reading it. It's as simple as that. Now, if you don't mind, I'm tired and would like to go to bed."

"I'd be tired, too, if I spent all my time fighting a losing battle."

Mallory gave Freddie a warning look.

Freddie held up a hand. "All right. I can see you're going to be stubborn, so I'll let it go until tomorrow. But don't think I'll forget."

"Of course not," Mallory muttered under her breath.

"Sweet dreams," Freddie said with a smile that promised mischief, humming as she headed toward the adjoining door.

Only after the door had clicked shut after Freddie did Mallory's brain register the tune her friend had been humming.

"Here Comes the Bride."

CHAPTER EIGHTEEN

Dexter felt as though he were at the bottom of a fifty-car pile up.

He stared out his office window, following Mallory's every move as she meandered through the garden, as she did each morning.

And each morning he stood at the window, watching her, never letting her see him, hiding behind a self-imposed wall, doomed to spend his life looking out, bound to the strictures of his birth.

He tortured himself. He knew it, but couldn't stop. He had become like a man possessed, committing the smallest details to memory; Mallory leaning down to sniff a rose or brush her fingertips over the smoothness of a petal, making him die a bit more inside as he wished she would touch him with the same wonder, to feel her sweet caress one more time.

For three long days, he had tried to shake the dull ache that had encompassed his entire body.

Three days since the night he had stood with Mallory on the battlements and lied to make her believe he wanted her to leave.

Three days that he'd had to live with her nearness, the hint of her soft perfume teasing his nostrils, the enticing way her lips moved when she spoke or her hips swayed when she walked.

Three days of enduring the businesslike mien she wore when she taught him new dance moves, or made him read lines of poetry, or watched him mutely as he bought his first pair of contacts.

Three days of understanding the meaning of hell.

When had things gone so horribly wrong? And why did he so desperately want to bridge the gap?

"Vhat's the matter, my boy? You're looking vorried."

Dexter flinched imperceptibly at the reminder that he was not alone to brood.

He turned to face the person speaking to him, chiding himself for forgetting about his guest, a man who, in many ways, had been more of a father to him than his real father.

Gustav Renker had been his science professor from his days as a lonely lad at Eton. At times, Gustav had been his only friend.

Even though he was reaching his seventieth year, his white hair sticking up in cotton tufts—making him look like Albert Einstein—and one eye beginning to cloud with the onset of a cataract, the man was still as sharp as a tack and as active as ever. He had told Dexter more than once over the years that Austrians were made of strong stock. That had, indeed, turned out to be the case.

"I'm sorry, Gustav. I have a lot on my mind at the moment."

Gustav nodded. His gray eyes, though older and a bit duller, had seen much and missed little. "Are you sure you don't mind my staying for a few days? I passed a lovely inn a short vays back. I imagine they'd have a room for an old man."

"I have more rooms than I know what to do with." And with Mallory's aloofness, the house seemed twice as large. "I welcome your company— and the opportunity to beat you at a game of chess. I have to salvage my pride from the last trouncing you gave me."

"I accept your offer and your challenge." Then he gave Dexter a look he well remembered, one that had made many a youthful prankster confess their wrongdoings. "So tell me, my boy. Vhat is troubling you?"

Dexter was only mildly surprised by the question. He never could get anything past Gustav. "What makes you think anything is troubling me?"

"I could hear it in your voice during our last telephone conversation, and I can see it on your face now."

"Is that the reason for your unscheduled visit? To see if I was falling apart?"

"Can't a teacher visit his favorite pupil?"

"Ex-pupil. It has been a long time since I was in school."

"Ah, but that doesn't mean there is not a great deal yet to learn. Now, tell your old professor vhat is on your mind. Is it the research?"

Dexter thought to lie, but Gustav had an uncanny

knack of seeing through deceptions, as he had in
the days when Dexter had been in his class, a boy
born too smart for his own good, seeing himself
in the eyes of others, knowing he never quite fit
in.

"No. It's not the research." Dexter almost
wished it was.

He couldn't get Mallory out of his mind. The
way she had looked at him when he had told her
he wanted to finish their project so she could go
home had cut right through him, lacerated him
in a way nothing else had.

He damned himself for lowering his guard for
even a moment and allowing her to crawl into his
heart, making him want something he couldn't
have—making him wish two hundred years of Harrington tradition never existed.

One week. One week was all he had left before
he had to kneel before Sarah and pledge his heart
to her forever.

Seven damn days until Mallory would be gone
from his life, hating him for what she would discover . . . while he hated himself for being too
much of a bloody coward to tell her the truth.

A hand, marked by age, came to rest on Dexter's
shoulder, comforting in its surprisingly strong grip.
"Vhat is it, my boy? Is it the lovely voman you vatch
so intently through the vindow?"

Dexter shrugged and eased away from Gustav,
afraid to let his mentor see the downfall of the
man he had once called his most gifted student,
who he believed had so much to offer, but not just
to the world of science. But to life. It seemed to
Dexter that he had offered little to either.

"I've made a terrible mistake," he murmured,

his gaze roaming over the endless books on his shelves—books that covered every conceivable topic in the field of human sexuality. Yet they all seemed to lack one very important element, an incontrovertible human element. Love. It had taken Mallory to fill that gap in his education.

"Vhat mistake have you made? I cannot imagine something so terrible."

Dexter raked a hand through his hair, grimacing as he faced his friend. "I think I've fallen in love."

The old man's eyes lit up. "Vhy that's vonderful! Love is a grand thing, my boy. If you have found it, you should hold onto it vith both hands." Gustav clasped his small yet hearty hands together to emphasize his point.

Dexter dropped into the chair beside him and sighed. "It's not that simple." He hesitated. "I've fallen in love with the wrong woman."

"If you love her, how can she be the wrong voman?"

"Because I can't marry her." The words came out of Dexter's mouth without conscious thought, making him pause.

Did he want to marry Mallory? Would he do so if he were free to live as he pleased? Would she want him?

He shook his head. Did it really matter what her answer would be? Or his? He had a responsibility to uphold, tradition to honor, his parents' last wish to fulfill, and he could not hurt Sarah by walking away now. Her friendship meant too much to him.

Gustav's wrinkled brow creased in thought. "And vhy is it that you cannot marry this girl?"

"I am bound by duty to another woman."

"Duty to whom?"

Dexter shrugged. "My parents. My name. Two hundred bloody years of tradition."

"Ah, tradition." Gustav settled himself onto the couch. "My family had many customs, a vay of life ve clung to vigorously. But that vas before ve found ourselves prisoners in a concentration camp, captive to the vhims of soldiers, having no rights of our own. You learn to survive, to grow strong, living for the day vhen you vill be free once more."

Gustav extracted an antique wooden pipe from his inside jacket pocket. Dexter remembered that pipe well. How the smell of the smoke had comforted a young boy away from home, forgotten by his parents.

Gustav stuffed the bowl, methodical as always. Dexter smiled to himself when he saw what his mentor used to light the tobacco: the engraved silver lighter Dexter had given him as a gift the day he graduated from Eton, an exact replica of Dexter's own, the one he had used to light his and Mallory's ascent through the secret passageway.

Gustav puffed contentedly for a moment, his expression faraway. "Freedom. You don't realize how precious it is until you no longer have it." He slid a glance Dexter's way and gestured with his pipe. "Do you know vhat vas the one thing I vowed I vould never give up to anyone again should I ever be released from that camp?"

"What?"

"The joy of making my own decisions. Never vould I let another human being dictate my life to me. And I have lived by that creed all these many years."

Dexter understood what his friend was trying to do, but it didn't change his situation. "I wish things were that simple, but I can't set aside my duty that easily."

Gustav waved a dismissive hand. "Pssh! Duty smuty. You always vere a hardheaded lad, stubborn to a fault."

Dexter frowned. "I don't think I was hardheaded."

"Hardheaded and serious minded. You need to relax, my boy. Experience new horizons." Gustav leaned over the arm of the couch, a twinkle in his eye as he said in a conspiratorial whisper, "I may have reached my twilight, but there is still a fire in my heart and a spring in my step. I do not spend all my time contemplating recombinant DNA and the marvels of the opposable thumb, you know."

Dexter chuckled, glad his old friend had come to visit. Gustav had renewed his spirit. But more than that, he had renewed his hope. "No one can say you're not an original piece of work, Gustav."

Gustav nodded sagely and blew a smoke ring; it made a saintly halo around his head that belied the wicked glint in his eyes. "Thank you, my boy. I do my best. And I vill impart one more bit of visdom I learned from a vise man called Forrest Gump. He said, 'Life is like a box of chocolates. You never know vhat you're going to get.' This I have found to be very true."

"Hmm." Dexter nodded. "Interesting analogy."

"Indeed." Gustav puffed away. "Oh, and let me not forget the most important point! Something my students told me vhich has served me vell during those times vhen I needed to forget my vorries."

"And what was that?"

His face a mask of seriousness, he replied, "Life is short, so party hearty."

Dexter quirked a brow. "A most intriguing concept," he murmured, contemplating the full definition of partying hearty.

The door to his office swung open then.

"Oh, pardon me," a female voice apologized. "I didn't mean to barge in."

Dexter glanced up and found Mallory's mother framed in the threshold, knob in hand, embarrassment staining her cheeks.

He could see where Mallory got her beauty. Her mother was still an attractive woman.

He suspected that Barbara Ginelli was in her mid to late fifties. Her complexion was marked only by a few wrinkles around her eyes and mouth. And like Mallory, her mother was petite—perhaps even a bit shorter.

Yet it was the sadness in her eyes that Dexter noticed most, a sadness that seemed to cling to her, one that he recognized because he had glimpsed it in Mallory's eyes once or twice.

Dexter rose from his chair, Gustav following suit. "Is anything wrong, Ms. Ginelli?" he asked, feeling odd calling anyone but Mallory by that name.

"No, no. Everything's fine." Her flush deepened. "I've just lost my bearings again." She shook her head. "You'd think by now I'd know my way around."

Dexter smiled. "It takes a while, trust me. What can I help you find?"

"Well, I was to meet Adele in the solarium for our morning coffee. I think I took a left when I should have taken a right. I'll retrace my steps. I'm sure I'll have more success this time. Again, my apologies for interrupting.'' She turned to go.

Dexter opened his mouth to call her back, but Gustav spoke up before him. "No apologies necessary, dear lady. Ve vere just finishing our conversation. Vere ve not, Dexter?" Gustav turned to him, the look in his eyes warning Dexter to agree or face the consequences.

Dexter smiled to himself. Clearly Gustav had a fire in his heart—and it seemed Barbara Ginelli had ignited the flames. "Gustav is quite right. We are finished." Then to tweak his friend's nose, he said, "I'd be happy to show you the way to the solarium."

Dexter took a step toward her, but Gustav laid a hand on his arm, rather forcefully, in fact. "No, you stay here, my boy. I know you have many things to take care of. I vill show the lady the vay to the solarium." Turning up the charm, he said to the lady in question, "If you don't mind the company of a doddering old man, that is?"

"You? Doddering?" She treated him to a bright smile. "To my eyes, you're in your prime."

Gustav briefly glanced Dexter's way and wagged his eyebrows before moving across the room with a decided spring in his step. "I'll talk to you later, my boy." He waved a hand over his shoulder, his gaze focused on the lovely lady waiting for him in the doorway, to whom he very gallantly held out his arm. "Perhaps after we find the solarium, you'd like to visit the garden with me? It is most splendid this time of year."

Mallory's mother inclined her head and looped her arm through his. "I'd like that."

Together, the couple set out for their destination. Dexter could only wonder where they would end up—and hoped Mallory didn't blame him if it happened to be in Gustav's bed.

Mallory. Now that he was alone, Dexter contemplated the sage words his mentor had imparted to him.

Life is short, so party hearty.

Perhaps that was exactly what he needed to do. Enjoy himself. But more importantly, he should try to enjoy whatever time he had left with Mallory. Since she had arrived, he had only shown her his serious side, which, granted, was pretty much all he knew. But this would be his last opportunity to prove he could be different, fun, and he didn't want to waste it.

It was time to put all he had learned to good use.

CHAPTER NINETEEN

Mallory could only gape at the stranger in front of her, certain her chin would have swung around to the back of her head if her chest didn't currently hold it in place.

It wasn't every day the Earl of Braden sported a diamond stud in his earlobe.

A real-life, genuine, this-will-only-hurt-for-a-minute diamond stud. The professor. *Her* professor. The staid, no-nonsense, I-don't-know-you-well-enough-to-be-so-informal professor ... wore an earring! An earring! It defied explanation!

"What have you done to yourself?" she asked, the brilliant gem winking at her as they stood in the foyer, a bright path of afternoon sun spilling in the open front door.

"It's an earring," he replied.

Mallory shook her head. Sometimes the man could be as dense as the Amazon jungle. "Yes, I can see it's an earring. The question is, why do you have one?''

Had she awoken in a parallel dimension? Would cows be floating in the air if she looked outside? Would the sky be green and the grass blue? Would a spacecraft be hovering in the driveway?

He shrugged. ''I wanted one.''

As if the earring wasn't enough, his entire outside packaging had changed, as if a fashion-conscious Tinker Bell had sprinkled fairy dust over him making him into Cinderfella.

He wore a fitted white T-shirt that showcased a well-muscled chest and six-pack abs, and an indecently snug pair of jeans hugged his lower half. Mallory hoped he didn't turn around. The man's buttocks encased in faded blue Levis would surely be her undoing.

Dexter also had the distinction of being the first earl she had met wearing a pair of cowboy boots— black, to match the supple leather biker's jacket completing the ensemble. His silky dark hair brushed the top of the jacket collar, a single heart-breaking lock slanting across his forehead.

''I don't understand this, Professor. What is going on?''

''What is there to understand? I've made a change. Don't you like it?''

Why did he have to look at her in that expectant, vulnerable James Dean–type way? The sort of expression that said, *I'm on the edge and fragile. Be gentle.*

''Yes, I do like it,'' Mallory replied, her voice lacking conviction, which he noticed.

''But?''

"Well, you're just not . . . *you* in those clothes. I don't really know who you are."

"I'm still the same man underneath."

What a thought. Now he was not only rich, smart, sweet, charming, boyish, generous, caring, and built better than the gods of Olympus, but he was also sexy, handsome, uninhibited, and dressed better than her.

Where-oh-where was the justice in that!

"When did you—"

"Do all this?" he finished for her.

She nodded.

"Yesterday."

So that was why she hadn't see him the whole day. He had been out becoming a new man. She had been surprised when Cummings came to tell her that Dexter had to cancel their meeting. Dexter had never missed one of their meetings and frowned at her when she was two minutes late.

"The girl who pierced my ear suggested some other spots I could pierce," he said conversationally.

Mallory could well imagine. In New York, people were very inventive, and somewhat overzealous, about impaling their body parts. "Please tell me you didn't pierce anything else."

"No. Too many piercings would look overly gratuitous, as well as being quite painful."

Mallory sagged with relief. She just might faint if she found out he had nipple rings.

"However," he went on, "I did stop at the tattoo parlor after my piercing, which was conveniently located in the back of the piercing establishment. I had the tattooist—named Malice, by the way— emblazon *Bad to the Bone* across my right arm."

"You didn't!"

The corner of his lip curved up into a teasing half grin. "I'm only joking."

Joking! The man who once said, *I don't understand this propensity you have for senseless tomfoolery*. Was the moon in the seventh house? Had Jupiter aligned with Mars? And why was that song suddenly running through her head?

"I still don't understand what would make you go to this . . . extreme."

He stared down at himself. "I don't think it's extreme."

"For a man whose family hasn't changed their style of clothing since before the *Titanic* sank, I'd say it's extreme."

He frowned at her. "Freddie said I looked great."

"Freddie?" When had he started calling her Freddie instead of Ms. Feldman? "Freddie went with you?"

"Yes. She seems to have a thing about clothes. I also remembered her talking about going shopping with that Simon fellow. You know, the one with the cannons."

How would she ever forget?

"Well, it seemed only right to ask an expert, just as people consult me as an expert in the field of—"

Mallory held up her hand. "I know." Why did he have to keep mentioning his expertise? She had only to look at his face to think about it . . . and think about it.

Mallory felt a pang of hurt resurface. Every day since that night on the battlement, she found it more and more difficult to be with Dexter. And every day since, he had been sweet to her, and she hated it. But she didn't hate him. Perhaps it would be easier if she did.

Now, seeing him changed, she knew he no longer needed her. He had accomplished what he had set out to do. Was this his way of telling her she could leave?

For four days, she had done well keeping her feelings in check. Now all the emotion she had held back threatened to overwhelm her.

Abruptly, she turned on her heel and headed back the way she had come, not exactly sure what she intended to do. Sit in her room all day and cry? No, she had done enough of that. She refused to become one of those weepy females who were lost without a man—and this particular man had never been hers to begin with.

She had barely taken three steps when a large, warm hand grasped her upper arm, stopping her before she started up the stairs.

A scowl marred Dexter's normally smooth brow as they stood face-to-face once again. "Where are you going?"

"Does it matter?"

"Yes, I . . . I thought we were going to do some more, er, research."

At that moment, Mallory was sick to death of research. She wanted to be more than just research to this man! "Why don't you ask Freddie to tutor you?" Mallory hated how she sounded: petulant, petty, and jealous. But she couldn't help it.

"I don't want Freddie. I want you."

I want you. Never had Mallory heard those words spoken to her. She wished she could savor them, but they served only to confuse her. One minute she thought Dexter liked her, cared for her perhaps, and the next minute he withdrew.

Mallory wasn't sure when exactly she had begun to care for him, but she had discovered how strong her feelings were the night he had confirmed that his work was still the most important thing to him. She had crumbled inside. That was when she knew she loved him.

Mallory started as long, lean fingers cupped her chin and tipped her head up, Dexter's gaze searching hers. Her heart beat in thick, painful strokes thinking about the day she would leave this man, a day that seemed very close at hand.

"I'm sorry," he murmured, gently brushing her hair away from her face.

Those two words battered Mallory. "What are you sorry about?"

The look in his eyes was so pained that Mallory wished he would let her help him, let her inside, if only a little. "For whatever I did to upset you. For things I've said. Things I haven't said." His gaze dropped to her lips. "Things I wish I could say."

Mallory felt tears prick the backs of her eyes. What did he wish he could say? And why couldn't he say it? She had to know. Whatever it was.

A loud burst of laughter echoed through the front door, cutting her off. When a second uproar came a moment later, she asked, "What's going on out there?"

Dexter, she discovered, was still staring at her lips. "What?" he murmured, appearing oblivious to the noise.

Mallory swallowed as he inched closer to her. "O-outside."

"It's nothing." He took another step toward her.

Two of Dexter's nothings went flying past the open front door, a laughing woman eluding the hands of her male pursuer, who yelled, "Don't worry, love. It won't hurt a bit!"

Mallory quirked a brow at him. "Nothing, eh?"

Dexter sighed, the forlorn expression on his face almost comical. Then he took her by the hand. "Come with me," he said, and tugged her out the front door.

The sight that greeted Mallory made her stop abruptly, which nearly got her pulled off her feet as Dexter kept moving. She barely noticed his hands at her waist, righting her, as she focused her attention on his Rolls Royce—which was currently stuffed with at least twenty people.

Limbs dangled everywhere, arms hanging out one window, legs from another, and what looked suspiciously like someone's rear end pressed against the glass of the front window.

"What is going on?" she asked, staring up at the handsome stranger beside her, who seemed to be getting a great deal of amusement out of the abuse his car was taking. "What are they doing?"

"When we were returning home from our shopping trip, Freddie asked me how many people I thought could fit into the Rolls. I hadn't a clue, so I suggested we gather up some people and find out."

"This was your idea?" Mallory knew her expression was incredulous.

He nodded. "I thought it would be fun. In a way, I got the idea from you."

"From me? I've never crammed people into a car."

"You asked me once if I had ever done anything silly."

Mallory remembered what his response had been and how her heart had gone out to a young boy whose parents had denied him the opportunity to be a child. "So this is your idea of being silly?"

"Well, it is rather ridiculous, wouldn't you agree?"

It wouldn't be so ridiculous if the antic was pulled by anyone other than Dexter. "I don't believe it." She shook her head. "I just don't believe it."

"Perhaps we can set a new world's record." He nudged her gently in the side. "Would you like to see if we can fit?"

See if they could fit?

May the Lord forgive her. She had created a monster.

Nevertheless, she couldn't deny him. His smile was too sweet. His eyes too alight with promise. His body thrummed with the excitement of a re-strained youngster.

Mallory threw up her hands. "Why not?"

He beamed and grabbed her hand again.

Reaching the side of the car, Mallory spotted a number of Dexter's servants, glimpsing Quick's face crammed amid a pile of bodies, and a bur-gundy sleeve with gold piping that appeared to belong to Henley, Dexter's valet. And was that . . . her mother's blond hair poking up near the back window? And Genie's blue-nailed hand groping someone's buttocks?

Mallory started as Dexter's hands settled at her waist. She glanced over her shoulder. He gave her a reassuring nod—and then a shove into the car.

Mallory laughed as male voices hooted and

female voices giggled, and various grunts and groans ensued as she found herself packed more closely into a group of people than anything she had ever experienced on a New York subway.

When her body twisted around, she saw Dexter still outside, smiling but looking a bit unsure of himself. She strained over three bodies and grabbed his hand. "If I do it, you do it."

His grin broadened. "If you insist, Ms. Ginelli." Then that big, beautiful frame headed straight toward her, bodies wiggling, more laughter and groans and good-natured fun.

Mallory felt sorry for whoever had climbed into the car first. She imagined they would find at least one person who needed medical attention. She could just see someone trying to explain to the paramedics how the injuries occurred.

"Well, um . . . twenty-eight people were lying on top of him."

Mallory chuckled at the thought, but her amusement was diverted when Dexter's body jammed full length against hers. His arms encircled her waist, pulling them closer together. Whether he did this because of space constraints or because he wanted to, she didn't know. What she did know was that it felt right.

He stared at her mouth, and she wondered if he wanted to kiss her as much as she wanted to be kissed. He slid his head closer. Her eyelids fluttered shut. . . .

And then the muffled groan of someone saying they were suffocating brought the moment and the revelry to an end. Mallory tried to staunch the disappointment she felt.

It took at least ten minutes to untwine the mass

of humanity shoved into Dexter's Rolls, everyone laughing and clapping each other on the back until twenty-four people had been counted. Now Mallory knew the answer to the question . . . *Just how many people can fit into a Rolls Royce?*

She thought she had the final count until two mussed and rather flattened looking bodies were peeled from the floor of the car. Two bodies that had lain face-to-face, thigh to thigh. Two people who now wobbled side by side.

Freddie and Cummings.

As their senses returned, the two enemies faced each other, their movements coordinated as if they were squaring off before a duel. Blue eyes narrowed at brown. Brown eyes followed suit.

"Gentile," Freddie jabbed.

"Shrew," Cummings retaliated.

"Pompous crumpet eater."

"Insecure little witch."

"Bite my Butterfinger, Brit."

"I'd rather starve, Yank."

Another moment of glances that promised retribution passed. Then they both pivoted on their heels and headed in opposite directions.

Mallory shook her head and chuckled.

"That's nice."

She glanced over her shoulder to find Dexter standing behind her, so close she could smell the subtle blend of his cologne, and feel his body grazing hers, reminding her of the moment in the car, the desire that had overwhelmed her—that still overwhelmed her.

How she wanted to lean back against his chest and feel his arms wrap around her waist, to know what it was like to be cherished and protected, if only in her mind. If only for a moment.

"What's nice?" she asked, realizing she was just standing there staring at him.

"Your laugh," he replied in a husky tone. "It's beautiful."

"Thank you," Mallory murmured, afraid to say more, to look too closely at how she felt at that moment. Her emotions were in turmoil, like a wildly pitching ship being tossed from one swell to the next.

"Let's go somewhere," he suddenly announced. "Just the two of us."

The two of them? Alone? She couldn't.

"I want to do something with you," he went on, as if sensing her reluctance. "Something other than research."

Something other than research. Mallory had never heard anything so lovely. "Like what?"

His brow furrowed, as though the answer to that question was the most difficult problem he had ever been asked to solve. Then, suddenly, he smiled—and it was devastating.

"How about a picnic? I'll have the cook pack us up some of that chicken we had last night along with a loaf of French bread and Brie. I'll grab a bottle of wine from the cellar, and we'll be off. What do you say?"

An afternoon alone with Dexter. She had spent so many afternoons alone with him, but never without the research. It was always propped between them like a wall.

Mallory thought to ask him why he wanted to go on a picnic when only a few days ago it seemed as if he were desperate to have her gone. But did she want to give up the opportunity to be with him, no barriers, just a man and a woman on a warm summer afternoon? Perhaps the new Dexter felt differently about her. Perhaps. . . .

"Mallory?" he prompted, bending at the knees to look into her eyes, that come-hither smile on his face. "Will you come with me?"

The way he looked at her, so expectantly . . . How could she say no? "Yes," she replied. "I'll come with you."

He rubbed his hands together. "Stay right here. I'll get everything we need and be back in a flash." Then he jogged off toward the front doors, his silky dark hair flying in the breeze, the sunlight streaking it with gold. Mallory stared after him, lost in her thoughts.

"Boo!"

Startled, Mallory clapped a hand to her chest and swung around to face the perpetrator. Her sister—who clearly still possessed a knack for untimely arrivals. "Genie! You scared me half to death!"

"If you hadn't been staring at Dexter's ass, you might have heard me walk up," Genie crudely retorted.

Mallory frowned. "I wasn't staring—Never mind. What are you doing?"

"Talking to my sister. Is that a crime?"

Mallory wondered at Genie's less than friendly attitude. She might have thought Genie was angry at her because they hadn't spent much time together since she had arrived. But it was Genie who had been too busy to do anything with her, not vice versa.

Genie had gotten a glimpse of Quick, and hormones had kicked in. Every time Mallory spotted her sister, she was with the young and handsome butler. Clearly Genie was infatuated. Again.

Even so, her sister hadn't been acting quite like herself from the start. Mallory was worried—and when it came to Genie, it seemed as though she had spent her entire lifetime in that particular state.

Yet for a short while Mallory had only herself to worry about, and she felt a twinge of guilt for having enjoyed the freedom so much.

"Is something the matter, Genie?"

"What could possibly be the matter?" The barely suppressed anger in Genie's green eyes belied her words. "I'm here in England with my sister the famous romance writer. I'm sleeping in a castle, eating like a queen, being waited on hand and foot, and basically getting the royal treatment, thanks to you. *Always* thanks to you. So what could be wrong?"

"Obviously something is."

"And if so, are you going fix it like you fix everything?" The animosity radiating from Genie was like a physical force, slamming into Mallory.

"Is it Bruno? Has there been more trouble? Mother said—"

"Mother said! Mother said! Since when did you two become such pals?"

Pals? Was that what they were? Certainly there had been a time when Mallory might have said she and her mother were friends, but those days were long gone, buried beneath the weight of old memories.

"She's worried about you, Genie. I am, too."

"Well, you can stop worrying. I'm not a little girl

anymore. I don't need you to come to my rescue. So just leave me the hell alone!" She pushed past Mallory and raced for the front door, nearly knocking Dexter over as he came out with a mammoth picnic basket in one hand and a large plaid blanket tucked under his arm.

"What's the matter with her?" he asked, nodding over his shoulder as he walked up.

"Nothing," Mallory murmured, trying to hold back the torrent of buried emotions threatening to break free from the place where they had been locked for ten long years. Would the memories always haunt her? Would she never be free of them?

"Are you all right?"

Mallory nodded, forcing back the need to go after Genie. For as long as she could remember, she had been the one to fix things, to make things right. Well, not today. Today was for her.

"So where are we going?"

"I know a spot along the riverbank about five miles from here. I used to go there when I was a boy. I would lie out on this long, flat boulder and pretend I was a lizard baking in the sun."

Mallory quirked an eyebrow. "I thought you Harringtons never did anything silly?"

"And a week ago I would have been willing to bet I never did. But today it came back to me. When I thought about the picnic, the memory returned. Odd, huh?"

Not so odd, Mallory thought. Some memories were like that, returning when they were least expected—and sometimes when they were least wanted.

Banishing the thought, she plucked the blanket from underneath his arm. "Ready to go?"

"More than ready. We only have one problem."

Only one? she wanted to say. "Which is?"

He flashed her a sheepish grin. "I don't know how to drive."

CHAPTER TWENTY

"Watch out for that"—Mallory bounced in her seat—"pot hole!" She clutched the dashboard for dear life, struggling to be heard over the car stereo belting out some repetitive refrain that was completely unrecognizable as the English language.

Why had she told Dexter she would teach him how to drive? What insanity had possessed her to take responsibility of a man trying to change everything about himself in a day and then compound the issue by going out in his very, *very* expensive car? She was mad!

"Turn the wheel to the left! The left!" They narrowly missed a towering tree that looked as if it had survived many years of natural disasters—until Dexter came along and scared its leaves into dropping early.

Mallory grabbed the edge of the wheel when

Dexter decided to punch the gas pedal. "Slow down! You're going to get us killed!"

"Don't be a front seat driver."

"That's backseat driver!"

"Not if you're in the front seat." He turned his head and gave her a wink, his momentary inattention promptly causing them to veer off the road again.

"Let me drive. You don't have a license!" Not that that little fact had stopped him when he plunked his big body behind the steering wheel and refused to budge. "We'll get arrested!" Then she and her sister could compare rap sheets.

"Relax. We're almost there."

"Relax!" Mallory gaped at the man whose backbone had, until today, been so rigid it wouldn't bend in gale-force winds. "I think I've aged ten years."

A devilish grin curved his lips when he glanced her way. "And may I say you look quite fetching for your advanced age."

Oh, why did the man have to choose now to become carefree? "If you don't stop—"

"Well, would you look at that," he said, effectively cutting her off.

Mallory glanced around, expecting to see her spirit floating above her dead body. She was relieved to find nothing out of the ordinary. "Look at what?"

Dexter chuckled softly. "We're here—and all in one piece no less." He drew the car to a nominally jarring stop. "Not too bad for a novice, eh?"

"I'm driving on the way home," she told him in a voice that brooked no argument, but he wasn't listening. He had already hopped out of the car and was retrieving the picnic basket from the backseat.

"It's been years since I've been here," Mallory heard him say as she got out of the car on wobbly legs and moved around to his side. "I have a memory of carving my initials in a tree down by the stream."

Now that her heart rate was returning to normal, Mallory took a moment to look around her, awed by the beauty. She had never seen such vivid shades of green, rolling green as far as the eye could see and trees that reached for the sky, dappled sunlight filtering through the tall branches making a kaleidoscope of gold patchwork on the ground within the woods.

"Come on," he urged. "Let's look for that tree."

Ten minutes later, they had their blanket spread out next to the stream beside the large, flat boulder Dexter had mentioned, the picnic basket untouched as they searched for the infamous tree.

"There it is!" Mallory called out. "I found it!"

Dexter came over to her, and side by side, they examined the handiwork of a young boy. "Well, I'll be damned," he said. "It's here. I thought perhaps I had imagined it."

Mallory stepped closer to the tree, trying to make out the words written below Dexter's name. "Dare to dream." She glanced over her shoulder. "Did you write that?"

He shrugged, looking uncomfortable. "The scribblings of youth."

A very wise youth, Mallory mused, tracing each letter with her index finger. *Dare to dream.* What had happened to the young boy who had written those words?

Mallory turned to face him and leaned back against the tree. "Why did you stop coming here if you loved it so much?" she asked, though she suspected she already knew the answer.

"Who says I loved it?"

"I can see it in your eyes."

He shoved his hands in his pockets, an endearing trait that always gave away his reticence to speak about a subject. "My parents didn't like me to come here. My mother said the son of an earl doesn't frolic in a stream like a guttersnipe. She also didn't like it when I got my clothes dirty."

Mallory hated to think it, but she knew if Dexter's mother were alive, she wouldn't like her very much. The woman had treated her son in such an impersonal way, almost as if he were another one of her artifacts—one she had lost interest in.

"When I have children, I'll let them play in the dirt." She smiled to herself. "We can make mud pies together. I always wanted to make a mud pie."

"So why didn't you?"

She bent down and plucked a buttercup. "Mud isn't easy to come by in New York City. Muddy water, yes. Stand too close to the curb on a rainy day and you'd get a healthy dose of city sludge in your face."

A smile curved one corner of his lips, bringing out the dimple in his cheek. "If I ever come to New York, I'll remember not to stand too close to the curb."

Her enjoyment of the day faded at his words. *If I ever come to New York.* It really was all coming to an end, wasn't it?

She pushed away from the tree. "We better eat that chicken before it gets cold."

Dexter's hand on her arm stopped her. "It's already cold."

"Oh. That's right." Mallory glanced down at the tiny yellow and purple flowers beneath her feet, hoping he would release her. She couldn't bear it when he stood so close—couldn't bear wanting to touch him and knowing it would be one more memory that would return to New York with her while he stayed in England. "I'm famished," she lied, her appetite having left her.

He hesitated and then released her. Mallory ducked away, wondering how she would share a blanket with him, watch him eat, talk inanities, and think about the path she had chosen, the one that had brought her to Dexter—the same one that would take her away.

She knelt down and busied herself removing the food and dishes from the basket. She felt his presence behind her. Her hands stilled for a moment before she shook herself and continued. She made a plate for him and put it as far away from her as she could.

"Any farther and I'd be sitting in the stream."

Mallory glanced up to find Dexter across the blanket from her, a hint of amusement in his eyes. "What?"

He pointed to the plate. "You sure you want it there? How about another three feet? Then I can eat in the water."

"I'm sorry. I guess my mind is just . . . preoccupied."

He sat down, a forearm propped across his bent knee. "I noticed. Do you want to tell me about it?"

Tell him about it? Tell him that he was the reason

she was preoccupied? No, there was no place for that here. No place for it at all.

"There's nothing to tell." She busied herself with pushing the food around on her plate. The pop of the cork in the wine bottle made her jump.

"Sorry." He flashed her an apologetic look as he poured the rose-colored wine into a glass and handed it to her. Then he held up his glass. "What shall we toast to?"

Mallory swirled her wine and then touched her glass to his. "To those who dare to dream."

His eyes caught and held hers. "To those who dare to dream," he murmured, clinking his glass to hers, his eyes never leaving her face as he put the glass to his lips. "So do you want to tell me what's on your mind?"

Mallory had hoped he would let the matter drop. "Nothing really."

"Is it your book?" he said as if she hadn't spoken.

Her book. She had barely looked at it since she had arrived. For once, she had focused on something else, discovering a need her books could never fulfill.

"No, it isn't my book." She nibbled on the crusty French bread, but could taste nothing. Her mind was elsewhere, swirling around the topic she had to broach, a topic they both had been avoiding. "I was wondering what day to make plane reservations."

He stopped eating, but didn't look up. "There's no rush," he said quietly.

No rush. Why did he persist in confusing her? Hadn't he told her only a few short days ago that he wanted to finish their project expeditiously so she could go home?

"You can't say you need me anymore. Just look at you. You're the man you wanted to be. No woman could resist you now."

He glanced up, angry blue eyes impaling her. "I didn't do this to be irresistible to women."

"So why did you do it? You never did tell me."

He looked away. "I did tell you."

Yes, he had. Research. Always research. Perhaps she was looking for another reason, something that would make more sense of her trip—and what she had found once she had arrived. "So is our project to be the topic of your next paper?"

"No. I would never do something like that."

Of course he wouldn't. She had known that even as she asked the question. "You must love your work quite a bit if you would go to all this expense and trouble."

"It was worth it." His words seemed to hold a double meaning, but then he had always been a puzzle, one whose pieces never fit together twice. "But there are things in this world that I love besides my work . . . things both beautiful and rare."

Mallory gazed out over the gleaming water of the stream, wondering what it would be like to be one of the things Dexter loved, to realize she was worthy of the love she had longed for most of her life, love she didn't seem to deserve once her father was gone.

Across from her, Dexter pushed his plate away and stretched out, leaning back on one elbow, his wineglass clutched in his hand. Mallory tried to concentrate on the chunks of watermelon that had completed their meal, but she couldn't stop looking at him, his long legs extended, his big body encompassing much of the blanket, his profile as perfect as a Greek coin.

He slowly swiveled his head toward her, the crystal blue water of the stream no match for the brilliance of his eyes, leaving her unprepared for his question, yet not surprised that he had turned the tables on her.

"Tell me about your parents."

Like him, Mallory felt no desire to talk about her parents. "There's nothing to tell." She pretended great interest in the chicken leg on her plate.

"I seem to recall saying the same thing to you, yet my answer didn't satisfy you."

Fair is fair, he was telling her. Fine. "My father left when I was fifteen, and you know my mother. He was a truck driver, and she was a substitute teacher. And that's about it. As you can see, my parents weren't nearly as interesting as yours."

"I don't think my parents were interesting." His gaze drifted. "I thought everyone else's parents were interesting—or perhaps the word is *normal.*" The last word held a bitter edge.

Normal. It seemed like an eternity since Mallory's life had been normal.

Dexter picked up the wine bottle and tipped it to her glass, refilling the little bit she had drunk. "Your mother is very nice."

Mallory nodded and took a sip of her wine, thinking about what Genie had said, how she had asked when Mallory and their mother had become friends, as though they were enemies.

Once, they had been very close. But a piece of her mother had died the day her husband left with no warning and no good-bye. After that, a part of her had shut down, and she had closed her heart to caring too much. Perhaps they all had.

Mallory glanced up to find Dexter regarding her intently. "Your mother and Gustav are enjoying each other's company," he told her, his voice sounding tentative, his eyes watchful, perhaps wondering how she would feel about her mother and Dexter's old teacher spending time together.

"I noticed." Mallory had sensed a change in her mother, a diminishing of her sadness, a lowering of her guard. Yet Mallory didn't think the change was solely due to her mother's newfound friendship with Gustav.

There were a few times when Mallory thought that perhaps her mother wanted to talk, to exchange more than just their usual quota of meaningless words. But they had been glossing over all the important topics for so long that Mallory didn't know if she wanted to open up, to take the chance of scratching old wounds, to expose her barely mended heart.

"Does the idea of Gustav and your mother bother you?" Dexter asked.

"No," she replied honestly. No matter what may have transpired over the years, her mother deserved some happiness. Mallory would not deny her that.

A contemplative silence fell over them both. Then Dexter sat up abruptly.

"What is it?" she asked. "What's the matter?"

"Let's go for a swim."

Mallory could not have been more surprised if he had suggested they eat a mouse. "A swim!"

"That's right."

"But we can't!"

"Why not?"

"We have no swimsuits, for one." And seeing Dexter with water glistening off his body was an image she could well live without.

"All Adam and Eve had were fig leaves," he said, pushing to his feet, yanking off one boot and then the other.

Next, he shrugged out of his black leather jacket, spun it around his head, and flung it like some Chippendale Dancer doing a striptease. The jacket landed in an ignoble heap next to a tree stump.

When he went to peel his shirt off, she stammered, "W-what are you doing?" as though it was some sort of mystery.

"Going for a swim." He hauled the shirt over his head and sent it flying the same way as his leather jacket, leaving him naked from the waist up—and leaving Mallory trying to catch her breath.

Large bands of muscles crossed his chest, coiling and flexing beneath smooth skin that tapered down to a taut stomach where the jeans hugged his hips.

He propped his fists on those hips, and his arms reminded her of a mountain range, high peaks and low valleys, veins skimming the surface like hidden streams.

"I'll make you a deal," he said.

Mallory's riveted gaze snapped from his silky brown nipples to his face, praying he would think the color in her cheeks was due to the warmth of the day. "A deal?" she squeaked, and then cleared her throat.

"If you throw me in first, then I'm yours to command. But if I throw you in first, then you have to tell me whatever I want to know. What d'ya say?"

Mallory blinked. Who was this man? "What has happened to you?"

"What do you mean?"

"I mean, who are you and what have you done to the real Dexter Harrington?"

He laughed. "I'm a scientist, Ms. Ginelli. I improved on the original formula, that's all."

Improved. Like he was a bottle of shampoo or a can of soup? People were always improving things she liked exactly the way they were.

"I don't understand how this transformation came about so quickly," she said. "If you will recall, you were reticent about the project from the start."

"I guess you can say I found my motivation."

"Your motivation?" What did that mean? And why did he have to stare at her like that? With his eyes saying she should know something she didn't.

Could it have been Freddie that brought about this sudden change in Dexter? Mallory wondered, experiencing a healthy dose of jealousy. Freddie had that way about her, an ability to command men's attention, like a modern-day Cleopatra.

Dexter shrugged. "A friend told me something that made a lot of sense. It opened my eyes—and my mind. I was like a sponge after that. One thing I learned surprised me a great deal."

"What was that?"

"Women's magazines can be insightful tools to use in understanding the female mind."

Mallory's jaw dropped. "Are you telling me that you have been reading women's magazines?"

He nodded. "I learned several useful things. For example, in one article, a woman said that relationships were liked Porsches, easy to get into but hard to get out of. I found that rather intriguing—

although I don't think I would have used a Porsche for my analogy when a Rolls is by far a better automobile."

Mallory couldn't help smiling as a hint of the old professor came through in his words. "I see. What else did you learn?"

"Well, it seems females have a fascination for men's chests. They find them very sexy, it being a toss-up between a sprinkle of hair and hairless." He looked down at his chest and then at her. "What do you think?"

"Think?" He wanted her to use her brain at a time like this? With him standing half naked in front of her like a male model waiting for his photo shoot? "About what?"

"About my chest?" His muscles rippled with the slight movement of his arms. "Would you call it sexy?"

The man had to ask? Even women who liked other women might change their minds seeing Dexter's bare chest. "It's a very nice chest." Better than nice, but wild horses couldn't drag that out of her.

He digested her response with a "Hmm," and then rubbed a hand over the chest in question. Mallory swallowed. The man just didn't know his appeal.

"There are other things women want besides sexy chests," she said, though she doubted many women would throw away a man who had one just to prove a point.

"Yes, I know. I read that, too. They want a sense of security, self-worth, and unconditional love."

Once again, he seemed to be looking at things like the scientist and not the man, recognizing the components, but perhaps not understanding how the pieces fit together.

"A little bit of mystery is nice as well," she told him.

A small frown puckered his brow. "Mystery wasn't in there. I'll have to write that one down."

Mallory smiled inwardly. "Don't write anything down. Just be yourself."

"Being myself is what got me—" He stopped, his frown deepening. "This transformation is what we intended," he said, a gruff note to his voice. "So count yourself a success."

A success? She didn't feel like a success. "I didn't do this to you."

"Perhaps not entirely." His voice lowered, his eyes searching her face. "But without you, it would never have happened."

Why did she wish it hadn't happened, and that things could go back to the way they had been?

He reached out and took her by the hand, hauling her to her feet. "Now, let's swim."

He was back to that again? "I think you've gone mad."

"No." He smiled. "Not mad. Just warm. Come on." He tugged her toward the water.

"I'm not going in there."

"Prepare to lose the bet."

"Dexter! Stop!"

They stood at the water's edge, and he turned to face her. "I like the way that sounds."

"What?" she asked, telling herself it was only exertion making her breathless.

"My name on your lips. I think this is the first time I've heard you say it."

Perhaps because she had stopped thinking of

him as the professor or the earl, and started thinking of him as just a man.

Without warning, he scooped her up into his arms and trudged into the water. "Put me down!" she shrieked.

"As you wish, my lady." He released her abruptly, and she plunged into the cold water, her hair band coming off, sending her black tresses over her face so that she came to the surface looking as though a huge wad of seaweed had sucked her up.

She sputtered and swiped the hair from her eyes, glaring at her tormentor. "You . . . you . . . oooh!"

The corners of his lips twitched; then he lost the battle to contain his amusement and tipped back his head, his roar of laughter echoing through the woods.

Mallory tried to stay angry, but it really was too funny. A small chuckle bubbled up. She slapped her hand over her mouth, but the laughter would not be contained.

Dexter sobered first, enchanted by Mallory's smile and the way her eyes lit up when she was happy. In all his years of being a scientist and all his research and all the accolades he had received, nothing measured up to the joy he felt at making Mallory laugh. That sweet sound filled a void inside him like nothing else ever had.

He wanted her, heart, body, and soul. She was so close, her clothes drenched and clinging to every curve, her NYU T-shirt molding her breasts, hard peaks straining against the material, making his gut clench with desire.

A bead of water rolled down her neck tormenting him. He watched it slide around the curve of her throat, dip into the hollow at the base, linger for a moment, and then slowly ease over her collar-bone and wind a path down her chest, disappearing into the valley between her breasts. How he longed to follow that drop of water with his tongue.

Perhaps she sensed his unbridled need because she walked backward in the water, eluding hands that would have reached for her and pulled her close.

She moved to the opposite bank and sank down on a rock near the water's edge, her eyes never leaving his. Then she said something he knew he would never forget. "You are so beautiful."

Her words slammed against him, blasting away the last layer encasing his heart. He stood before her, humbled, awed—and so damned scared he would ruin everything.

"Mallory . . ." Her name was a hoarse rasp of sound.

Her gaze skimmed down his body, making the blood run hot through his veins. Desire that matched his own was reflected in her eyes when they met his. "Your parents must have been glori-ous to have made you."

Dexter tensed at her words. Why did it always come back to his parents? No matter how closed-mouthed he was on the subject or how obvious he was about not wanting to discuss them, she would not let it go. She probed until he wanted to rage at her to stop, or kiss her into forgetfulness. No one had ever been this interested—in him, his life, his work. And never had he wanted to share any of it. Until now.

And he knew then that, for better or worse, he had to share his secret and exorcise its influence from his life, a secret he had never told anyone, not even Cummings.

"I don't know what my parents looked like," he said, taking the first step.

A puzzled frown knit her brow. "What do you mean you don't know?"

"I don't know because I never met them." Dexter stared down at his reflection rippling in the water at his waist, wondering if somewhere in the world there was a face similar to his.

"Are you saying you were adopted?"

"No . . . I only wish I had been. Maybe then I would feel normal, as though I fit in somewhere in the scheme of life, had roots, even if it meant my biological parents didn't want me or couldn't raise me for some reason."

"What are you saying?"

"I'm saying that what you see before you is an experiment."

"An experiment?"

Dexter ran his fingertips over the water, banishing his image. "I was created in a lab, much like Frankenstein's monster. My parents couldn't have children. But far be it for them to adopt some needy child. No, they had to make their own. They wanted to build the perfect son. Someone who had the body of an athlete and the brains of Einstein. They were scientists after all. It wasn't in their nature to do anything half measure—or expect anything less than perfection."

Bracing himself, Dexter glanced up at Mallory. What he saw buffeted him. There was no horror in her eyes, no pity. Just simple curiosity.

"So you're a test tube baby, then? That's not so odd."

"No, I'm what you'd call a biological milkshake. They mixed a little of this, a little of that, shook it all together and waited to see if their creation would be a success. My parents were happy with the general outcome—if not disappointed in some regards." Disappointed by having a son who didn't want to walk the path they had chosen, didn't want to be burdened with the responsibility of being the only son, the one who had to carry on the Harrington tradition. He wasn't even really a Harrington after all.

He didn't know what he was.

"Did you think I would be horrified by your revelation?" she asked, the softness of her voice and the understanding in her eyes only making his pain redouble. He didn't want her kindness. He wanted her to walk away, leave him be, stop making him yearn for things he couldn't have.

"I belong in a scientific sideshow," he said in a bitter voice. "They can put me in between cloned sheep and conjoined twins. Meet the offspring of genetic tampering."

"Really, you act as if you're half man/half horse or have a third eyeball or another head growing out of your shoulder. Face it, you're made of flesh and blood just like the rest of us."

"You don't understand."

"Then explain it to me, because the only thing I see before me is a man—an exceptional, gifted, compassionate man."

Mallory's words reached that cold place inside him, a place he had longed for someone to touch. Yet it came too late to change how he felt about himself. "You don't know what it's like to wonder about everything you do, to ask yourself if your thoughts are your own or if they were created just like everything else. I had multiple female donors and multiple male donors. Nameless, faceless people. Handpicked specimens who I don't know and who couldn't care less about knowing me." He raked a hand through his hair. "Who am I? That question has plagued me all my life."

"I know who you are," was Mallory's simple, quiet reply. "You're a brilliant scientist, a man who cares about his friends, who loves animals, who couldn't learn how to rumba if his life depended on it, but who'd be a shoo-in at the Indy 500. In short, a man who has terrible taste in bow ties— and I do mean terrible."

Dexter didn't want to smile. He didn't want her words to ease even a fraction of his pain. Yet she always managed to do just that. "Terrible, huh?"

She shrugged, mischief lighting her eyes. "Well, maybe that red one isn't too bad."

"I'll have to remember to wear it more often, then." God, how he wanted her, needed her. He was drawn to her, like a moth to a very beautiful, very elusive flame. He didn't want to deny himself any longer. She was like a drug he couldn't live without.

He eased through the water toward her, his rational, scientific mind clouded over with passion, an ache only this woman could soothe. Her eyes widened, and she stared up at him through a fringe of thick, wet lashes as he came to a stop in front of her.

He didn't think about what he was doing, and he didn't need any instruction. He had discovered the secret behind what a woman desired from a man. His heart. And Mallory had his, no matter what the future brought.

He took her hand and lifted it to his chest. Then he cupped the back of her head and leaned down to brush his lips against hers, his heart slamming against his ribs as her tongue met his, heat sluicing through him in a torrent of sexual demand.

He coiled an arm around her waist. She eased slowly upward, her chest skimming along his as she rose to her feet, her nipples tormenting him even through her shirt. He cupped her buttocks and pulled her tight against his arousal, wanting her to know what she did to him.

He kissed her, kissed her in a way he had never kissed another woman, kissed her the way he had dreamed about since she first pressed her lips to his in his office.

His mouth moved over hers with urgent demand, deeper, tongues dueling, wanting to taste, to touch. He couldn't get enough of her.

Her soft moan registered in his brain. It was the sweetest sound, yet it brought reality back with hurtling force. He couldn't do this. He couldn't take something from Mallory he didn't deserve.

He released her and stepped away. He saw the hurt in her eyes, the confusion. The need. It matched his own, but he was powerless to do anything about it.

"I'm sorry," he said, his voice hoarse with desire. He clenched his hands into fists to keep from touching her. "Please forgive me. I don't know what came over me."

He swung around, the water cascading away from him, sounding loud and harsh as he pushed toward the opposite bank, trying to outdistance the hunger burning through his gut like acid.

"Dexter." He tensed, her soft voice stopping him. But he couldn't face her, couldn't stand to see the passion-induced look in her eyes. He wondered what he had done to make God punish him so, to bring Mallory to him when he couldn't have her, to torture him with a glimpse of something that could never be. "Look at me," she quietly beseeched.

Dexter steeled himself as he slowly turned to face her. But no amount of mental or physical preparation could save him from the power of this woman.

A slight tremble shook her, yet something told him it wasn't from the chill of the water. Her gaze did not waver as she moved toward him, her brave, indomitable spirit shining like a beacon. It took all the strength he possessed not to shy away from her, afraid she would touch him.

Afraid she wouldn't.

She stopped in front of him. Her gaze swept over his face, as though memorizing every feature before meeting his eyes. "Do you remember when I told you about choosing a path?" she asked.

He nodded, recalling every word, just like all the things she said to him.

"Wherever life leads you," she murmured, "it will be because you made the final decision. And it doesn't matter how you came to be here. It just matters that you're here."

She never ceased to amaze him, this angel-faced city girl. He had always thought himself smart, believed it to be the only tangible thing in his life, and yet he couldn't see the same simple truth that

Mallory saw so clearly. She made him want to believe in himself—the man, not the scientist. She dared him to reach for something he wanted.

His heart beat in slow, painful strokes as he took her hand in his, his fingers entwining with hers. He slipped his other arm around her waist, bringing her closer, her free hand sliding up his chest, scoring his flesh with heat.

"I'm choosing a path," he told her.

"And what are you choosing between?" she asked, her breathy voice making him burn.

"Between asking if I can touch you, caress your skin with my lips, press your body against mine . . . or walking away and doing the honorable thing."

Mallory rose up on tiptoe and curled her hand behind his neck, her fingers sliding upward into his wet hair as she whispered against his lips, "Let me see if I can help you decide."

CHAPTER
TWENTY-ONE

Mallory had never felt so bold, so uninhibited as she did at that moment in Dexter's arms. She wanted to hold on and never let him go. God, how she loved the feel of him, the hard, exquisite expanse of him, the sweet, hot taste of his lips, his hands touching her.

She wrapped her arms tighter around his neck, pressing her body close, reveling in the warmth of his mouth, the glide of his tongue, the intensity of his desire. It pulled her along, swept her up in a maelstrom of intoxicating sensation.

The glide of the water over their bodies was its own pleasure, swirling at her hips as he cupped her buttocks and brought her closer to the hardness between his legs.

He ravaged her mouth, leaving it bruised and swollen as he worked his way down her neck, no spot unexplored. She threw her head back to give him better access even as a small voice asked her what tomorrow would bring. Regrets? Self-recrimination? Or joy that she had reached out and taken what she wanted no matter what the future held? She didn't know, nor did she want to.

He lifted her. She wrapped her legs around his waist and rubbed against him, reveling in the groan that rumbled deep in his chest.

"How long I've waited for this . . . for you." His breath was warm against her already fevered flesh. "Take this off," he growled when her shirt got in the way of his exploring lips.

Mallory could no more deny him than she could deny herself. She wanted his mouth on her, wanted to see his expression when she was without barriers.

With exquisite slowness, she shimmied out of her wet, clinging shirt, her nipples showing dark against her simple cotton bra. A moment of insecurity made her hesitate.

"You're perfect," he said in a husky whisper, banishing her doubts . . . as his teeth banished her bra, clasping the front closure skillfully, setting her free, exposing her to his hungry gaze. "Better than my wildest dreams."

Nervousness made her speak. "I thought you were a novice at this."

Dark, satiny blue eyes lifted to hers. "Not a novice. Just clumsy."

He was far from clumsy. Everything about him seduced her, the way his eyes caressed her, his hands, his mouth . . . his body, the friction exquisite torture.

"Women have always made me nervous."

"You're not nervous now."

"I know, but I feel different with you, able to be

myself. You don't expect the world's best lover or a bumbling scientist. You accept me for who I am . . . I think you always have."

Mallory swept her fingers through his hair. "Always."

He smiled wickedly. "Good. Now perhaps I can practice some of the techniques I've learned over the years. There are some benefits to being a sex doctor. Would you like to find out?"

Would she like to find out? It seemed as though she had been waiting her whole life to find out. The words he had once spoken to her came rushing back.

I know the erogenous zones, where to touch and for how long, how to build the desire. What things to do to bring the greatest pleasure.

Every inch of Mallory's body went up in flames. And as his gaze devoured her, she found the strength to say, "Why, Professor, do you think that's prudent?"

"Oh, yes, Ms. Ginelli . . . very prudent." Then he lowered his head and took her nipple in his mouth.

Mallory's body went boneless as his lips closed around her aching peak, and she was thankful his strong arms held her tight. Every tug of his mouth sent the pleasure spiraling downward, liquid heat building at the core of her. He teased each nipple until they were rigid and begging for his touch.

Mallory wanted to touch him, to lay her tongue against those silky brown pebbles and do to him what he was doing to her, but he wouldn't let her. All she could do was clutch his shoulders as he suckled and rocked her against his erection.

Then he slid his hand down the front of her

jeans, having unbuttoned and unzippered them without her even knowing it. His fingers slipped beneath her cotton panties.

Mallory arched back as he touched her where no man had ever touched her, easing between her slick folds and massaging the swollen and sensitive nub, driving her wild as he flicked it with the edge of his nail, increasing the tempo and then suddenly rubbing in circles, bringing even more exquisite pleasure.

She panted like a wild thing, moaning his name, pleading, demanding, feeling the wet path of her tears run down her cheeks as the pressure built until she cried out, her nails digging into his shoulders as wave after wave of intense release made her convulse.

"Dexter," she rasped.

"Ssh." He feathered kisses over her cheeks, his mouth washing away the salty path of her tears, tears she couldn't believe she had shed. But she had been lost in the moment.

Without removing her legs from around his waist, he walked them toward the bank and to the long, flat boulder he claimed to have sunned himself on as a child. Now he laid her upon it and looked at her. Her nipples drew into tight buds at his scrutiny.

She had never wanted a man as she wanted Dexter. And Mallory knew she had finally reached that place in her life, a crossroad. She had to make a decision: to give her most precious gift, her virginity, to Dexter or not.

She had always told herself that she would not sell herself cheap, that she would give her body only to the man she loved. In that moment, the answer seemed so clear. Perhaps more clear than anything had been in her life.

She loved Dexter. Perhaps he didn't love her back. Perhaps he didn't know how. He had never been shown love; how could he be expected to know how to give it?

She held out her hand to him. A small frown creased his brow as he stared at her, looking uncertain. She prayed he would not deny her offering.

He hesitated and then took hold of her hand, encompassing her fingers within his embrace. He bent down and kissed the back of her hand as if they belonged to another time, a time when gallantry ruled the day. Her heart swelled with love for him.

She tugged him forward, wanting to feel his body against hers. He resisted. "What—"

He pressed a finger to her lips. "Ssh. Let me make you happy."

"But you've—"

He effectively silenced her by taking her nipple in his mouth. Her words shattered into little pieces and floated away. Those large hands moved down over her ribs, gripped the waistband of her jeans and began peeling them off. They clung to her like a second skin.

He reached her ankles and ran into the barrier of her sneakers. With a sinful smile, he removed first one, then the other, tossing them over his shoulder. They plunked into the stream. He tugged off her jeans, leaving her clad in only her wet cotton panties and white socks.

He gazed at her panties, and Mallory tried not to move; but she couldn't help herself. If he didn't touch her soon, she might go mad.

Beads of sweat dotted her brow and the valley between her breasts as he laid his hands on her calves, his fingers stroking her skin with a feather-light touch, moving upward with torturous slowness, until he used only the index finger on each hand to lightly skim her inner thighs. At last, his hands abutted the nest of curls between her thighs.

Mallory squirmed, and he obliged her silent plea, slipping one finger beneath her panties and parting her moist folds. The first touch of his finger against her engorged nub made her back arch, and a low moan escaped her lips.

Her eyelids fluttered open, viewing the canopy of trees above her through passion-hazed eyes. She glanced at Dexter's handsome face, his jaw gritted with the control he forced himself to maintain, all his muscles tense.

Her gaze skimmed downward, over his chest and stomach to the long, hard length straining against the zipper of his jeans. She reached out, wanting to stroke him, but he took hold of her wrist, stopping her.

"Please," she begged, her voice not sounding like her own.

He shook his head, but said nothing. He used his free hand to pull her panties off. Then he pinioned both her wrists at her sides and eased her slowly toward him so her legs dangled from the sides of the boulder.

Then he knelt down between her thighs, and the world exploded in a vibrant array of colors as his mouth and tongue replaced his finger, stroking, sucking, flicking the very tip of her clitoris.

Mallory didn't know when he had released her wrists. She was lost to the sensation. But his hands were not idle. They caressed her stomach and moved inch by excruciating inch toward her breasts, cupping, shaping, sweeping a thumb over her nipples to tease her.

When he removed his hands, she thought she would die. But he needed them to put her legs over his shoulders, bringing his mouth tighter against her, opening her, increasing the erotic torture.

His hands returned to her breasts, rolling her nipples between thumb and forefinger. Her head jerked back and forth, her hips writhing, the pleasure culminating until the heat exploded through her veins and she climaxed again.

Her head rolled to the side, her body limp as a satiated sigh escaped her lips. She smiled to herself, remembering how nonchalant and clinical Dexter had been about how he could make a woman feel and what the outcome would be.

I know what things to do to bring them great pleasure, *which would, of course, culminate in multiple orgasms.*

His boast had not been an empty one.

He stretched out beside her on the sun-warmed boulder. Mallory turned toward him and laid her head on his shoulder, smelling the hint of cologne on his neck. He hadn't missed a thing when he had made his transition from old Dexter to new. Yet Mallory knew she would love him in his tweed and smelling like musty old books.

His eyes were closed, one forearm draped over his brow, allowing her the opportunity to admire the muscles in his chest and stomach. He flinched when she laid her hand on his chest, cracking open one eye and glancing down at her.

"Hello," she murmured, lifting slightly to brush her lips over his.

"Hello," Dexter replied, his voice hoarse from the control he had exerted to keep himself from making love to Mallory, something he wanted to do more than anything. He longed to plunge into her warmth, to find what had been missing from his life all these years. He knew the answer was there waiting for him. He need only reach out for it. But he couldn't.

He couldn't make love to Mallory, not knowing the secret that hung between them. In good conscience, he couldn't touch her as he so desperately wanted to. But if he had to feel her body pressed to his much longer, he wasn't sure what he would do.

His dishonesty had caused this, and he had passed up all the chances he had had to tell her the truth about Sarah. His reasons had been entirely selfish. He couldn't let her go.

Every time he had thought about telling her, he convinced himself another day wouldn't hurt, another hour, and now it was another minute . . . just another minute. Why hadn't he listened to Cummings and been honest with her from the start?

Probably because she had captured his heart the moment she had snuggled against his chest that first night, sighing and content as she was now, her cheek pressed against his chest in the same way, making his gut constrict with need.

He wanted to be the man she wrote about in her books, the man who existed in her mind. He wanted to be her hero. But he couldn't be that man when he had Sarah to think about. Sarah, who was waiting for him to fulfill an unspoken promise.

Dexter tried to close out the yearning Mallory roused in him as her hands smoothed across his chest, a finger swirling around his nipple and then gently gliding across. He clenched his hands to keep from reacting, to keep from hauling her on top of him, unbuttoning his jeans and taking her there, on top of the sun-dappled boulder, claiming her in a way that was as old as time.

She leaned up on her elbow, her silky black tresses caressing his arm, his shoulder, whispering across his chest, making every fiber of his being come alive. He watched her head descend, the tip of her pink tongue sliding out of her mouth to tease his nipple. His body reacted as if he had just been branded with a cattle prod.

Her mouth closed over her treat, and he jammed his eyes shut, vowing that in one more moment he would end the torment . . . just one more moment.

He had never been touched in such a way, never savored and enjoyed. To women, he had been some odd fascination, like a newly discovered species at the zoo. But with Mallory, he felt . . . loved.

"Dexter," she murmured as her lips trailed up his chest, planting sweet kisses on his collarbone, her tongue skimming over the pulse at the base of his neck, which had beat erratically before she had even touched him.

Her mouth brushed his chin before tasting his bottom lip and then the top. Then that sweet mouth fused to his, teasing him with the silky-sweet thrust of her tongue.

His fingers unclenched, and he cupped the back

of her head, his lips slanting over hers fiercely, trying to convey what he couldn't say.

She eased on top of him, her breasts skimming lightly over his chest. She lifted slightly and rubbed her nipples tantalizingly against his heated flesh. Sweat dampened his hair and rolled down his back.

"Mallory," he groaned, trying to find the words he needed to stop what was happening. He was quickly losing control.

She straddled his hips then, fitting herself snuggly over his erection, sweeping her hair down his chest and belly as she slowly sat up. She gyrated her hips, and he was in agony.

He thought he shook his head, but couldn't be sure. What he did know was that he had to touch her. He cupped her breasts. They were more beautiful than his limited imagination had envisioned: pert, upthrusting, and fitting perfectly into his palms.

She tossed back her head and moved over him faster as he played with her nipples. He couldn't make love to her, but that didn't mean he couldn't give her pleasure. He loved watching her face, seeing the desire in her eyes, the light flush that pinkened her skin when she climaxed.

He eased a finger between her moist cleft and found her swollen nub. She gasped and then moaned deep in her throat as he moved against her. He had never heard a sweeter sound. She arched her back, her hands clasping his knees as his finger slid back and forth, the tempo increasing with each sweep.

She cried out, her whole body tightening, those beautiful breasts thrusting up toward the sky, a slim beam of light swirling over the pink tips.

Dexter tried to resist, but at the first convulsion, he slipped a finger into her, his teeth gnashing with need as her inner lips closed around him . . . again and again and again, wet heat flowing over him like honey.

Slowly, her eyelids opened, and he was struck with the full force of those golden hazel eyes, and he knew he was lost, completely and utterly lost.

Her hand went to the waistband of his jeans and undid the button. Quickly, he caught her wrist. "What are you doing?"

She glanced at him, a sweet, mischievous grin on her gamine face. "I want to touch you . . . there."

Why did she have to say it like that? With a delicious ache in her voice? She made him want to forget all his promises, forget he had obligations, forget his life and stay with her, here in these woods, build a cabin, be a farmer. It was a nice dream, but he was too damn pragmatic, too much the scientist, too much the thinker to believe it would be so easy.

"I think we had better go."

The smile slowly slipped from her face. "But . . . why?"

Dexter heard the unspoken question in her voice, the one that asked if she had done something wrong. She didn't know the problem was with him, not her.

He knew he would tell her everything; but he had to find the right words and the right time, and this was not it, not when they had just shared something so special.

He didn't want to ruin the memory with talk of another woman or recriminations. This might be the last time Mallory would even look at him, touch him like she cared, and he wanted to preserve that moment.

Tonight he would tell all. He would use the rest of the day to figure out the hows and whys. A small voice warned he was merely putting off the inevitable, but he refused to believe that was what he was doing.

"I think we should get back. I have some ... work I need to do."

"Work." The word came out an accusation, as if she could see through him and knew he was keeping something from her, or that she thought he believed his work was more important than her. Nothing was farther from the truth.

She scooted off him, and he hated himself, hated himself more than he ever had all the years he had known he was different. She grabbed up her shirt and yanked it over her head, forgetting her bra, which Dexter suspected had sunk to the bottom of the stream.

Dexter tried not to look at her breasts, the way the shirt hugged their contours, those sweet, hard pebbles pressing against the material, making him yearn to touch them again, to remember their weight in his palms and the silky smoothness of her skin.

They walked back to the car in silence. He let her drive, his sense of adventure having deserted him when reality and his dishonesty had come between him and Mallory.

Mallory stared straight ahead, each mile measuring the length of her nerves. Once more she had left her heart open to be wounded. She had offered herself to Dexter, and he had tossed her aside. Was all the emotion she saw on his face and in his eyes just part of a game, a component of the project?

I have no intention of making love to you.

He had once said those words and had followed them to the letter. Had the time at the stream been his way of saying thank you for her tutoring? A bonus of sorts? Tossing her a morsel of what she couldn't have?

Or could it have been his way of proving to himself that everything about him had changed and that he had become every woman's fantasy?

Her body still tingled from the touch of his hands, his mouth. He had imprinted his memory in her heart as indelibly as he had imprinted it in her mind. Yet he had only left her wanting more, yearning for the one thing he would not give. Not to her.

The car had barely stopped at the front door when Cummings emerged. A shiver of foreboding ran down Mallory's spine at the look on his face.

Obviously Dexter had seen it, too, for he was out of the car first. "What's the matter?" he asked, meeting his friend between the car and the front door.

"Have you seen today's newspaper?"

"No, I didn't have a chance to read it this morning. Why? What's happened?"

Cummings's expression was grim as he handed Dexter the newspaper tucked under his arm.

Dexter glanced apprehensively at his friend and then at Mallory before snapping open the paper. The headline was as vivid as a beacon on a moonless night.

A CURE FOR WOMEN'S IMPOTENCE?

Dread filled Mallory as she scanned the full-page

article, a color photo of Dexter placed squarely under the headline. Her gaze drifted downward to the small picture in the corner of the article to a face she saw every day.

Her own.

Under her picture, it read, *World-renowned sex scientist reveals secret formula to New York romance writer.*

"It's all over the television as well," Cummings said.

When Mallory's gaze lifted, she found Dexter staring at her, pain and accusation filling his eyes. He said nothing to her. Instead, he tossed the paper to the ground and stormed into the house, heading straight for his office.

Mallory chased after him. His roar of anguish echoed down the high-ceiling hallway, yet she entered the lion's den anyway, Cummings hot on her heels.

Dexter swung around upon hearing her enter, books and papers scattered around him; the binder was nowhere in sight. "Why?" he demanded.

"Dexter, I didn't—"

He slashed his hand through the air, the wild look in his eyes cutting her off more effectively than words. "I trusted you like I've never trusted anyone. I let you read my research because I foolishly believed you were interested."

"I was!"

"Don't lie to me!"

Cummings stepped forward. "Dex, look, you don't—"

He pointed a finger at Cummings. "Stay the hell out of this! It was your damn advice that brought her here."

Cummings's jaw worked furiously, and Mallory feared the men would come to blows. Without thought for her safety, she stepped in front of Cummings. Dexter's eyes narrowed on her face, and she knew her action had only made things worse.

"Dexter, please listen to me," she beseeched. "I don't know how the newspapers got the information about your research. I swear."

"You don't know?" Disdain twisted his lips. "Shall I enlighten you then? Remind you of the binder I placed in your hands? Reenact the scene, perhaps? What will it take, do you think? Because I remember everything vividly. I don't believe I'll ever forget."

"You know I would never hurt you like that." She took a tentative step toward him. He stepped back. She reeled as if he had dealt her a physical blow. "I understand how much your work means to you."

"You never gave a damn about my work! And you never gave a damn about me, did you? It was all a ruse so you could get your hands on that material."

"No!" She shook her head. "I didn't even want to see it!"

"That's not what I remember. You seemed very interested to me. Obviously you're a superb actress. Was everything else an act as well?"

Mallory knew what he was asking, and it hurt her to no end. "No, it wasn't an act. I care—"

"Don't!" he warned. "Don't say it." He raked a hand through his hair. "Just tell me, is this what you planned from the start? Have you been deceiving me all along?"

"I never deceived you about anything!" Mallory

thought she saw a momentary wavering in his eyes. Regret, perhaps? Or something deeper? "I won't lie and say I knew nothing about what you were working on. My editor told me a little bit about your research before I came here."

"So you cooked up this scheme with your editor?"

"No! Of course not!"

"What happened then? You got here and decided the information was just too convenient to pass up? Especially since I put the binder in your hands and practically forced you to read it? Did you think that was an open invitation to let the world know about my work?"

"If you'd just listen." But she knew he had passed judgment the minute he had opened the paper. Still, she had to try. "I will admit that my editor suggested I interview you, find out about your research, but I told her I wouldn't do it."

His laugh mocked her. "Oh, so you're noble now? Is that what you're telling me?"

"I'm telling you the truth."

"The truth." His expression hardened to a razor-sharp edge, changing him into a man she hadn't seen before. "You mean you didn't sell yourself to me to pay off your sister's bookie?"

The blood drained from Mallory's face. "How . . . How did you know about Bruno?"

"I told you once I'm a stickler for research. How do you think I got you to come here? I knew your sister owed considerable money to this Bruno character. I don't do anything without knowing what I'm getting into."

Mallory forced back the tears building. She would not cry. Not in front of this cold, heartless man. "How dare you accuse *me* of using *you!* I was never anything more to you than a guinea pig to use in your precious research. So don't you dare point the finger at me!"

"I never lied to you about your role. You knew what I wanted from the start."

Emotions threatened to choke Mallory. "Yes . . . I knew. And I was a bigger fool than you will ever be."

The anger in his eyes seared her to the bone. He picked up one of the scattered books on the floor and hurled it toward the mantel, smashing a teakwood clock. Mallory flinched as the clock shattered, pieces arcing into the air.

Cummings lunged toward Dexter and manacled his wrist. "Damn it, Dex! You don't know that Mallory did anything! You're accusing her without any proof."

"So are you telling me that you sold my information to the papers, Cummings? Is that what you're trying to say?"

"You know me better than to ask such a question."

Dexter wrenched his arm from Cummings's grip. "I do know. So that leaves the only other person I showed my research to." He swiveled his gaze to Mallory, his eyes colder than the North Sea, as he said, "Namely you, Ms. Ginelli."

A bitter wind blew through Mallory's heart.

"Stop this before it's too late," Cummings urged.

Dexter stalked to the window, watching the molten globe of the sun descend behind the horizon.

"It's already too late." His voice was toneless. "It's been too late from the first moment I laid eyes on her, from the second I allowed myself to forget who I was and what promises I had made."

CHAPTER TWENTY-TWO

Mallory stared out her bedroom window into the starless night sky, no trace of a moon in sight. A storm was brewing, wind beginning to lash the trees, chill seeping in through the stones, the first fat drops of rain splattering against the sill.

Yet the storm outside could not match the one inside her as Dexter's accusation battered her, his words playing over and over again in her mind.

You mean you didn't sell yourself to me to pay off your sister's bookie?

He had known about Genie all along, and he had used that weakness against her. He was not an innocent victim, and she would not beg him to believe that she had told the truth. It was a losing battle anyway. Everything pointed in her direction. Besides, if her word was not good enough, then what was?

Angrily, she swiped away the tears coursing down

her cheeks. She would not cry, not for a man who trusted her so little as to believe her capable of such treachery.

Now there would be no more delays, no more wondering when the end would arrive. It *had* arrived. It was time for her to go home.

She made plane reservations for everyone, asking for the earliest departing flight, hoping there would be something the next day, disappointed to find out there wasn't.

However, luck was with her. An early morning flight was available the day after tomorrow, the plane only half full according to the reservationist because a Star Trek convention had been cancelled at the last minute. Mallory could just imagine spending six plus hours with a bunch of Trekkies subjecting each other to the Vulcan death grip.

She moved to the mirror, absently running the brush through her hair, intending to put it up as she always did to keep the unmanageable mass off her face.

Her hand stilled as she remembered what had happened to her last hair band, how it had been washed away as she plunged into the stream, coming to stand face to chest with Dexter when she surfaced. He had run a gentle hand over her hair, telling her how beautiful she was, his gaze devouring.

Mallory closed her eyes and blocked out the thought even as she knew she would never erase the memory of Dexter's caress or the way he made her feel.

She tossed the brush down and headed for the door, intending to find her family and tell them the time had come for them to return to New York.

She paused, her hand on the doorknob as a rustling noise came from underneath her bed. A second later a small, furry body came flying out and launched itself at her leg.

A scream died on Mallory's lips when she realized it was only Rosie, Dexter's monkey. Apparently Rosie had decided to renew her acquaintance in much the same way as she originally introduced herself, only this time Mallory wasn't sleeping—and Dexter wasn't standing before her.

Mallory plucked Rosie from her leg as the mischievous monkey began playing with her shoelaces, probably intending to tie them together.

Hoisting Rosie in her arms, Mallory looked her uninvited guest in the eye. "May I ask what you're doing here? This is not your room." Then again, it wasn't Mallory's either. She pushed aside the wistful feeling that swept over her. "I'll be gone soon, and you can have your playroom back. Okay?"

Rosie chattered away, her small, lion-shaped face animated as she fiddled with Mallory's necklace, testing it with a finger and then deciding to see what it tasted like.

Mallory tugged the necklace away. "I'd like to keep this if you don't mind."

Rosie was unperturbed at losing her toy as she quickly found another one. Mallory's hair. She wrapped a hunk around one black but very humanlike finger. Then Mallory's hair went the same way as her necklace, into Rosie's mouth.

Mallory couldn't resist a smile. "When was the last time you ate?" she asked, retrieving her hair. Rosie bounced against her arm and flapped the skirt of the adorable dress she had on—complete with underwear in a matching red rosebud design. It was the cutest thing Mallory had ever seen. "Is this outfit for your new boyfriend?"

Mallory remembered Dexter telling her that he had just integrated Rosie with a few of her fellow tamarins. He had said it was time she reestablish herself with her kind. Rosie also had to choose a mate. Dexter hoped to some day return Rosie to her homeland and set her and the other monkeys free.

With his animals, Dexter could be the kindest, most compassionate man. Humans, however, were a different story. The sadness Mallory thought she had banished descended once more.

She padded over to the bed and set Rosie down in the middle. "I have to go, but you can stay here and play if you want. Just keep out of my underwear, all right?"

Mallory turned to go, but Rosie wrapped her spindly arms around her thigh. "I'm glad you like me now, but I have to find my family. Perhaps we can play later."

Clearly Rosie didn't like that plan. She began slapping her hands on the bed and chattering shrilly. Then, like a sprung coil, she leapt from Mallory's bed onto Genie's cot and heaved the blanket over her head.

Mallory laughed as Rosie's little body bobbed beneath the blanket. Mallory could just picture her sister's expression should she enter the room at that moment and see her blanket levitating. Genie would certainly believe that the boogieman did indeed haunt Braden Manor.

"All right, young lady, that's enough." Mallory strode toward the cot to save Genie's personal belongings from the wrath of an impish monkey. Rosie thought it was all great fun and began to thrash about like a hyperactive two-year-old, which she just so happened to be.

Mallory went to lift the blanket off Rosie's head when something fluttered to the floor, a piece of paper that had been tucked underneath the mattress. Mallory picked it up, and discovered it was a copy of a packing slip for express mail. She recognized her sister's handwriting immediately and almost as quickly noticed the recipient's address.

The *London Times*.

Contents: one binder.

The blood drained from Mallory's face. Genie had taken the binder. Genie had sent it to the newspaper. Genie had been the poisonous wedge between Mallory and Dexter.

How had her sister known about the important information contained in that binder? It didn't make sense. There had to be a mistake. Mallory hadn't discussed Dexter's research with anyone but Freddie, and Freddie wouldn't say anything.

Then a memory tickled the back of her mind of *where* she and Freddie had discussed the binder. Right here in her bedroom; Genie on a cot not ten feet away. But her sister had been asleep. Or had she?

Mallory shook her head. Genie would not do something so despicable. She wouldn't stoop that low. But then, hadn't she been arrested for stealing more than once?

Mallory wanted to banish the thought, to find an excuse for Genie's actions as she always did, but she couldn't. Not this time. She could no longer save Genie from herself or continue to be her sister's scapegoat.

Genie's problems had been steadily escalating. Mallory just never imagined—or perhaps never wanted to believe?—that her sister would give her such a backhanded slap. It didn't matter that Genie had stolen from Dexter and not her. Genie had to have known her actions would hurt Mallory as well.

Pain and anger built inside Mallory like a slow-burning fire. How could Genie do something like this to her after all she had done to help her? Couldn't her sister have left one small corner in Mallory's life unblemished by deceit and lies?

She swung around and headed for the door. The added despair of Genie's betrayal heaped on top of Dexter's defection numbed Mallory to anything but the need to lash out.

She opened the door and nearly collided with her sister. Genie jumped back, saying, "Geez, Mal, where's the fire?"

Just seeing her sister made the floodgates of Mallory's long sequestered hurt and anger burst open. "Is there no level to which you won't sink?" she bit out, tired of being the mat her sister wiped her feet on, tired of waiting for the next shoe to drop. Just plain tired of it all. "Does absolutely nothing faze you anymore? Or have you grown so uncaring that anything goes? Even screwing over your own family?"

"What are you talking about?"

Mallory waved the paper in Genie's face. "Does this look familiar?"

Her sister swiped the paper from Mallory's hand. "What are you doing snooping around my bed?"

"You have some damn nerve to be castigating other people for snooping when you're nothing but a dirty little thief! How could you, Genie? How could you take Dexter's research and give it to the newspapers?"

Genie tried to push past Mallory and enter the room, but Mallory wouldn't budge. "Get out of my way!"

"Go to hell."

"I don't owe you any explanations!"

"No, you owe me a damn sight more than that."

"Well, join the fucking club."

Mallory was stunned by the coldness in her sister's voice. "What's happened to you? You've gotten hard, Genie. Does nothing matter to you anymore?"

"Where've you been, Mal?" Genie asked in a mocking tone. "I stopped caring a long time ago."

Mallory saw the stark reality of that truth in Genie's eyes. "Even about your own family?"

Genie scoffed and turned her back on Mallory. "Especially about my own family."

"Why, Genie? What did we ever do to you? We did everything we could to help you."

"Perhaps I'm tired of trying." Some of the fire had left Genie's voice. "Perhaps I'm tired of everything."

Mallory moved to stand in front of her sister. "I know I haven't been very easy to talk to these last few years."

Glinting green eyes lifted to impale Mallory. "Ya think?"

Mallory laid a hand on her sister's shoulder. "I'm sorry that I haven't made more time for you."

Genie shrugged off her hand. "Oh, get off it,

will ya? I'm sick of the saint act. Mallory the perfect. Mallory the talented. Mallory, Mallory, Mallory!"

Genie's callous dismissal renewed Mallory's anger. "And I'm sick of your stunts. I'm not bailing you out anymore."

"Then don't! Just get off my back."

"Fine. But you owe Dexter an explanation. He's been nothing but kind to you, and this is how you repay him?"

"Why are you making such a big deal about that stupid research? The world would have known about this stuff sooner or later." Genie eyed her, her look calculating and distrustful. "You love him, don't you? That's why you're so upset."

"Let me make it clear that what I do or don't feel for Dexter is none of your business. I'm upset because I care about you—even if you don't care about yourself."

Genie held Mallory's gaze for one second and then looked away. "Well, what's done is done and it can't be undone."

"But you can make amends with Dexter."

"What's the point?"

"Self-respect?"

"Self-respect." Genie shook her head. "That's a good one."

Mallory wanted to shake her sister, to make her open her eyes and see how she was destroying her life. "Every time I think that you are going to turn yourself around, you disappoint me."

"So what else is new?"

"Was it for the money? Is that why you did it?"

"And if it was? Would that be a surprise?"

Mallory felt her tenuous control slipping. "You owed Bruno money again, didn't you? Didn't you!"

she demanded when her sister clamped her jaws together.

"Yes! Are you happy now?"

Mallory squeezed her eyes shut. "I can't believe it." She shook her head. "After all the times I've rescued you from that slimy worm, you do this."

"I don't need you to rescue me! I can take care of myself."

Mallory's eyes snapped open. "Then, why don't you? For God's sake, Genie, why can't you stop doing these things?"

"I don't know!" her sister shouted. "Why can't you stop being little Ms. Fix It? You are so self-righteous. You think you know what's best for everyone. Well, you don't! I don't need you to tell me how to run my life!"

"I've never tried to run your life, but God knows you need someone to do it with the way you're screwing it up."

"Maybe if you hadn't sent Dad away, I wouldn't have had so many problems!"

The barb hit its mark. Mallory felt the old yet familiar constriction of her chest, the pressure that wound its way around her whenever her father was mentioned.

"That shut you up, didn't it?" Genie prodded viciously. "Because you know I'm right. Your big mouth ruined everyone's life!"

"I did what I thought was best."

"*I did what I thought was best,*" Genie mimicked in a cruel voice. "Who made you fairy godmother? You were only fifteen years old."

"And you were only seven!"

"Yes, I was only seven years old and fatherless.

Thanks to you! I never got to know him. You took that away from me."

Mallory didn't know if it was better to shake Genie or hug her close, to remind her sister of the days when they had been friends or simply let go. But the days Mallory wanted to recapture were so long ago, a lifetime it seemed, and now the past had come back to haunt them.

"Could it possibly be that you don't remember what happened?" Mallory asked, unable to believe that her sister might have forgotten the ugliness that had severed their family completely—and irrevocably.

"You just wanted to get rid of Dad because he loved me more than you. You hated that he spent more time with me, that he read to me and sang me to bed at night and let me cuddle in his lap and . . ." Tears clogged Genie's throat, her pain heart-wrenching. "I hate you," she said in a ragged whisper.

Mallory stepped toward her sister, wanting to comfort her; but Genie darted back, glaring at her as if she was the enemy, and Mallory knew that in Genie's eyes she was.

Her sister needed a vent for her anger, and for ten long years, Mallory had taken the abuse, perhaps hoping her sister would get over the rage. Mallory could now see that the rage had only festered.

They could no longer hide behind silence.

"Genie, you know why Dad left."

Anguish etched Genie's face. "Leave me alone! I won't listen to you anymore!"

Mallory took a deep breath, searching within herself for strength, knowing she would need it now more than ever. "He left because I threatened to tell the police about what he was doing to you."

Genie clapped her hands over her ears. "I don't want to hear this!"

"I told him if he ever touched you again, I would kill him."

Wildly, Genie shook her head. "No! He didn't— I was his princess!"

Tears Mallory had refused to shed all those years ago began to course down her cheeks. "He molested you, Genie. He did things no father should ever do to his daughter."

A shocked gasp filled the air. Mallory's gaze jerked toward the sound to see a figure emerge from the shadowed embrace of the dimly lit corridor.

Her mother.

Her mother, who had never known that horrible secret.

"Have you ever noticed what a great antiseptic alcohol is?" Dexter asked in a slurred voice, slanting a glance at the man who had come up beside him. "Especially if applied internally and in liberal measure." Perhaps he would tie a lime around his neck and let himself sink to the bottom of a bottle of Corona—Mallory's drink of choice. It seemed apropos.

"It depends on vhat you are trying to numb," Gustav replied, concern evident in his eyes, pity Dexter didn't want to see. "It von't vork on a guilty conscience . . . or a vounded heart."

A wounded heart. Was that why he hurt so much? Dexter wondered, looking down the slope of the hill he and Gustav stood atop, his gaze drawn to the west where he and Mallory had spent their afternoon beside a lazy stream, where he had allowed himself to get closer to her, not only physically, but mentally and emotionally as well. Something he had vowed he wouldn't let happen.

He couldn't make out anything in the blanket of darkness, yet he could see the valley in his mind as if it were daylight. He could picture Mallory's beautiful face alight with desire, her breasts rising and falling as he stroked her, her liquid heat covering his fingers as he built the fever . . . a fever that still raged in him even now, unabated and pounding at him for fulfillment.

The weather matched his mood. Wind began to whistle through the trees, steadily picking up, the smell of rain in the air, thunder brewing in distant clouds, keeping tempo with the emotion churning inside him.

He laid a hand against the gnarled trunk of an ancient beech tree. Two memorial plaques sat at its base. He wasn't sure what drew him to this place, to his parents' makeshift gravesite. Perhaps it was just a need to get out of the house.

Or perhaps he had come to exorcise his demons.

"My heart's not wounded," he finally said. "Just my pride." Just his soul.

Dexter held up the scotch bottle and shook it; disappointed to see it was almost empty. It didn't matter. He had a cellar full of alcohol. He could stay drunk until he was ninety-nine, or until he had forgotten Mallory's treachery, whichever came first. The thought of her made him ache, so he put the bottle to his lips for another slug.

"You lie quite convincingly, my boy."

Dexter narrowed his blurry eyes on Gustav. "Don't analyze me, Gustav. You're not Freud. Just leave me alone to get drunk in peace."

Gustav looked up into the night sky spread out before them like a huge movie screen. "You alvays vere a master at complicating things."

Dexter's laugh was self-mocking. "God forbid I should do anything the easy way. Right?" Or let himself think that maybe someone special and rare had come into his life, that perhaps happiness was finally within his reach.

For a long moment, they stood silent, both staring up into the sky. Dexter spotted Orion, the giant hunter, pursuer of the Pleiades, the seven daughters of Atlas metamorphosed into stars. Lover of Eos, the goddess of the dawn—and finally killed by Artemis, the virgin goddess of the hunt and moon. Poor bastard was done in by a female. Dexter understood how that felt.

Dexter hoped Gustav would leave as quietly as he had come, let him enjoy his bout of self-pity, yet he knew his mentor too well to think that would happen.

Gustav turned to him. Dexter could feel those probing gray eyes searching his face, looking beneath the surface. "So vhat happens now?"

"Nothing happens."

"And vhat of Ms. Ginelli?"

Dexter's jaw worked. "What of her?"

"You know she'll leave."

"I know." Dexter averted his gaze, not wanting Gustav to see the truth, to know that a large piece of his heart would go with Mallory when she left. He hated himself for wanting her to stay, for wanting to tell her that he was the one who had fallen short of the mark.

"So vhat vill you do then?"

Yes, Harrington, what will you do? "I'm leaving for London tomorrow to see Sarah."

"So you intend to follow through on the marriage proposal, do you?"

"Of course." But did he intend to follow through? Was that why he was going to London? Or was he going to tell Sarah that he could never be a good husband to her, not when he loved another woman?

He wouldn't know what he would say until he got there, until he saw Sarah. Whatever he decided, he had to talk to her. She deserved that much. He had been running away when he had come to Wales, knowing Sarah was right in the middle of the social whirl in London, too busy to press him for that final commitment.

Gustav shook his head. "I thought you had forgotten such foolishness. After I saw the change in you . . ."

Dexter glanced down at his attire. He hadn't changed out of the clothes he had worn to the stream. He still had on the jeans, T-shirt, and black leather jacket. What had he really hoped to accomplish with all this? It didn't seem worth what he had gained . . . and then lost.

"The clothes don't change the man, Gustav." Dexter had learned that the hard way.

"I vasn't speaking about the clothes. I vas speaking about you. You're different."

"I'm no different than what I've always been. A boring scientist." Why had he ever thought he could be something he wasn't? Maybe because he had so desperately wanted to change . . . but not for any of the reasons he had first imagined.

"You may vant to believe that nonsense; but you are not the same man, and I think that has everything to do vith the vivacious Ms. Ginelli. You think she betrayed you, my boy, but something tells me you don't believe it, not completely. So the question is, vhy have you used this incident as an excuse to sabotage vhat the two of you have?"

Dexter shoved away from the tree. "I did no such thing. We didn't have anything to begin with, so there was nothing to sabotage."

"Oh, you most assuredly did have something—something very special. My eyes do not deceive me. You love her. You said as much. Vhat compels you to deny it now?"

Dexter opened his mouth to discredit Gustav's claim, yet he would never be able to convince his friend that he didn't love Mallory anymore—not if he couldn't convince himself.

Deep down, he was so damn scared he shook with the fear—the fear of not living up to Mallory's expectations, of not being the man she wanted, needed, the fear of disappointing her.

He didn't want to be a man every woman desired. Only this one woman.

Gustav laid a comforting hand on his shoulder. "She didn't betray you. Had you seen the heartbroken look in her eyes as she flew past me in the hall, you vould know she vould never have done such a thing to you."

Dexter saw his world collapsing around him the harder he tried to hold on to what was left. "Let it go, Gustav. This is my life."

Gustav nodded sagely. "This is true, and yet I

cannot help but vonder vhen *you* vill finally understand that.''

Dexter understood. It had taken Mallory to show
him what he was missing, what he could have and
what he was giving up because of damnable stubbornness and misplaced honor. He had repaid her
with accusation.

Gustav turned to go, yet he paused and said over
his shoulder, ''The love ve hold back is the one
that follows us all the days of our lives. Remember
this, my boy.''

Dexter watched as the night swallowed Gustav,
knowing that no words were as true as the last his
friend had spoken. If he let Mallory go without
telling her how he felt, he would regret it for the
rest of his days.

He knelt down next to the memorial plaques,
the only thing he had left to remember his parents
by, as their bodies had never been recovered from
the sea after their plane crashed.

He pulled away some of the grass creeping over
the edge of their grave markers and then dusted
away the leaves and debris partially covering the
words, the pledge each and every Harrington had
lived by.

Duty, honor, and above all, respect.

For three decades he had tried to live up to that
creed, to fit into the mold, wanting desperately to
feel like he truly was a Harrington and not some
laboratory-generated misfit.

Yet he realized then that it was not just the desire
to be a true Harrington that had guided him, but
a yearning to find out where he belonged in the
world.

At long last, he had finally found his place, his

reason for existing. Mallory. He had been made to love her, and if she would give him another chance, he would make every day as magnificent as the sunset falling over Braden Manor.

"Dex?" a voice called out. "Are you up here?"

Dexter rose and stared into the darkness that had swallowed Gustav a short time ago. Cummings suddenly appeared, dashing under the protective covering of trees as the heavens opened up, and rain began to fall.

"What are you doing?" Dexter asked.

Cummings ran a hand through his damp hair. "I was planning on performing an ancient Indian rain dance, but as you now see, it's unnecessary. What do you think I'm doing? I was looking for you."

"Well, you've found me."

"I see that. Hiding, are we?"

Dexter sighed inwardly. It seemed he was destined not to get any peace. "What do you want?"

"What do you think?"

Dexter had a good idea. But the last thing he needed at that moment was another person berating him over his behavior with Mallory. He had been the star of his own ass-kicking contest since she had run from his office. "Look, I know you're just trying to help, but I want to be alone. All right?" He needed time to figure out what he was going to say to Mallory.

Cummings rubbed his thumb and forefinger together and held them up in front of Dexter's face. "Do you know what that is? It's the world's smallest violin, and it's playing just for you."

"I get the picture, now leave off."

"I didn't run up that hill for my health, old man.

I've got things to say, things I should have said before."

Dexter felt his patience beginning to slip. "I'm not in the mood for whatever it is."

"Well, boo-hoo. Because I'm not leaving until I've said my piece."

Dexter folded his arms across his chest. "So say it."

Cummings didn't hesitate. "I'm sick of your stupid sense of duty."

"So you've told me."

"And I'm damned pissed that you hurt Mallory."

"Mallory is none of your business."

"She may have qualms about defending herself, but I don't. She's a wonderful woman, and I'm starting to think you don't deserve her."

Dexter clenched his hands at his sides. "And you do, I suppose?"

"Maybe I do," Cummings returned, a challenge in his eyes.

Just thinking about another man touching Mallory made Dexter feel volatile, like a stick of dynamite waiting for a spark. "If you know what's good for you, you'll stay the hell away from her."

"Or what? You can't have it both ways, Dex. Either you want Mallory or you want Sarah. Choose."

"You overstep your bounds dictating to me."

Cummings's jaw tightened. "Oh, yes, let me not forget that I'm only your employee. An employee certainly shouldn't speak so forthright to his boss, right? A friend, on the other hand, could say what he pleased if he saw another friend ruining his life."

Dexter glared at him and then stepped away,

sweeping a hand roughly through his hair. "Damn it! Why do you push me?"

"Because someone has to. I don't want to see either of us with any more regrets."

Dexter understood regret; it had dogged him since his parents' death, and he couldn't bear to live the rest of his life feeling that way about Mallory.

"Look, I realize I treated Mallory badly, and I plan to rectify that. I just have to figure out how."

"An apology might suffice—although if I were her, I'd use you for target practice."

A grudging smile curved up the corner of Dexter's mouth. "Thank you for the vote of confidence," he said dryly. "Now, if you're done beating me up, I have to go hunting."

"Hunting for what?"

Dexter started down the hill toward his house. "For a white flag."

CHAPTER TWENTY-THREE

"Please tell me it's not true."

Mallory felt heartsick as she looked at her mother's bloodless face. She had never meant for her mother to find out this way. She had never meant for her to find out at all.

"Don't listen to her!" Genie cried, tears streaming down her face as she pointed an accusatory finger at Mallory. "She's lying!"

"No, Genie." Mallory shook her head sadly. "I'm not." She only wished she was. But she had seen everything, had witnessed her father entering her sister's room, the hour after midnight. Mallory remembered it as if it had just happened.

She had been about to head to the kitchen for a glass of warm milk to help her sleep when she had spotted her father in the hallway, slipping quietly into Genie's room, the door making barely a sound as he closed it.

Mallory pressed her ear to the door, heard a mewling sound of protest come from her sister, and a shiver of foreboding ran down her spine.

Quietly, she opened Genie's door and saw her father sitting on the edge of her sister's bed, unbuttoning Genie's pajama top, peeling it back with deliberate care. His hands began to caress Genie in a way that no father should ever touch his daughter, least of all a seven-year-old child. Any love Mallory had felt for her father had withered and died on that night.

Mallory had ached with the secret, wanting to tell her mother, yet having made a solemn vow to her distraught sister she would never do so. But seeing the pain and withdrawal in her mother had chipped away at Mallory's heart until there was a hole she doubted anything would fill.

How she had wanted her mother to know that she had not been a bad wife, had not done anything to push her husband away or make him leave, but rather that he had been a coward, a conscienceless shell of a human being who had sneaked away with his tail between his legs.

Mallory wasn't sure where she had dredged up the courage to confront her father that night, to tell him to get out and never come back, unless he wanted the whole world to know he was the lowest form of humanity, more than just a pedophile, but a man who would fall so far as to sexually molest his own child, whose actions had left scars that had yet to heal.

Perhaps it had been Genie who had given Mallory the strength to do what she had to. Her sister's gaze had found her standing on the threshold, fear in her young eyes—eyes silently beseeching for help. Eyes that would never again hold the sweet innocence of youth.

That night Mallory slept in her sister's room, their arms wrapped around each other, comforting in their despair even as they started the process of trying to erase the memory from their minds, hide it as if they should be the ones who were ashamed.

That night Mallory had become Genie's champion—and the only person who would ever know her sister's awful secret.

Now everything was out in the open.

"Why didn't I know?" her mother asked in a raw voice. "Why didn't anyone tell me that Frank . . . that he . . ." She drew in a quick breath, her hands shaking as she spoke. "All the years I've spent wondering what happened, asking myself what I might have done to send him away, and foolishly hoping he might return one day." Her voice caught on a sob. "All that time wasted loving a man who didn't love me in return only to find out he didn't deserve my love—and he didn't deserve the two wonderful daughters I had given him."

"He's gone now," Mallory said, choking back emotions. "We can't continue to let him affect us, to color our lives so that we are helpless to move forward. If we do, he will have won, and I damn well won't let that happen. I just want us to heal. To be whole again."

"As do I," her mother softly agreed. She closed her eyes briefly, and when she opened them, they were lit with a hint of the fire that had once burned so brightly inside her, fortifying her as she walked toward Genie. "I'm sorry, Genie. So dreadfully sorry. I should have been a better mother to you."

She glanced at Mallory. "I should have been a better mother to both of you. If only I had opened my eyes, maybe I would have seen your pain and not been so selfish in my own. Can you ever find it in your heart to forgive me?"

"Nothing happened!" Genie cried, still trying to hold onto a lie, the agony etched on her face tearing at Mallory's heart all over again, revealing the hurt child inside the young woman.

Mallory's legs trembled, and she felt they might not hold her upright. She prayed for strength. As though God had heard her plea, she felt hands at her waist, keeping her steady.

"It's all right," Dexter murmured in her ear. "I won't let go."

Mallory turned her head and gazed up into his handsome face, the look in his eyes promising to hold fast, asking her to trust him. He mouthed, "Forgive me."

Forgive me. Two words that soothed the pain of his accusations. Two words that gave her the strength she needed. Now Mallory prayed she could give that strength to her sister and help her through this ordeal.

"He's gone, Genie. He can't hurt you anymore."

"It's not true." Genie shook her head. "It's not. Daddy wouldn't do that to me . . . He wouldn't."

"Please, Genie, let go of the pain," Mallory softly pleaded. "I'll help you."

"Help me!" Genie's laughter had a hysterical note to it. "I don't want your help! Do you hear me? I'm tired of being your weak little sister!"

"You were never weak. You were a defenseless child. How could you fend off your own father?

You should never have been put in the position to do so. You were a victim, Genie.''

"I was weak! I was!" Her voice caught on a sob. "If I had only been stronger . . . more like you; then . . . maybe I could have . . .''

She dropped her head into her hands and slowly sank to the floor, her deep, heart-wrenching sobs tearing through Mallory like a knife. Her sister had never cried that terrible night and hadn't shed a tear since. She had locked it away, denied the memory. Until now.

Mallory went to her sister and knelt down on the floor, wrapping her arms around her. Genie stiffened and then went limp, laying her head against Mallory's shoulder and weeping brokenly. Her mother knelt down on the other side of Genie and pressed her cheek against her daughter's hair.

And in the quiet stillness of that hallway, they began to rediscover what they had lost so long ago.

Faith. Friendship.

And hope.

Mallory found Dexter waiting out in the hallway when she closed her bedroom door, having finally gotten Genie to sleep, tears still wet on her sister's eyelashes as she drifted off into an exhausted slumber.

Mallory felt emotionally drained and physically numb, nothing left inside her to give. Yet, for the first time, she felt a spark of hope, a feeling that perhaps everything would be all right.

"You didn't have to wait up," she quietly told him. Yet she was glad he had. She wanted to see him. She needed his strength, yearned for him to pull her close and let his warmth seep into her chilled bones and take away the hurt that still lingered inside her.

He pushed away from the wall and met her in the middle of the hallway. He nodded toward the bedroom door. "Is Genie all right?"

Mallory nodded. "She's sleeping. I think now that everything is out in the open, she can begin to move past this, or at least I pray she can." Mallory stared down at her hands. "She has so much to offer."

"I think a lot of that is because of you."

Mallory shook her head. "I wish I could have done more. I don't even know how long it was going on. But I should have known. I was her sister."

Dexter put his finger beneath her chin and tipped her head up. "Your own mother didn't even know, so how can you blame yourself?"

"Because Genie and I were close once." Mallory willed away the tears that longed to fall, tears that like her sister, she had refused to shed. "She always trailed after me, looked up to me. But I failed her."

"No. You didn't fail her. You saved her." He swept away loose tendrils of her hair with his knuckles, and Mallory shivered from the force of that simple caress. "Any man who would do that to his own flesh and blood should be drawn and quartered. But now you have to take your own advice. Let go of the pain. I'll help you," he softly added, using words she had once spoken to him to ease his despair.

"I thought you hated me."

"I could never hate you. I can only hate myself for being so ready to accuse you of something I should have known you could never have done. God, I'm so sorry. I don't know what came over me. I've never been such a hothead, never felt so out of control . . . until you came along.''

"It seems I have a knack for destruction."

"That isn't what I meant. What I was trying to say was that I haven't felt much of anything. I've been existing, but not really living. You don't know it, but you didn't just save Genie tonight . . . you saved me as well."

"Please don't say any more." Mallory didn't want to hear his words. She couldn't bear it if he put her aside again.

He smoothed a length of her hair between his fingers. "Gustav was right," he said, his voice a husky rumble that made her weak.

"About what?"

"He said I was trying to push you away."

"I see." Mallory stared at his shoulder, too afraid to look into his eyes, fearing that what she hoped to see would not be there.

"Don't you want to know why I was pushing you away?"

"Why?" she whispered.

"Because I realized I was falling in love with you."

His words whipped the air from her lungs, leaving her voice raw as she said, "Don't say something you don't mean."

"I do mean it. I think it started when you whammed me with your pillow when we first met or maybe it happened when you threatened to knock me senseless with that paperweight or perhaps it was when you practically forced me to eat a jalapeño." He made a face and she laughed. "Or it could have been—"

Mallory put a hand over his mouth, muffling his words. "I get the picture."

The eyes that looked into hers were wicked as his tongue began to make circles on her palm. Her mouth went dry, and her stomach tightened, desire rippling through her.

"I think," she said, trying to catch her breath, "that you lied, Professor."

"About what?" he murmured, clearly distracted as his tongue moved down one finger and up the next.

"About wanting to learn what women desired. I believe you've known all along."

"Not women," he corrected. "One woman." He coiled an arm around her waist and brought her tight against his chest, his mouth lowering to hers as he murmured, "You."

Mallory smiled against his mouth . . . and then she was lost to a kiss so heady, so heated with sensual promise that if the world never righted itself, she would be very happy.

And yet, she couldn't completely blot out the memory of how he had acted when they had been at the stream, his withdrawal, both physically and emotionally.

He must have sensed her hesitance because he pulled back and stared down at her. "What's wrong?"

"This afternoon you didn't . . . you wouldn't . . ."

"Make love to you?" His voice was tender. "I wanted to, so damn much I ached with the need."

"Then, why?"

"An attempt at nobility, I suppose." He sighed

and shook his head. "I think our parents harmed us more than they helped."

Mallory nodded, yet she felt as if she had grown wise beyond her years in the past few hours. "That may be true, but we are all fallible. We wouldn't be human if we didn't make mistakes." She had made her share of them. "Sometimes we expect too much from the people we care about. Sometimes we expect too little. And those we look up to might have looked up to someone, too, someone who failed them, and the cycle of pain just keeps going."

"My family did things the same way for generations. We built tradition out of bricks, stacking them one on top of the other until the bricks were so far reaching there was no way around the wall or over it."

"I know." Mallory understood how destructive walls could be. "I realize that I didn't really know my father, what his life had been like. He kept much to himself. I just assumed he was the strong, silent type. I see now that I mistook silence for strength when they didn't go hand in hand. I will never condone what he did to Genie, but I can't say that I haven't forgiven him. I only hope Genie can find forgiveness in her heart and move on. For her own sake."

"I hope so, too." Then almost tentatively, he said, "Did he ever . . ."

"Do to me what he did to Genie?"

He nodded.

"No. He had always been good to me. I don't know what changed him. I doubt I ever will. But I refuse to allow myself to become another victim."

"Genie is very lucky to have you."

"Maybe I'm lucky to have Genie. She's taught me a lot about being brave, and about surviving. But the biggest thing I learned is that secrets can be destructive."

Dexter's face clouded for a moment. "Yes ... secrets can be destructive." He paused and then said, "I have a confession to make."

She waited, but when he said no more, she prompted, "What?"

"Well, I ... I seduced you. At the stream."

Mallory attempted to look aghast. "You seduced me, Professor?"

He nodded, a contrite yet utterly charming half grin on his face. "Umm-hmm. A full-out, strategic plan to assault your senses and batter down your resistance."

Mallory pulled down his head so she could whisper in his ear, "I have a confession, too. You wouldn't have met with any resistance, so all your planning was in vain."

His grin broadened. "None?"

"None," she murmured.

He ran his fingers absently through her hair. "I wanted to be alone with you. I couldn't stop thinking about touching you, but I wanted everything to be perfect. I didn't want to disappoint you."

"You could never have disappointed me."

"I didn't want to take the chance. I haven't been with a lot of women, you see. So I thought if I did more research, I could do it right."

Mallory's heart swelled to bursting for this handsome, endearing man who professed to love her. He had done so much for her, admitted things most men never would. She had been blessed.

"The day I ran into Freddie in town," he went

on, "she picked out a whole bunch of movies for me, macho flicks she called them. And every night, I watched a different one."

For the first time, the mention of Freddie's name in connection with Dexter didn't make Mallory feel jealous. "She did, huh?"

"Yes. I watched quite a few with a rough-around-the-edges chap named John Wayne who walked rather oddly, almost as if the ground was slightly tilted. And I saw two movies with a brutish fellow who kept saying, 'Yo, Adrian.' I'm not sure what 'yo' refers to, but Adrian didn't seem to mind."

Mallory laughed. Her professor was in rare form. "Rocky, you mean?"

He nodded, clearly perplexed. "What an odd name to call a child."

Smiling, Mallory shook her head. If anyone had ever told her she would someday fall for a serious minded Ph.D. who wore tweed and felt the need to analyze everything and everyone, she would have called them crazy.

"Did you learn anything new from these movies?" she asked, pressing closer to him.

His hand smoothed over her buttocks as he murmured, "Care to find out?"

"Oh, yes. Most definitely."

He moved against her and she could feel the proof of his desire for her. She remembered his hands on her, his mouth suckling her . . . then sliding lower. An urgency to feel him inside her made her throb. This was right. She knew it.

"Dexter . . ." Boldly, she laid a hand against the bulge straining the zipper of his jeans.

"Mallory," he groaned. "Wait . . . I have another confession to make."

Mallory put her finger to his lips. "Ssh. No more confessions."

"But I really must—"

"Later. Right now I want you to take me to your bed."

"You do?"

"Yes," she whispered, feathering her lips against his jaw. "I do."

"But—"

She glanced up into his eyes. "Don't you want me?"

"More than you'll ever know," he returned without hesitation.

He gazed down into her eyes for one more second, fighting something within himself. His own need perhaps? The same fear of disappointing her? She didn't know. All she knew was that she needed something only Dexter could give her.

Then, as though his control had finally snapped, he scooped her up in his arms and carried her down the hallway, to his bedroom, shoving open the door with his foot and kicking it shut with a resounding slam that told her quite clearly there would be no turning back.

With an inherent gentleness that seemed at odds with such a big man, Dexter placed her in the middle of his bed.

The mattress sagged as he came down beside her.

Mallory rolled up against him, and he wasted no time taking advantage of her nearness. His lips came down on hers with possessive fervor, taking and giving all in the same breath.

Half his body lay across hers. She tore at his shirt, wanting to feel his skin, stroke those velvety brown nipples. His muscles bunched and flexed as he helped her with the buttons, a hint of his subtle cologne tickling her nostrils. She kissed his shoulder as soon as he was free of his shirt. Gently, she grazed his skin with her teeth.

Dexter groaned as Mallory ground her hips against his, feeling on the brink of losing control, the heat that had begun building that afternoon at the stream now at the boiling point.

God, he had thought about this moment for weeks, and now, instead of taking things slowly, he wanted to wrap Mallory's legs around his waist and plunge into her, deep, hard, to hear that sweet whimper, his name a moan on her lips.

He had promised himself that he wouldn't give in to his desire, not until he had spoken to Sarah, explained what had happened, that another woman now owned his heart.

He prayed Sarah would forgive him for his fall from grace. He would do everything in his power to make it up to her. He loved her. But as a brother loved a sister. If he married her, he would only make her miserable, and that he didn't want. First thing tomorrow morning, he would go to London to speak to her.

Tonight, however, belonged to Mallory.

Her fingers scored his chest; her lips followed suit. He eased back a bit to allow her access. His eyes clamped shut as her soft mouth found his nipple and gently sucked, her hands massaging his back and then moving down to cup his buttocks.

"This," she murmured huskily, "is a work of art." She gave his backside a squeeze.

Dexter chuckled softly, and then said in the most

serious voice he could muster, "Please, madam, refrain from your playful antics. That is not a toy."

She tilted her head back and smiled up at him. "Call me madam one more time and I'll . . ."

He quirked a brow. "You'll what?"

Her tongue slid out and circled his nipple, kissing it gently before she replied, "I'll have to torture you mercilessly until you remember my name."

Dexter wrapped his arm around her waist and pulled her up so that they were face-to-face. "You are one woman I will never forget. *Mallory*," he whispered, his mouth lowering to hers, his fingers deft on the buttons of her shirt, warm hand sliding the material off her shoulders before he cupped her breast, teasing her nipple through her bra.

When he slipped his hand beneath her bra, the sensation jolted her, right at her core, blood beginning to rush through her veins, nerves jumping in her stomach as his mouth replaced his fingers.

Her hips bucked against his. She was not sure if she could take more of the sweet torture he had given her at the stream. She needed him, on top of her, inside her, deep and filling. Now.

"God, you make me crazy," he said, his voice thick with desire. His hand slid down her stomach and underneath the waistband of her loose-fitting pants. He cupped her through her panties. How she wanted his touch there, just as she wanted to touch him . . . there.

She popped open the button of his jeans and eased the zipper down. He was hard and big, big enough to momentarily concern her. She was not so naive that she didn't know how things worked, but the pain. . . .

The thought floated away as his hands eased

beneath her panties, a single finger slipping between her cleft to stroke her clitoris. Mallory knew he would never hurt her, not intentionally, and she wanted him so desperately her fear was fleeting.

She smiled as she slid her hand over his erection, his low moan causing an answering response in her.

She slipped her hand inside his boxers and found him, and he was just as she had imagined. Silk over steel, and so very hot.

"Don't," he begged. "Or I won't be able to control myself long enough to pleasure you."

"Everything about you pleasures me." She trailed kisses along his jaw, continuing to stroke him as he stroked her, her finger smoothing over his tip, finding evidence of his desire for her. She wanted to taste him.

Boldness thrummed through her veins as she put her hands against his shoulders and pushed him back. Worry crossed his brow, but she whispered, "Ssh. Do as you're told and you won't get hurt."

Then she took over, exposing the long, hard length of him, manacling his wrists and keeping them prisoner at his sides, even though she knew she could never pit her strength against his.

Yet he submitted.

And she tasted him, wrapped her mouth around his shaft and let instinct guide her, remembering how he had used his mouth in a similar way. She needed to know if he loved the feel of her mouth as much as she loved the feel of his. His deep, guttural groan told her he did. His body jackknifed when she cupped him.

Then he moved so quickly that Mallory barely had time to blink before she found herself on her back, his big, muscular body enveloping hers.

And her wildest dreams took flight.

Each caress was sinfully delicious, more than her imagination could have described when she put her fantasies to paper in her books.

Mallory's back arched as Dexter took her nipple into his mouth, drawing the sensitive peak higher and higher with each tug, his tongue circling and flicking without releasing his hold.

His fingers teased the other tight bud. She writhed against him, fanning the flames of his desire, pushing his passion to the brink and his control to the edge of its endurance.

Dexter felt frenzied, yanking off her pants, tearing at her panties and spreading her legs wide to slide a finger between her wet folds. She was tight. And hot.

He began to stroke her, fast then slow, back and forth, bringing her to a fevered pitch, feeling her body tense and spreading her thighs even wider to increase the sensation, matching the rhythm of his tongue on her nipple to his finger on the engorged nub between her mound.

She panted and cried out.

His head dropped to her shoulder, his moan mingling with hers as he slid his finger inside her again and felt her sheath contract from her orgasm. He had never felt so alive, so powerful, as he did at that moment.

She wriggled her hips in silent plea, wanting the consummation as much as he did, seeking surcease in the joining.

He positioned his shaft where his finger had

been, sinking into her warmth only a little bit, death and rebirth clashing as her inner lips clenched around him.

"Are you sure?" he asked, praying for strength as he remained still.

She smiled. It devastated him, broke him down, and built him up again. His heart hammered against his ribs as a long-dormant dragon came to full, flaming life inside him.

She cupped his cheeks. "Yes," she breathed, passion-filled hazel eyes gazing up at him. "I'm sure."

Dexter closed his eyes briefly and prayed. *Please Lord, let me be worthy of her.*

Then he took her wrists, pinioning them above her head, and drove into her . . . to find he had been her first. Sweet Jesus, the gift she had just bestowed upon him, giving him what she had given no man.

"Mallory . . . God, I—"

She laid a finger against his lips, the look in her eyes reflecting what was in his heart, as she murmured, "Don't stop now, Professor. Class isn't over yet."

CHAPTER TWENTY-FOUR

Mallory woke up hugging a pillow tightly, a sliver of warm sunlight slanting across her face. She cracked open an eyelid, disoriented at first. Then she smiled, remembering where she was.

Dexter's bedroom.

The drapes were drawn, wrapping the room in cozy darkness except for a single beam of light that had found a part in the curtains.

Mallory rolled over onto her back, taking the pillow with her, wishing it was Dexter instead. She sniffed, breathing in a hint of his cologne and the scent that was uniquely his.

A delightful soreness centered between her legs. Dexter had made love to her over and over again until dawn was about to break on the horizon. He had shown her every delight he could offer, making her body hum with ecstasy.

The man was insatiable. Her smile grew wicked

just thinking about it, and her body tingled from the memory of his hungry caresses. She wanted him back, wanted to spend the day letting him show her more of the wanton splendor he had promised as her eyelids drifted shut.

Where had he gone?

Mallory felt too languid to rise just yet. Instead, she surveyed Dexter's very masculine room, complete with walls of mahogany wainscot, a desk as large as the one in his office, more bookshelves, and an array of expensive yet exquisite artwork. The professor had very good taste.

"All right, lazy," she said to herself. "It's time to get up, find your man and drag him back to bed."

Her man. How she loved the sound of that. But she liked the idea of tossing him back into bed much, much better.

Smiling at the thought, Mallory eased her legs over the side of the bed, wincing slightly from the night's amorous activities. Her feet didn't touch the floor. Not surprising, though, considering whom the bed had been made for. Then she glanced to her left and spotted an envelope propped against the lamp on the nightstand.

She plucked it off the table, knowing immediately it was from Dexter. She remembered the last note she had gotten from him. Could this be another invitation? Perhaps he wanted to return to the stream, but this time let her do sinful things to his body.

Heedless of decorum, she ripped open the back flap and pulled out the note written in Dexter's familiar script.

To Whom It May Concern:

*I bequeath my body, in its entirety, to Mallory
Ginelli to do with it what she will—and I can only
hope she will do what she will again and again.
All I humbly ask in return is that she love me as
I love her.*

Mallory smiled, knowing those were two requests
she would not have a problem fulfilling.

*And should Ms. Ginelli read this note, I would
like her to know that I will be thinking about her,
wanting to touch her, to lay my tongue upon the
spot that makes her cry out my name, to feel her
body pressed tightly to mine, needing her like no
man has ever needed a woman. And I will feel this
way for the remainder of this day and for every day
hereafter. Upon my return, I will have matters of
the utmost import to discuss with her.*

> *Until then, all my love,*
> *The professor*

Mallory held the note to her heart, feeling like
a girl in the throes of her first crush, knowing she
would tuck the letter, envelope and all, away for
safekeeping.

She wondered briefly where Dexter had gone
and why he had not told her he was leaving. But
more importantly, what did he mean by "matters
of the utmost import"?

He couldn't be referring to marriage . . . could
he?

Mallory rose from the bed and padded to the
window, excitement beginning to pour through
her as she pushed open the drapes. Marriage to

Dexter. She hadn't even thought about the possibility.

But now that the idea had presented itself, her answer seemed clear. If he asked, she would say yes. But would he ask? She had no clue how he felt about marriage. Perhaps he was one of those men who believed in living together. Maybe that was what he planned to discuss with her.

What would she say if he only wanted to live together? Many couples did it, and of course it made sense, giving her and Dexter more time to get to know each other. Yet, in a way, they had lived together for nearly two months, and she loved him more every day.

Another thought struck her. If he did propose either marriage or living together, would he want her to live in England? Or would he live in New York? She loved England and would be happy to stay with her prince in his castle, but what would happen to her newly reestablished bond with her family?

Mallory wanted to build on that tenuous relationship, but how could she do that long distance? Genie still needed her, and Mallory suspected her mother did as well.

And one more thing gnawed at her. Dexter's fear of flying. Would he never be able to come with her if she went to New York to visit her family?

Mallory decided it was best to stop thinking and time to get dressed and find out where Dexter had gone. She smiled when she saw that he had picked up her clothes from where they had been thrown in her mad dash to be free of them and draped them neatly over the top of a chair. That was her professor.

Mallory glimpsed a piece of artwork jammed in between his desk and the wall, then noticed the empty space she suspected it had once occupied.

She shimmied into her jeans and hooked her bra, curiosity making her slide the picture out of its spot. It was a stunning oil painting of a young woman whose eyes glittered like two amethyst gems. Certainly nobody's eyes could be that spectacular.

A frown creased Mallory's brow, and she wondered why the portrait had been hidden. Had it even been hidden? Or had it been there for a while? She had been too caught up in her passion the night before to remember if it was hanging up or not. Could Dexter not have wanted her to see it? If so, why?

Her stomach tightened as a memory surfaced. Slow dancing to a romantic song in Dexter's office, he had asked her if she had ever loved someone with all her heart—and she had asked him the same. Yes, he had replied.

Could this be the woman he had once loved? She was beautiful, perhaps more so than Freddie. Mallory could never compete with such a woman.

But did she have to? Dexter loved her now. And maybe this woman didn't exist or was only a relative, though she bore no resemblance to Dexter or anyone in the numerous portraits that graced the walls of Braden Manor.

Mallory shook off her unease and slid the portrait back. She was allowing herself to speculate, one of her worst habits.

She shrugged into her shirt, determined to banish her worries. Yet, even as she left Dexter's bedroom, she knew thoughts of the mystery woman would shadow her.

"Where is everyone?" Mallory murmured to herself, frowning as she looked around the empty hallway. She had yet to see Cummings or Freddie or her mother or Gustav or Genie or Quick. Had they *all* gone out with Dexter?

She glanced at her watch. It was almost noon. She had slept much later than usual. Everyone had probably gone about their business for the day. She shrugged and turned around, heading toward the kitchen to get some food.

She had barely gone ten feet when the doorbell rang. "I'll get it," she called out, certain no one else was going to get it.

Moving to the door, Mallory swung it open to find a young woman standing there, dressed impeccably in an expensive suit that emphasized a trim figure, her long auburn hair flowing over her shoulders. Yet it was her eyes that captured Mallory's attention.

They were, indeed, as spectacular as depicted in the portrait in Dexter's bedroom.

"Hello," the woman said in a lovely English accent.

"Hello," Mallory returned, feeling as if a mighty hand had wrapped around her chest and squeezed. Why did the sight of this woman worry her so? Belatedly, she remembered her manners. "Won't you please come in." Her movements were stiff as she stepped aside, stifling the urge to slam the door and bolt it.

The young woman smiled. "Thank you." Then

she floated into the foyer, moving with the elegant strides Mallory associated with the wealthy upper crust. She turned to face Mallory and held out her hand. "My name is Lady Sarah Benton. How do you do?"

Mallory hesitated, and then shook her hand. "It's nice to meet you, Lady Benton. I'm Mallory Ginelli."

"Please, call me Sarah. Lady Benton is my mother."

The woman was too nice to dislike. As well, she possessed none of the airs Mallory would have expected from an aristocrat. "Call me Mallory."

She nodded. "I must say, the picture didn't do you justice. You're very pretty."

"Picture?"

"In the newspaper." Sarah dug into her purse and pulled out the folded front page. Opening it, she pointed to Mallory's snapshot. The newspaper had used the photo that was in all her books. "That's you, correct?"

"Yes. That's me." A dull ache centered in Mallory's chest as she remembered the pain that article had caused. Yet, in the end, the article had been the impetus to the renewed bond between her and her family, and the relationship between her and Dexter. Perhaps it was true that good things could come from something terrible.

Violet eyes studied Mallory. "I must confess to a good deal of surprise at finding you answering Dexter's door. According to this article, it was you who gave the newspaper the information about his research."

The woman's use of Dexter's name bespoke long

familiarity. Who was she to him? "That article is all a big mistake."

"Oddly enough, I'm inclined to believe you. I'm glad I don't pass judgment easily or else I may have felt it necessary to take you to task for doing something so despicable to Dexter. I know how close he keeps his work, allowing very few access, even me. How is he, by the way? That is the real reason I came. I was worried about him."

"He's fine." Who was this woman?

Sarah glanced around. "Is he here? I'd like to see him."

"No, he's not here. I'm not sure where he is."

She made a small moue of displeasure. "If I know him, he is probably off to find the culprit who stole his research." She shook her head and sighed. "Well, I brought an overnight bag. Perhaps you and I can talk further after I've put my things away?"

An overnight bag? A sense of foreboding washed over Mallory. This woman obviously knew Dexter very well. She was familiar not only with his research, but with his home as well. Clearly she had been a guest before. The question was, had she stayed in one of the numerous guest bedrooms . . . or in Dexter's bedroom?

Mallory wasn't sure what to do. Part of her was desperate to ask the woman to leave. Yet, if Sarah was Dexter's friend, how would it look if Mallory threw her out?

"I'd love to talk further," Mallory said tentatively. "But this is not my home. So I hope you don't mind if I ask you how you know Dexter."

"Oh, I'm sorry. How rude of me. I've spent a

lot of time here over the years, so I guess I just expect everyone to know I'm Dexter's fiancée.''

The world stopped moving in that moment, and Mallory reeled from a blow unexpected and devastating. Dexter's fiancée? He was getting married? Was this the matter of ''utmost import'' he wanted to discuss with her? *I love you, Mallory, but I'm marrying another woman?*

The girl put her hand on Mallory's arm. ''Are you all right? You're looking a bit pale. Would you like to lie down?''

Mallory shook her head, praying words would come, that she could dig past the numbing pain the woman's admission had caused. ''No . . . I'm fine. Thank you.'' She hesitated and then asked, ''How . . . How long have you and Dexter been engaged?''

''Well, we are not officially engaged, but we've been planning on getting married since we were both children.''

Since they were children.

Mallory told herself that just because she and Dexter had spent one night together, one monumentally beautiful, earthshaking, life-altering night together, that didn't mean a fairy-tale ending was a given. People slept together all the time. One-night stands were the thing. Why should she be any different? She had probably been a last fling before Dexter settled down.

So, knowing all that, why was the pain still so intense? And why did she feel as if she had lost her footing once again and might never regain it?

But more than that, why had she allowed herself to believe that after a lifetime of waiting, she had finally gotten her own happily ever after?

"W-where are your bags?" Mallory asked, feeling as if she existed in a haze.

"I only have one bag. Let me retrieve it from my car." She started past Mallory, but hesitated, concern evident on her face. "Are you sure you're all right?"

Mallory forced a smile onto her face. "Fine."

Not looking entirely convinced, she nodded and then disappeared out the door.

Mallory took a deep breath and closed her eyes, willing back the pain, wishing she could hate Dexter, wanting to hate him for his deception, trying to block out every tender caress and every softly spoken word.

Had he even loved her? Or had he just used those words as a ruse to get her into bed? Perhaps he had learned more than she had taught.

Lady Sarah came back then. "Would you walk me to my room, Mallory?" she asked, a gentle smile on her face.

Mallory nodded, too numb for protests.

They ascended the stairs and headed down the long corridor, Sarah leading the way, her steps unwavering, confirming that she knew exactly where she was going. She had been coming to Dexter's home for years, after all. They had been planning on marrying since they were children. Why had Dexter neglected to tell her that small fact?

"Have you known Dexter long?" Sarah inquired, her gaze mildly probing.

Mallory shook her head. "No. Only about two months." Yet she had believed she had gotten to know him well during that short time. Now she realized she didn't know him at all. "But I'm leaving to go home tomorrow."

Until that moment, she had forgotten about the plane reservations she had made. She should be glad she hadn't canceled them.

She should be.

"Have you been staying here all that time?" Sarah then asked.

Mallory didn't know what to say. She knew how she would feel if her husband-to-be had had another woman living in his house for such a long time. Yet she didn't want to hurt Sarah. Another life didn't have to be ruined.

"Yes, but with a friend of mine. She came along to keep me company while Dexter and I were doing some research." Mallory hoped the girl would not probe into the subject of their research.

Sarah let out a small sigh. "Dexter does love his research. Sometimes I think he loves it more than anything else."

Mallory hadn't expected to feel a kinship with this girl. But it couldn't be helped. They had both taken a backseat to Dexter's work. "I'm sure he loves you very much."

"I know he does," she murmured, a hint of sadness etching her face. "And I love him, too. I've known him for so very long. He has always been wonderful to me."

The words cut Mallory to the quick, but she would never let on that Dexter's deceit had broken her heart so thoroughly that she doubted she would ever completely mend.

"He's always been there for me," Sarah went on. "Tending my scraped knees when I scrambled after him as he climbed the crags, or standing up for me when his parents railed at me for dirtying my dress." She turned to look at Mallory. "His parents were, well, rather strict."

"So I've heard."

She looked surprised. "He told you about his parents?"

"Yes."

Sarah stared at her for a moment. "He never talks to anyone about his parents. I even had a hard time getting him to open up, and I've known him forever. He's my best friend."

Mallory willed back the tears that threatened to fall. "You're very lucky to have such a good friend," she murmured, wishing Dexter had cared enough about her to have been a friend.

Sarah nodded. "Yes, I am lucky. Any woman would be proud to have a husband like Dexter." A hint of something Mallory couldn't quite discern lingered in Sarah's remark. "I've never met a man so sensitive to others, and yet so pained inside."

Mallory understood, for she had seen the same thing. And she had wanted to be a balm to that pain. Yet another woman would take her place.

"Sometimes I wonder if . . ." Sarah hesitated.

"Yes?"

She shook her head. "Never mind. It's not important."

Mallory did not push. Instead, she looked at Freddie's bedroom door as she and Sarah passed it, wishing she knew where Freddie was, wanting to talk to her, even though Mallory felt too raw, too hurt, to tell her friend much of anything.

Suddenly the door flew open, and Freddie's irate voice echoed into the hallway. "How dare you ask me such a thing, you . . . you *man!*"

Cummings came shooting out into the hallway. Shoes in hand, pants half zipped, and wearing a jacket with no shirt underneath. He stopped dead in his tracks upon seeing the two of them.

"Sarah?" His mouth dropped open.

Freddie appeared in the doorway next, pillow in hand. And Mallory discovered where Cummings's shirt had gone to. Freddie was wearing it. What was going on?

"Take that!" Freddie flung the pillow at Cummings's head. "And don't you—" She stopped abruptly, finally realizing they were not alone. "Oh, hello, Mal," she said, as though it was just another day and she had not been caught in an indelicate situation with a man she claimed to loath.

Cummings cleared his throat, his gaze darting between Mallory and Sarah and then finally settling on Dexter's intended. "What are you doing here, Sarah?"

"Nice to see you, too, Jonathan."

Jonathan? Freddie and Mallory mouthed in unison. Good Lord, Cummings had a first name.

Cummings still looked flummoxed. "I'm sorry. I'm just surprised to see you. Did you, er, tell Dex you were coming?"

"No. But after I saw all the television and newspaper reports, I simply couldn't stay away. I was worried."

"I see." Then Cummings glanced down at himself as if remembering his state of undress. He grimaced. "Let me get, er . . . Why don't I walk you to your room?"

"But—" Sarah began, only to have Cummings loop his arm through hers and practically drag her away. She glanced over her shoulder, an apologetic expression on her face. Then they disappeared around the corner.

Leaving Mallory to face Freddie. She quirked a brow. "Do you mind telling me what just happened?"

Freddie's expression turned mulish. "Not unless you plan on telling me why you look like your dogs just died."

Mallory didn't want to talk about Dexter. The pain was too fresh. Besides, the truth was in her eyes for the whole world to see. Words were unnecessary.

"I plan to leave tomorrow. I made plane reservations for everyone." Yet Mallory was not so blind, nor so naïve, that she didn't understand what she had just witnessed between Freddie and Cummings. "Will you be coming with us?"

"What the hell kind of question is that? Of course I'm coming with you. I mean, there's no reason for me to stay here." Freddie's voice wavered slightly. "No reason at all."

Mallory nodded, wondering if Freddie knew just how much she understood that sentiment. There was nothing left for either of them here.

Dexter walked in the front door the following morning to find three pairs of eyes fastened on his face: Cummings, Gustav, and even Quick. Each of them wore identical expressions of accusation.

"What is going on?" he asked.

"Good God, man," Cummings snapped, moving forward with an agitated stride. "Where have you been? I called you at least twenty times. Didn't you get any of my messages?"

"First of all, you know where I've been. In London." Although his trip had been a bust. Sarah was nowhere to be found when he arrived at her home, which had prolonged his stay. He hadn't wanted to leave until he had talked to her; but every time he went back to her town house on Grosvenor Square, she was not there, and all her butler knew was that something urgent had come up and he didn't know when she would be returning.

Why hadn't he called to let her know he was coming? Probably because he had expected her to be home. Moreover, he had been too eager to discuss their future, tell her how he felt and let her know about Mallory, to wait.

Now that he had failed, he couldn't move forward with his plans to ask Mallory to marry him. He had to make things right with Sarah first.

"What about my messages?" Cummings prodded.

"I didn't get any of your messages because I stayed in a hotel a block away from Sarah's instead of at my place. I didn't want to traipse back and forth across town."

"Couldn't you have at least called and told a body what you were doing?"

The serious look on the men's faces made Dexter apprehensive. "Why are you all staring at me like that? Has something happened?"

The men glanced at each other, and then Cummings said bluntly, "The women have left."

It took a moment for the words to sink in. "Left? What do you mean left?"

"As in not here. They're gone. Packed up their things last night, called a cab, and are now on their way to Heathrow as we speak."

Dexter raked a hand through his hair. What the hell had happened? He had left a perfectly content, sleeping Mallory yesterday morning, having made love to her with a fervor he had never before experienced, hoping to imprint the memory in her mind until he returned and could take up where they had left off, but this time with a ring on her finger.

Dexter strode between the men, agitated and confused. Then he swung around to face them. "I don't understand. Why did Mallory leave?"

"Hello, Dexter," a soft, familiar voice called from the landing behind him.

Slowly, Dexter turned to face the woman he had gone to London to see. "Sarah?"

She walked down the stairs, coming to a stop on the last step. He moved to greet her. She took his hands in hers. Her smile was sweet, yet sad. "I came to see how you were. I read the article. Are you all right?"

The last thing Dexter cared about at that moment was that bloody article or his work. "I'm fine. The thing in the paper was all a misunderstanding."

"That's what Mallory said."

Mallory. God, what had he done? As soon as he saw Sarah, he knew that somehow Mallory had found out about his deception. That would explain her flight.

Tell Mallory the truth or let her go.

Cummings had tried to warn him, but Dexter had not heeded his friend's advice. Now it was too late. He had lost her.

"I went to London to see you, and you came to Wales to see me. We must have passed each other on the road." Yet he felt no irony, only a keen sense of despair.

Had he passed Mallory as well? He had been in such a rush to get home once the morning had come and Sarah had still not returned. He had just wanted to hold Mallory in his arms.

"I hope you don't mind my showing up like this," she said.

"You know you are always welcome here."

"I know," she murmured. "You truly are my best friend."

Dexter felt a pang of remorse hearing Sarah's words, words that only made it harder for him to do what he had to do. Not just for his happiness, but for Sarah's as well. Look what his deceit had wrought. Mallory had left him. He couldn't continue the lies with Sarah, and the first lie would be that he loved her.

"You still have time to go after her."

Dexter snapped out of his musings. "What did you say?"

"I said, you still have time to go after her. She only has about a half hour start on you."

"But—"

"If you don't, it will be the biggest mistake of your life."

"What are you telling me?"

"Dexter, I've known you all my life, and for all that time I have waited to see the look that is in your eyes right now. But that look is not meant for me. What's more, I saw the same look in Mallory's eyes. She loves you. And you know what? I like her. I really do. All I want is your happiness, and I think she makes you very happy."

"But what about us? We're supposed to get married."

She graced him with a tender smile. "I know, and I hope you won't hate me if I tell you that I don't want to marry you. My reasons for coming here weren't entirely because of the article. I wanted to talk to you . . . about us."

Now *that* was ironic. "I could never hate you." Then he blinked. "You don't want to marry me?"

She laid her hand gently against his cheek. "No," she murmured. "It was fear of losing your friendship that kept me from saying anything before this. I couldn't bear it if I hurt you. I guess I had hoped that someday I would grow to love you as a wife should. But I . . . I don't think I ever will. And now I see that you don't care for me in that way either."

"I didn't mean to fall in love with Mallory," Dexter vowed, taking hold of Sarah's hand. "It just happened."

"Oh, Dex. Do you think I believed you planned to love another woman? I know you far too well." A hint of color stained her cheeks as she quietly added, "And if we are making confessions, then let me say that I, too, have found someone I love with all my heart."

The truth of her statement showed clearly in her eyes. They sparkled with burgeoning excitement. "You can't imagine how wonderful it is to know you've found the one person who is meant for you and you alone." She chuckled then. "On second thought, I imagine you can."

God, did he ever, but he feared he might have bungled his only chance. "What about your parents? You know how they feel about duty and tradition." They were as much sticklers as Dexter's parents had been.

Sarah straightened, tossing her shoulders back. "I'm a modern woman, Dexter. I'm ready to start some traditions of my own. Now"—She pushed at his shoulders—"go get Mallory."

He hesitated. "What if she won't have me?" Even if he should catch up to her in time that was no guarantee he could make things right.

But what would he do without her? He couldn't lose her, not now when he had just found her, now when he was free to love her as she deserved to be loved.

Sarah pressed a hand to his chest. "Let her know what's in your heart . . . and perhaps take that big bunch of roses out of the vase on the table over there."

Dexter leaned down and kissed her cheek. "Thank you."

She smiled gently and whispered, "Good luck . . . and Godspeed."

CHAPTER
TWENTY-FIVE

"Good morning ladies and gentlemen, and welcome aboard British Airways Flight 175, nonstop to New York. Our flying time is approximately seven hours and forty minutes, and we will be cruising at an altitude of thirty-five thousand feet. The outlook for the weather is hazy at present. Ron Jacobs is your captain, and I'm Clarissa Markinson, the head flight attendant. We will be taking off momentarily, so please fasten your seat belts and enjoy your flight."

Mallory reached for another Kleenex, hating herself for weeping like a baby as she gazed out at that despicable tarmac. If she never flew again . . . then she would probably never see Dexter again.

Lord, what was the matter with her? How could she care for the dirty, rotten cad? She only hoped he treated Sarah better than he had treated her.

Sarah had asked her to stay, to wait for Dexter's

return, saying that there might be some things he needed to tell her, some very important things. But Mallory didn't want to listen to anything he had to say—and she couldn't bear to see Dexter in Sarah's arms.

Mallory sniffled. What had the captain said about the weather? Outlook hazy. Well, that was no surprise. That sentiment seemed to encapsulate her entire life. Hadn't that been what the genie in her Magic 8 ball had told her before she left on this cursed trip?

She plucked another Kleenex from the package and suddenly found three hands outstretched in front of her. She glanced up to find Freddie, Genie, and her mother staring at her, each with identical weepy faces.

"What are you all crying about?" Mallory asked them.

"I'm not crying," Freddie said defensively, though her voice sounded suspiciously tear-clogged. "It's my, er, allergies kicking in."

"And what, exactly, are you allergic to?"

Freddie's gaze darted around the first-class cabin. "Cheap upholstery. Do you see the material these seats are made of? Who knows what kind of germs are lingering around here."

Mallory's gaze then moved to her mother. "And you, Mom?"

"I'm not crying either. I just have something in my eye."

"I see," Mallory murmured, her regard coming to rest on her sister. "And what about you, Genie? Is it allergies or something in your eye?"

Genie shook her head. "Neither. I think I smell an onion."

An onion? Well, that was at least original. "My God, don't we all look pathetic mooning over a bunch of men."

"Yeah." Genie nodded. "Who needs 'em?"

"Not me, that's for sure," Freddie said in her I-don't-need-anybody voice. "They're all pains if you ask me—and they lie, too."

Mallory understood that. She had to refrain from saying "Amen, sister."

Freddie, however, was on a roll. "They make you think they're just a piddly secretary with a huge chip on their broad shoulders and then *bam!* They tell you they made a fortune buying a horse load of AOL stock in its infancy and they are a millionaire. And *then* they have the nerve to think you're fine with that after you love them as that piddly, pompous, pigheaded, pain-in-the-posterior secretary! Oh, and of course, you should marry them. Well, forget it! If I wanted a millionaire, I . . ." She frowned. "I guess I'd marry one."

Mallory had done nothing more than blink through Freddie's diatribe. "Are you trying to say Cummings is . . . rich?"

Freddie nodded and sniffled again. "Filthy rich. Disgusting, isn't it? Just when I liked the man as he was, he had to go and be rich. The rat."

Mallory couldn't believe what she was hearing. "And he wanted to marry you?"

Freddie looked miserable. "How dare he . . . or him . . . oh, whatever!"

"Why does he work for Dexter, then?"

She shrugged. "They're friends. A bunch of stupider men I've never met."

This was just too much, Mallory thought, doling out Kleenex. There they were. Four women weep-

ing like children. What did the other passengers
think? she wondered, blowing her nose.

"Mallory!"

Mallory jumped in her seat hearing the thunder-
ous roar of her name. The voice was familiar. It
couldn't be. It wasn't.

Slowly, she turned, but she wasn't able to see
over the top of her seat. She rolled around and
got on her knees, peering wide-eyed toward the
stairs that spiraled to the lower level of the plane
where a commotion brewed.

"Mallory!" the voice bellowed once more.

Then a handsome face that Mallory thought she
would never see again appeared. Dexter crested
the top of the stairs, his gaze swinging back and
forth, a flight attendant hot on his heels.

"Please, sir. You must take your seat. We'll be
departing any moment."

Dexter ignored her. "Mallory!" he hollered,
sounding as tortured as Brando in *A Streetcar Named
Desire.*

Then he spotted her. He didn't smile. He didn't
move toward her. No, he just stood there looking
utterly beautiful and wearing the most determined
expression she had ever seen.

Mallory pressed her lips tightly together. She
would not smile. And she would not cry. "What
are you doing here, Dexter?"

"I came for you."

A murmur swept through the crowd of passengers, reminding Mallory they were not alone. And
as her gaze crept around the cabin in slow increments, she saw that every eye was on her and
Dexter.

"And I came for Freddie," another voice said.

"Cummings?" Freddie squealed and then darted an embarrassed look around. "Oh, it's just you," she amended in a normal tone, trying to pretend she didn't care he was there.

"Damn right, woman," Cummings growled. "And I've had all the guff I'm going to take from you."

Freddie snorted. "Go away."

He gritted his teeth. "I swear, Freddie, you're going to marry me or . . ."

Freddie jumped out of her seat and glared at him, arms crossed over her chest. "Or you'll what?"

Cummings returned her glare for all of a second; then his anger deflated like a punctured balloon. "Or I'll have to give all my money to charity and take a job as a street cleaner."

Mallory never thought she would live to see the day when Freddie, tough-as-nails-Jewish-American-princess, Feldman would crumble. But today was the day.

"You'd give up all your money . . . for me?" The last two words came out a squeak.

Cummings nodded. "If that was the only way I could have you."

"Oh," Freddie wept, "you are the most wonderful, sweetest, adorable man in the world!" She ran to him and wrapped her arms around his neck, giving him a kiss that made the women sigh and the men hoot. When Freddie's lips left Cummings's, the man looked ravaged. "Now," she said with a devilish grin, "exactly how much money are we talking about?"

Cummings shook his head and hauled Freddie against his chest. The man had finally learned what it took to keep Freddie Feldman quiet.

"Please, you must take your seats," the flight attendant beseeched, even though she wore a wistful expression. "You're holding up the flight."

"Pssh," a voice said. "Vhy is the whole vorld in a rush these days?"

"Gustav?" her mother said, blinking as a spritely body squeezed between Dexter and an occupied Cummings.

"Hello, my dear." Gustav smiled, looking completely disarming dwarfed between the two giants. "I could not let you leave vithout telling you how I feel about you. You see . . ." He swallowed and put a finger to his collar. "Vell . . ."

Her mother rose from her seat. "You love me?"

He beamed and wagged his finger at her. "Yes, my girl. I do. Since I met you, the fire has returned to my heart . . . and other places," he added with a wink, causing her mother to blush. "I vant to show you my country and my home. I vant to spend whatever time I have left on this earth vith you."

Mallory's mother walked toward him, arms outstretched. "And I want to be with you as well." She hugged him close.

"A-hem," yet another voice said. "Do you mind not blocking the aisle?"

Genie popped up from her seat. "David? Oh-my-God, David!"

David? Mallory thought as Quick gently nudged aside the flight attendant. Another person with a first name.

Dexter's butler held open his arms for Genie. That was all it took for her sister to barrel down the aisle and throw herself into them—and wrap her legs around his waist—kissing him with all the passion and fervor of a soon-to-be eighteen-year-old.

And that left only Mallory and Dexter.

His gaze had not wavered from her since he had topped the stairs. Mallory's mouth went dry, her heart pounding so hard she thought it would come right out of her chest.

"If you people don't take your seats this minute," the flight attendant warned, "I'm going to have to ask you to exit the plane immediately."

"Fine," Dexter said, and Mallory's heart dropped. He was going to leave. Then he added, "Let's take our seats, gentlemen . . . and ladies."

Mallory blinked. It couldn't be. They weren't coming with them, were they? No, it wasn't possible.

"What are you doing?" she asked when Dexter came to stand in the aisle across from her window seat.

"If you won't stay here with me, then I'm coming to New York with you." Then, from behind his back, he produced a bouquet of roses, handing them to her with all the mastery she had taught him.

Mallory took them without thinking. "But you can't come."

"Oh, yes I can. It's a free world."

Several people moved from their seats so the four couples could sit together. It seemed no one wanted to get in between true love—or four very protective men. Even the flight attendant helped with the resettling of the dislocated passengers.

Dexter plunked down in the spot Freddie had just vacated and fastened his seat belt. He glanced up at Mallory, as she was still kneeling in her seat.

"Well, come on, Ms. Ginelli. People are waiting to go."

Still dazed, Mallory turned and sat down, staring at him. "But . . . You're afraid to fly."

"This is true." Sweat popped out on his brow as if to confirm his words. "But a man has to do what a man has to do. I believe it was John Wayne who said that. It seemed fitting for this situation."

The captain came over the speaker, telling everyone to prepare for takeoff. Dexter's face paled, and his hands gripped the armrests.

"Dexter, this is crazy. You have to get off."

He took a deep breath and turned to her. "The only crazy thing would be for me to let you leave without telling you how much I love you." He took hold of her hand. "You're my Ilsa, my Adrian, my Stella, my Scarlett."

Mallory shook her head, willing back the tears. "I won't listen to any more of your lies. I know all about you and Sarah."

"Then you know she doesn't want to marry me?"

"So that's why you're here? Because she turned you down?"

"No. I'm here because she knows I don't want to marry her either."

"You don't?" A single unrestrained tear rolled down Mallory's cheek.

Dexter tenderly brushed it away. "No," he murmured. "I don't. I told you about my family and how strongly they believed in tradition. The marriage between Sarah and myself was arranged a long time ago. But I never cared for her in anything other than a brotherly fashion. She felt the same way. She told me to come here, that I would be making the biggest mistake of my life if I let you go. I didn't need her to tell me that. I knew."

"But why didn't you tell me the truth?"

"Because I was a coward. I didn't want to lose you, but I didn't know how to change the course my life was taking. You showed me how."

"I did?"

He nodded, his face paling drastically as the plane began to taxi down the runway. "You asked me once if I wouldn't do whatever it takes to be with the woman I love. To not want to lose the only person who I knew in my soul was the one for me." He raised her hand to his lips, his blue eyes capturing hers. "Well, I've found that love, and I have no intention of letting it go. Marry me, Mallory. I'll be lost without you."

Tears streamed down Mallory's face. Could it be true? Had she at last found her own happy ending?

The intercom crackled, and then the captain spoke. "Morning, folks. Our weather forecast for the day has changed. It seems we will have sunshine and blue skies for the rest of our journey together."

Mallory closed her eyes and laughed. She had her answer.

And as the plane lifted off into the sky, she looked into the handsome, endearing face of the man she loved and said, "I'll marry you, Professor . . . but only on one condition."

"And what's that?"

"That I get to teach our children how to dance."

He smiled and leaned over to kiss her. "Anything you say, Ms. Ginelli . . . anything you say."

ABOUT THE AUTHOR

Before she discovered romantic fiction, MELANIE GEORGE was an executive search consultant. Her most important job, however, has always been that of mother, to both a soon-to-be-college-bound son and two precious dogs, who sit with her in her office day after day while she pulls out her hair and swears this is the last book she will ever write (which she knows is a lie, but someone sympathetic always buys it and she likes the attention.)

When she is not writing, she is trying to restore her hundred-year-old house and has come to the conclusion that paint speckles will more than likely be a permanent part of her person. She looks forward to the release of her next contemporary novel, TO DIE FOR, due out in November 2002, where she will explore a completely new avenue, dealing with the pain of sacrifice, the healing of old wounds, and what a couple will do when one of them is faced with their own mortality. Melanie enjoys hearing from readers. You can visit her at: www.melaniegeorge.com.

DO YOU HAVE THE
HOHL COLLECTION?